A Gifted Curse

By Brima Matthews

This book is a work of fiction–Any resemblance to actual people, both living or deceased, events or locations is coincidental.

Copyright © 2022 Brima Mathews

All rights reserved. No Part of this book may be used or reproduced in any manner whatsoever without written permission of the author, except in the case of brief quotations embodied in critical articles or reviews.

Cover design by Brima Matthews

ISBN: 9798362167851

A Gifted Curse

Dedicated in loving memory to my father and grandfather, who always encouraged me to dream big.

A Gifted Curse

To my sisters and children who put up with my occasional mania and excitement over this story, thank you from the bottom of my heart.

To my 10:24 friends, I am so grateful for your loving support – y'all are awesome<3

And thank YOU for choosing to join Hakan and Fannar on their journey.

A Gifted Curse

"In each of us, two natures are at war – the good and the evil. All our lives the fight goes on between them, and one of them must conquer. But in our own hands lies the power to choose – what we want most to be, we are."

– Robert Louis Stevenson

A Gifted Curse

Table of Contents

PREFACE X
Chapter 1: *A GOOD HEART* 1
Chapter 2: *FRIENDLY COMPETITION* 13
Chapter 3: *THE GIFTING CEREMONY* 27
Chapter 4: *CHOICES* 42
Chapter 5: *OUR TEAM* 58
Chapter 6: *TROUBLE* 70
Chapter 7: *EXPECTATIONS VERSUS DREAMS* 82
Chapter 8: *HOLD NOTHING BACK* 92
Chapter 9: *GOOD NEWS AND BAD NEWS* 114
Chapter 10: *THE TOURNAMENT* 128
Chapter 11: *SURPRISES* 148
Chapter 12: *AN ALMOST BEAUTIFUL MOMENT* 162
Chapter 13: *COMPLICATED DESPERATION* 176
Chapter 14: *UNAPOLOGETIC LOYALTY* 185
Chapter 15: *DISCOVERIES IN THE DARK* 202
Chapter 16: *BREAKING POINT* 212
Chapter 17: *FIGHTING FATE* 222
Chapter 18: *PAINFUL GOODBYES* 235
Chapter 19: *FIRE AND WATER* 244
Chapter 20: *AFTERMATH* 256
Chapter 21: *HAPPY BIRTHDAY* 274
Pronunciation Guide 284
Gift Guide: 286

PREFACE

In the midst of the chaos of 2020, as a way to stave off boredom and escape the heart-wrenching realities of life, I began writing a fan-fiction story. I would then read that story to a friend as she made her long commute to and from work, and by the end of the third chapter she insisted I should NOT post it online, but instead find a way to make it my own so I could publish it 'for real'. I laughed at her; I was convinced there was no way I could turn that story into something original that was worth reading. Shortly after that conversation, my life got crazy busy and stressful, and I stopped working on that fanfiction.

Every-so-often, though, my friend's words would pop back into my thoughts: "Damn girl! You're such a good writer you need to write something original!". So, towards the end of 2021, I sat down in my spare time and started trying to come up with something completely my own. I had mapped out a whole timeline and came up with mini-backstories of a bunch of characters, and by January of 2022, I had started writing. However, come chapter three I felt like I was pulling teeth trying to write the story, and was ready to give up.

In February that same year, I was watching youtube (as one does when one is stressed and burnt out trying to figure out one's place in the universe) when I saw a trailer that made me go "huh, that gives me an idea." I spent what felt like twenty hours a day for over a week working on an outline for a new story, and this time, something was different.

Everything just flowed and fit together and I had so much that was going to happen on the characters' journey that I realized I had not one, but three books in the massive outline. In march, I started writing and finally it clicked–I had found 'my thing'. I was excited to sit down at my computer every day and put more words on the pages, especially when one of my sisters (who was proofreading as I wrote) would demand the next chapter *right then* because she *needed* to read what happened next. Nine months of loving labor later, the first part of Hakan and Fannar's struggle-filled journey is complete...

Chapter 1

A GOOD HEART

"*Fannar!*" whispered a blonde-haired, blue eyed boy as he nudged Fannar's arm.

Fannar turned from the window he'd been staring out of to look at his brother, who gestured for Fannar to pay attention to their lesson. Fannar rolled his matching blue eyes, sighed and looked down at the digi-tab on the table in front of him – It was still at the top of the lesson page. He glanced over at his brother's screen to figure out where he was supposed to be and saw dozens of notes scribbled all around the text. Fannar frowned at his brother's diligent work and began looking back and forth between the devices. After a few fruitless scans, Fannar sighed again.

"Hey, Hakan," Fannar whispered, "what…"

"Third page, fifth paragraph." his brother quickly whispered back.

"Thanks," Fannar replied as he began counting.

"Mhm." Hakan grunted, more than a little annoyed at his brother.

Fannar quickly found the line they were on, but it didn't take long for his attention to drift away from the history lesson and back to his daydream. He looked over at his brother as he thought, watching him markdown notes as he listened attentively. Neither of them had exceptional aptitude for academy lessons, but that didn't stop Hakan from striving for top marks. Fannar just couldn't motivate himself to work like that yet. They were only sixteen–they had plenty of time to study all the boring stuff they needed to learn. Hakan didn't see it that way though, and Fannar, although he disagreed with it, understood his brother's reasons.

As the older of the King's two children, Hakan was the successor to the throne, and he wanted to serve the people of Ladothite well – even if it meant having to work twice as hard as most to master a lesson. Fannar, on the other hand, only had to worry about learning enough to be a good advisor to his brother... assuming his brother was actually serious about putting Fannar on his council when that time came.

Hakan looked over and did a double take when he realized his brother was staring at him, lost in thought again. The older prince dropped his head in defeat, and the younger smiled at him. As much as Hakan loved his brother, Fannar could irritate him like no one else could.

The two had as many similarities as they had differences, both in personality and appearance. They were both blonde, but Hakan preferred to keep his hair just above shoulder length, while his brother couldn't stand having his hair that long. Fannar also had rounder, softer facial features compared to his brother's long, sharp ones. The younger prince was also far more outgoing than Hakan, who tended to be fairly reserved around people he wasn't close with.

Suddenly, there was a loud slam at the front of the room as the instructor dropped a stack of books on his desk, making everyone jump and several students scream in surprise.

Chapter 1

"Who can tell me the name of the council member that drafted the peace treaty with Snow Valley that eventually facilitated its official entry into the kingdom?" the teacher asked, looking from student to student.

A boy with short, black hair sitting near the front of the classroom shot his hand into the air, while Hakan and a girl at the table in front of them timidly raised theirs. Fannar, on the other hand, sank lower into his chair along with the vast majority of the students.

The instructor sighed and pinched the bridge of his nose. "Anyone, besides Hakan, Amehllie, and Shammoth?" he asked, looking back up at them with an expression of amused disappointment.

No one raised their hands.

"Alright... since most of you seem too distracted by the Gifting Ceremony tomorrow," the instructor said as he started piling up papers, "I don't see any sense in continuing today's lesson. You're all dismissed for the day."

Half the class cheered, Fannar included, and they all started to gather their things.

"Hah-kah-an," a round-faced boy with bright eyes whined as he approached the brothers' desk, "you couldn't've just *pretended* to not pay attention? Just this once?" he asked his friend.

Hakan ignored him as he put his digi-tab and pen into his bag.

"Why should he, Joule?" the dark-haired boy who had raised his hand asked, giving Hakan a nod as he joined them.

"And you, Shammoth!" Joule exclaimed, pointing an accusatory finger at the dark-hair boy, "you're just as bad!"

"What's bad about doing what we're here to do?" Shammoth replied coolly.

"If the two of you could've just been underachievers for *one day*," Joule lamented, dramatically holding up a finger, "maybe we could have gotten out of the *entire* lesson instead of just half!"

Hakan rolled his head back and groaned as he slung his bag over his shoulder.

"It's not our fault we're not as worked up about the Gifting Ceremony as you and Fannar," Shammoth said.

"Hey! I'm not worked up!" Fannar protested, his deep voice cracking slightly.

Hakan raised his eyebrows, "You couldn't even make it through the first paragraph before you were daydreaming," he said incredulously.

Fannar made a face, and mocked throwing a punch at his brother, who easily dodged it, and both started to chuckle.

"Hey! If you boys insist on staying in my classroom," the teacher bellowed from behind his desk, "I'll resume today's lesson!"

"No, no!" Yelled Fannar, snatching up his bag and darting for the door.

"We're leaving!" Joule called, following right behind.

Hakan and Shammoth waved goodbye to the instructor and walked leisurely from the room after their friends who had raced away.

Fannar and Joule hurried down the wood clad hall to the sleek steel staircase that connected the four stories of the academy building. Rushing down the metal steps, they tried their best not to knock into any of the other students hastily making their way out. As they approached the

Chapter 1

bottom of the staircase, they jumped the last three steps, down to the concrete floor of the main level, and didn't slow until they reached the aged-oak main doors. They squinted against the bright sun as they sat down on the top of the stone steps to wait for their dawdling friends.

"You know," Joule began as he caught his breath from the sudden sprint, "this is one of those times I'm not so sure you two are really twins."

"Same," Fannar replied, smiling impishly, "but there's no convincing mom otherwise. She keeps insisting that she was there when we were born–she would know. She didn't like it much when I pointed out that Hakan and I were both there too, but our memories aren't as certain," he said and the two broke into a fit of laughter.

As their cackling eased, Joule looked back at the academy building. "Isn't he excited at all for The Gifting tomorrow?" he asked the prince.

Fannar scrunched his freckled face in thought, "I think Hakan's too nervous to be excited."

"Mm," Joule grunted pensively, "I bet he'll get something cool like Bror."

"Oh, I hope he doesn't get that one!" Fannar exclaimed, "Can you imagine what lessons would be like if Hakan could influence emotions like Bror? He'd make me happy about studying and I'd end up working just as much as him and Shammoth!"

"Aargh! No!" Joule cried, covering his face in exaggerated despair as Shammoth and Hakan finally caught up with them.

"What's wrong with you now?" Shammoth demanded of Joule.

"Oi! Hakan!" Joule shouted as he jumped up and grabbed the startled prince by the shoulders, "you need to

5

swear you won't ever influence our emotions for academy work!" Joule ordered as he shook his bewildered friend.

"What?" Hakan gasped, looking in confusion from Joule to Fannar and back as he tried to keep his balance.

"Joule, why don't you wait until Hakan actually has a gift before you make him swear not to use it?" Shammoth suggested as Hakan freed himself from Joule's grip, "For all you know he'll get luminescence. The worst he could do with that is glow too bright at night when you two try sneaking into the kitchen when we stay over at the manor."

"Don't mock! Those midnight snack runs benefit us all," Joule argued, giving Shammoth a friendly shove.

"Did you make Fannar swear not to use a gift he may not get, too?" Shammoth teased.

"I don't think he'll need to worry about me." Fannar said, a hint of sadness in his voice. "I'll probably get a boring, common one like healing or a heightened sense of taste."

"You might get the plant one like my brother!" Joule excitedly interjected, "That one's actually really cool now that I've seen him use it during spars."

Shammoth scoffed at them. "You two are worried about the wrong thing, as usual."

Joule raised his eyebrows and Fannar scrunched up his face again at the declaration.

"How boring or common the gift is doesn't matter," Shammoth continued, "the only thing you *should* be hoping for is that you don't get one of the 'terrible trio' gifts."

"Why should we worry? Foresight and fire are both really, really, rare," Joule retorted in annoyance, "and after Moritz' gift, I doubt we'll see *any* of the rare ones this year, let alone one of those."

Chapter 1

Shammoth shrugged. "Maybe... maybe not. Like Fannar said, getting a heightened sense is pretty common, just because he got all five heightened it doesn't necessarily have to count as a rare gift."

"He's the first one in recorded history to have all five at the same time though!" Fannar argued. "If anything, it's the rarest of the rare gifts!"

"Telepathy isn't rare, though," Shammoth countered, "and no one in our generation has gotten it yet."

"Gah! Why do you always have to be such a downer, Shammoth?" Joule groaned, changing the subject.

"I'm just being realistic," Shammoth answered, sparking another debate between him and Joule.

As his friends bickered, Fannar looked over at his twin, who had gone unusually quiet. He was staring, unfocused, past Joule at the bustling road. Usually, Hakan was just as boisterous as himself and Joule when they all got together. This–this quiet, subdued behavior–was really out of character, and Fannar didn't like it. Glancing around, he quickly racked his brain for a way to snap his brother out of the glum mood. "All this talking's made me hungry!" he announced as he stood and stretched, "why don't we all go and see what pastries Mr. James' got at the bakery today?"

"Yeah, but none for the dark cloud!" Joule said, tousling Shammoth's hair.

"Not the hair!" Shammoth shouted, taking a retaliatory swipe at Joule's head and missing.

Joule once again took off running, this time with Shammoth on his heels, weaving between the other pedestrians and the electropods driving down the crowded street.

Fannar put an arm around his brother's shoulder and the two strolled along after their friends. "You good?" he asked in a concerned voice.

"Yeah," Hakan said dismissively.

Fannar paused, studying his brother's expression. "Liar," he finally said.

A small smile touched the corners of Hakan's mouth. "I *will* be fine," he corrected, giving his brother a sideways glance who squinted back disbelievingly at him. "I thought you said you were hungry?" Hakan asked, turning his gaze forward again.

"I am! And don't change the subject," Fannar replied, stubbornly determined to get to the bottom of what was bothering his twin.

"Well… how are you going to solve your hunger," Hakan said with a mischievous smile, "if I eat all the pastries before you get there!" he blurted before darting off.

"Hey, hey, hey!" Fannar called as he trailed behind his brother.

The two ran through the capital city streets, weaving between the surrounding people and vehicles for several minutes until they reached the bakery where their friends were already seated inside, cheerfully eating danishes.

"Awe! What's this?" Fannar asked, giving the baby ferret on Joule's lap a little scratch on its head.

"It's Mr. James' new pet." Joule mumbled through a mouth full of food, petting the fuzzy creature with his danish-free hand.

"What happened to the rabbit he had last week?" Fannar asked sadly.

"I made him a nice pen upstairs in the office!" called a voice from the back room.

Chapter 1

A thin, aging man with graying black hair, and a cheerful smile emerged, wiping his hands with a towel. "I figured you two weren't far behind when Shammoth and Joule showed up," he chuckled, picking up a basket full of danishes and holding it out to the princes. "Take your pick!" he said, smiling.

"Ooh!" Fannar squeaked, quickly snatching up the biggest one.

Hakan gingerly picked up a smaller one with extra red filling spilling over the top and took a bite. "Strawberry?" he excitedly asked from behind his hand, eyes full of joy.

"Mhm. Thought I'd make something special since you all have the gifting tomorrow," James replied, "and I remembered one of you said something about strawberry being your favorite," he added, winking at Hakan.

"Thank you!" Fannar said sweetly, looking over at Hakan. Strawberry was his brother's favorite, and he had mentioned it months earlier when James had made a batch of strawberry cheesecake rolls.

"Thank you," Hakan said politely, though noticeably deflated.

"Now," James said, looking around at the four teenagers, "I'm sure you're all very excited, but I hope none of you are putting *too* much thought into your gifting."

Shammoth rubbed his nose with a finger as he looked between Joule and Fannar, who were making nervous noises and trying to avoid eye contact with the wizened man.

While the two pretended like they hadn't been thinking about the gifting at all that day, Hakan swung his leg, trying to focus his attention on the ferret that was treating Joule like a climbing tree.

"Hmm," James grunted as he surveyed the boys. "You'll get what ya get, so no point in letting yourselves fret." He pointed a finger and said, "especially you, Hakan."

Hakan froze mid-leg-swing, and looked up at him in surprise, "why me?"

"I saw the same look on your dad's face when he came in here the day before his gifting," James answered.

Hakan took another bite of his danish and resumed swinging his leg, hyper aware of everyone's eyes on him. "I don't know what you're talking about," he said in the most casual voice he could muster.

"Is that so? Well then, I guess you're *not* worried that you won't get a useful gift that'll help you serve as king?" James replied knowingly.

"Nope," Hakan lied, mouth full as he stared determinedly at the floor.

"Good. 'Cause like I told your dad: being a good king has nothing to do with the gift you get. Even if you go through the falls and don't get any gift, just like a bunch of the kings and queens we've had, what makes a good king is a good heart."

Hakan stopped swinging his leg, and looked at Mr. James, doubt etched into his expression.

"I've watched you boys grow up," James said with a grandfatherly voice, "I know sometimes you've got a smart mouth... but you, Hakan, also have a *good heart*. And that good heart is going to make you a good king one day."

"What are you talking about?" Joule exclaimed. "He's not just gonna be good, he's gonna be great!" he insisted, springing from his seat, ferret in hand, over to Hakan and wrapping his free arm around the prince.

"Yeah, you've got nothing to worry about! Now if you were a slacker like Fannar..." Shammoth teased.

"Hey!" Fannar groaned indignantly but laughed all the same.

Hakan smiled as Shammoth continued to poke fun at Joule and Fannar's barely-acceptable study habits. After a few minutes, James offered them all a second danish, which they happily accepted, before he returned to the back of the shop. The boys lingered at the bakery taking it in turns to build up Hakan's confidence, and it wasn't long before he was back to his usual, cheerful self.

"Hey," Joule suddenly shouted amidst their chatter. "Chasan's gonna help me with sparring practice when I get home, I don't think he'd mind if you all wanted to come over and practice too." Joule told them.

"As tempting as that sounds," Shammoth replied, sounding a bit sarcastic, "I have to work at my parent's shop today. We just got a shipment of new processors in, and they want me to help with upgrade orders."

"I'll come," Hakan answered as he stretched.

"Yeah, me too. Mom and Dad're busy with the preparations for tomorrow, so we don't have much else the rest of the day." Fannar told his friend.

"We should also go by the academy on our way and ask Ismat if he wants to come," Hakan quickly suggested.

"Yeah, and let's bring him one of these," Joule added, popping over and grabbing another large, well-filled pastry. "He shouldn't have to miss out on them just because he's got the bad luck of being a year behind us."

Joule wrapped the treat in a delicate sheet of paper as he struck up a conversation with Shammoth about work at the tech shop, which the two continued as they left the bakery.

A few steps into following the others, Fannar noticed his brother wasn't behind him. As he spun around searching, he spotted Hakan behind the counter, quietly paying for everyone's food.

When he realized Fannar had caught him, Hakan raised a finger to his mouth, quickly finished at the register, and hurried to catch up to his brother.

"You know, Mr. James isn't going to be happy that you did that," Fannar said in a hushed tone as his twin strode closer.

"Which is why I didn't ask for permission," Hakan replied quietly, a sly smile on his face. "Besides," he continued, with a slight air of triumph, "I was just doing what my good heart told me to do. He can't get mad at me for that after his little speech."

"He probably still will though," Fannar pointed out, smiling broadly at him.

"Probably." Hakan said, beaming back at his brother, and the two headed out after their friends.

Chapter 2
FRIENDLY COMPETITION

Joule, Fannar, Hakan and Ismat walked along the wide, stone-paved road into the southern residential district, the youngest happily eating his danish. As they wound their way deeper and deeper into the large area, Fannar marveled at the timeline the houses made.

The closer to the city's center, the older and more hodge-podge the neighborhood block. The homes on the oldest streets still had some of their original, now often moss-covered stone walls that were upwards of 500 years old. Most of these houses had been slowly added to as the years went by; Some had timber additions that showed signs of being heavily patched as parts deteriorated, while others had instead stripped away the rotted wood ad-ons, replacing them with more modern steel and glass architectural styles.

During the reign of Fannar and Hakan's great-great-grandmother, the kingdom developed a deep appreciation for the beauty of nature. This appreciation was most heavily reflected in how all the architects since her reign had striven to make new structures disappear into the surroundings – each generation more successful than the last. Fannar looked around block after block, each road looking less and less inhabited despite being as crowded as any other before it.

As the four teenagers came to the end of the road, they were stopped by a tall, steel gate built into an equally tall, plant-covered fence. Joule stepped forward and placed his index finger on the scanner at the center of the broad piece of steel, which made a series of beeps before retracting to reveal a large yard shaded by the full canopies of several old trees.

They walked down a cobblestone path from the gate, and up a short, stone staircase to a wooden deck at the front of the house situated in the center of the property. The home itself was divided into three sections; both side sections were built out of wood and stone, and covered with vines and pockets of plants growing wherever enough dirt had managed to settle into a crevice. The center-front and back of the structure were made entirely of glass, which gave them all a full view of the living space inside.

"Did we beat him back?" Fannar asked, noticing the sitting room on the other side of the window-wall was empty.

Joule shrugged as he opened the glass door. "Hey! Chasan! You home yet?" he called as they entered the sitting room.

An affirmative noise came from the other side of the long, wood-plank wall that separated the sitting room from the kitchen-dining area, and everyone followed Joule to the other side where they found the older teenager sitting on the far side of the marble-topped island, his mouth full of food.

"How are you eating already?" Joule demanded, looking at his older brother in disbelief, "All the classes release at the same time! You couldn't've beat us here by more than a couple of minutes!"

Chasan fixed his little brother with a cocky expression on his matching round face as he swallowed his food. "Did you run here?" he asked in a haughty tone.

"No," Joule said as if this was the most absurd question his brother could ask.

"That," Chasan said, picking up a piece of fruit from his plate, "is why I'm almost done eating, while you all," he continued, waving a finger at the four of them, "are only just getting here."

Joule clicked his tongue at his older brother as he walked over to the cabinets to grab four drinking glasses.

"So did you forget you asked me to help you work on your sparring today?" Chasan teased as he chewed.

"No," Joule huffed, filling the glasses with water and passing them out to the others, "we just figured you wouldn't mind a few more people."

"Oh really?" Chasan asked, eyebrows raised, turning to look at the other three. "And how much are you all going to pay for my elite training services?" he quipped with a smirk.

"C'mon Chasan," Ismat groaned, dropping his head back in frustration.

"Isn't the love and appreciation we have for you enough?" Fannar enthusiastically implored, putting on a pitiful face.

Chasan sat back and watched the prince's expression grow sadder and sadder as he stared at him. "Oh, alright, alright!" he finally shouted in exasperation as he tossed the last piece of food into his mouth.

Fannar exclaimed and they all flung their arms around their defeated friend, loudly yelling their thanks.

"Okay! Okay!" Chasan yelled through the chaos, smiling shyly as he began cleaning up his place. "You know, Fannar, one of these days that look isn't gonna work on me," he shouted gruffly as he freed himself.

"Well today isn't that day!" Fannar triumphantly proclaimed, smiling brightly at his friend.

After he had finished cleaning up, Chasan brought them all back out front, where he lined them up in an open grassy area and led them through a series of stretches and warm ups. As the practice proceeded, the younger four made an extra effort to be respectful and take Chasan's instructions and corrections seriously.

Despite sounding boastful, Joule's brother was indeed considered to be an elite fighter. He was the best in hand-to-hand combat in the Honor Guard – a junior division for seventeen-year-olds who wanted to join one of the Ladothite Kingdom Guard divisions when they came of age at eighteen – and was even able to take on some of the City Guards that were several years older than himself.

"Alright, formation drills!" Chasan called out as they finished their last warm-up. He paired them off and worked on these for nearly half an hour before he was satisfied with their improvements. "Much better!" Chasan announced as his friends finished their last set. "Now, time to spar… Fannar and Ismat first."

Following instructions, Hakan and Joule moved to stand on the sideline beside Chasan, while the other two walked to the center of the practice area, exchanging a high-five before they squared off. Since Ismat's fighting skills were advanced enough to keep up with Fannar's, it made for an exciting practice match filled with many gasps and cheers from the onlooking friends. After a suspenseful ten minutes, Ismat won the match, the two shook hands, and Chasan went over what they did well and what needed improvement.

"Alright, switch out," Chasan instructed as he went back to the sideline.

Hakan and Joule switched places with the others, took their ready stances, and Chasan called the start. Joule made the first move, sending a jab at his friend's face, which Hakan deflected before throwing a punch towards Joule's mid-section. As he blocked the punch, Joule moved to send a kick at the prince's leg and whooped with excitement when Hakan barely dodged it.

A few moments later, Joule feinted a kick before attempting a quick strike to his friend's stomach, but once again missed the prince by a fraction of an inch. As the match went on, this happened again and again; Joule would attack and Hakan would barely escape in time.

Eventually, Joule sent a kick at the prince's head, but as Hakan suddenly leaned out of the way, he used the momentum to fluidly drop into a swipe at Joule's knee. Hakan's leg connected, and as Joule fell to the ground, the prince brought himself upright to crouch over him, an open hand inches from Joule's neck.

Fannar and Ismat cheered with surprise, as Chasan looked thoughtfully at his brother, then Hakan. Just as before, he gave encouragement and critique, but something felt off to him about the match. He dismissed the feeling and switched them out again. This time around, Fannar emerged the victor against Ismat.

After Chasan gave them their respective compliments and criticisms, he again switched out the fighters. As the second round between Joule and Hakan began, Chasan focused all of his attention on the prince. The match progressed with a sense of Deja-vu. From the beginning, it seemed like Joule clearly had the upper hand, but once again, at the last second, Hakan unexpectedly outmaneuvered him and won.

"Let's change-up partners." Chasan told them. "Fannar with Joule; Ismat with Hakan. You two first," he said, gesturing to his brother and the younger twin.

Despite the fatigue from the back-to-back matches, Joule did well... until about half-way through when Fannar seemed to get a second wind and started to out-maneuver him, eventually winning the fight.

"Switch!" Chasan immediately called before Joule had even stood back up.

They all looked at each other confused.

"I said switch!" Chasan bellowed again, more sternly than before.

They did as they were told, taking it in turns to shoot their older friend curious glances, and the new match began.

As Chasan watched, Ismat would attack and–just like in the previous fights–Hakan would barely make it out of the way in time. He continued to study the prince closely and realized something about his expression: it never changed.

Hakan never betrayed any sign of hesitation, surprise, or frustration. Several times it looked like Ismat was about to end the match, however the prince continued to look unconcerned. The younger fighter, on the other hand, would become more visibly frustrated following each attack that Hakan suddenly escaped. Then a moment came as the two circled each other when Chasan finally, for a split second, saw a change in Hakan's face – he looked sad.

Before Chasan could process what he had seen, though, Ismat landed a strong kick to the prince's chest, who tumbled backward to the ground.

Chapter 2

"Hakan!" Chasan shouted, staring angrily at the prince as the other four gaped at him.

Ismat quickly backed away as he and the others watched Chasan advance on the older twin still sitting on the ground. He turned to exchange bewildered expressions with the other two who had also been shocked into silence by their friend's sudden, and it their opinion unwarranted, hostility. Although Chasan could sound a bit aggressive when he got excited, they had never seen him behave so crossly towards any of them.

"Why are you holding back?" Chasan demanded as he stood over his friend.

"I'm not," Hakan argued evenly, refusing to make eye contact with his friend.

"Is that so?" Chasan asked doubtfully, and when the prince didn't respond, he sliced through the air at Hakan's head.

Hakan threw himself backwards, flat on the ground to avoid the strike, and kicked a leg up towards his friend. As Chasan pulled away, the prince used the momentum to send his other leg after the first, flipping himself backwards, and up to a standing position. His friend spun, aiming a kick at the prince, but Hakan was ready and easily blocked it.

This pattern of attack and evade continued, the intensity of the fight being amplified with every move Chasan made towards Hakan, and it didn't take long for the fight to go far beyond the skill levels of the three on the sideline.

Suddenly, Hakan fainted a punch at Chasan's head before he dropped, spinning as he went. The prince had finally taken the offensive, surprising his friend who barely dodged the unexpected swipe at his leg. Hakan kept the momentum of his kick going as he spun himself back to standing, and locked eyes with Chasan – the anger was gone, replaced with an amused and satisfied grin. There was a momentary pause as they surveyed each other and planned their next move.

Alright Hakan, Chasan thought as he noticed the beads of sweat forming on the prince's forehead, *Let's see just how much you've been holding back.*

His friend kicked at the prince's mid-section, but Hakan was ready. Quickly locking his left hand around Chasan's ankle, the prince heaved, rolling his body like a whip parallel along his friend to strike him hard across his back.

Chasan fumbled momentarily from the force of the hit before turning back to face Hakan, who was already advancing on him again. He watched as the prince jumped and twisted his body, bringing down a powerful kick which Chasan was forced to awkwardly dodge. After barely steadying himself in time to block the blow Hakan had immediately thrown following the kick, Chasan let out an impressed chuckle at his friend.

On the sidelines, Fannar, Joule, and Ismat stood speechless, their mouths falling as far as they could without disconnecting from their jaws. The back and forth between the two had gone on longer than any of the matches, and they watched in awe as Hakan and Chasan's arms became a blur of attacks. Eventually, Chasan broke the stalemate, landing a strong blow in the middle of Hakan's chest. As the prince stumbled backward, Chasan rushed him, jumping into a series of well aimed punches and his friend finally went down. The prince lay sprawled on the grass, panting, Chasan's fist an inch from Hakan's face.

Chapter 2

"That was amazing!" Joule howled as he and the other burst into roaring cheers.

"Well done!" came a voice from the gate.

Chasan extended his hand to Hakan and pulled him up to his feet as the newcomer approached them. A graying, sandy-haired, middle-aged man, with clean-shaven face and well-tailored clothes had arrived during the fight and watched from the gate.

"Of course, I'd expect nothing less from you Chasan, but Hakan!" The man said exuberantly, facing the teenager who was still trying to catch his breath. "That was very impressive!"

"Thank you, Councilman Leal," Hakan said, inclining his head in a small bow to his friends' father.

Leal smiled brightly at Hakan as he spoke. "Your father was telling me at one of the council meetings recently how you're one of the top students of your year at the academy," he said, sounding impressed, "and after watching that match, I'm thinking you must be a top fighter as well!"

"No doubt," Chasan said enthusiastically, giving Hakan an encouraging nudge.

"Very good!" Leal said as he gave the prince a pat on the shoulder "You're growing into a well-rounded young man, Hakan. You're going to make a fine leader someday." He turned his attention to Fannar, still smiling, "and what about you, young man?"

Fannar's grin slipped a little, and he laughed nervously as he waved his hands in embarrassment. "Let's just say I'm not excelling like my brother," he answered.

"I see," Leal said, giving Fannar a knowing look as the younger prince stuttered and fidgeted uncomfortably.

"Sir," Hakan interrupted, trying to move Leal's attention away from his brother, "since Chasan is such a strong fighter, are you going to let him tryout for one of the Guard divisions this summer?"

"Of course!" Leal exclaimed. "I'm actually surprised, given his level of talent, that your father didn't make an exception to let him tryout for the Royal Guard early like he did with Bror a few years ago."

"Yeah, but a lot of the guards ended up giving him trouble because he got special treatment – that's why Moritz didn't even ask about it the next year; he said it wasn't worth the hassle," Chasan said dismissively.

"Still…" Leal started to say, but trailed off, glancing around at them all. "Hmmm. I'm guessing, given the grass stains and dirt that I'm seeing on everyone that you've *all* been sparring?" He inquired; his face riddled with suspicion.

"Yes, sir," they said in unison.

"Out of curiosity," Leal said, looking bemusedly at his sons, "did you two get your chores done before you started?"

"No," Chasan admitted guiltily.

"And am I also right in guessing the three of you have chores you're neglecting as well?" he asked, eying his son's friends.

"Yes, sir," Ismat, Fannar and Hakan said together, trying to suppress their own guilty smiles.

"Well, then," Leal said in a kind yet firm tone to his older son, "I think this would be a good point for you to call it a day." He gave Chasan a wink and headed towards the house, calling jovially over his shoulder as he climbed the steps, "straight to work after you say your goodbyes, boys."

"Yes, sir." Chasan and Joule replied and exchanged their farewells, before Fannar, Hakan, and Ismat made their way back down the cobblestone path and out the gate.

"So…" Fannar mused as they walked down the road towards the city's center, "When were you planning to tell us you could fight like that?" he said, grinning at his brother.

"Yeah, you were incredible!" Ismat added excitedly.

Hakan's ears turned pink from their praise. "It's not a big deal," he mumbled, looking down at the ground.

"Not a big deal?" Fannar said, almost screaming the words, "Chasan's never gone that hard on any of us before!".

"And you took him on for a solid ten minutes," Ismat added, still thoroughly impressed.

"No it was fifteen, at least!" Fannar enthusiastically insisted, "and you'd've probably gone longer if you hadn't already fought three times before that!"

"Hey," Ismat mumbled, suddenly looking crestfallen. "You let me win during our match, didn't you?"

"No," Hakan argued, still not looking at either of them.

"After seeing how you fought Chasan, there's no way I'd be able to beat you," Ismat contended, "I may be ahead for my year, but I'm nowhere near *that* advanced." He waited for his friend to respond, but Hakan remained silent, and Ismat let out a frustrated sigh. "I want to earn my wins, Hakan," Ismat told him sternly, "I don't want any of you going easy on me."

"You don't have to worry about me, Iz," Fannar said, cheerfully putting his arm around Ismat's shoulder.

"Oh I'm not," Ismat assured him with a chuckle, "You and Joule are too competitive when it comes to spars to throw a match just to save my feelings."

"You've really improved a lot this year, you know. I had a hard time beating you, that second time around," Fannar told him as he beamed encouragingly.

Hakan slowed to a stop, frowning at the ground, causing the other two to look at him with confused expressions. "I'm sorry, Iz." he said softly, finally looking up at his friend, eyes full of remorse.

Ismat smiled and stepped over to stand directly in front of the older twin. "You're forgiven," he said warmly. "Just don't do it again," he added with a smirk as he poked the prince in the chest.

They resumed their trek, and Fannar and Ismat went back to animatedly discussing Hakan's match with Chasan, pausing only briefly to decline an invitation from their classmates to join a game. Hakan had to listen to the two recounting their favorite moments of the fight right up until they parted ways, Ismat turning to head to the western residential district and the brothers continuing towards the market.

"You know," Hakan said a few minutes after they had left their friend, "everyone brought up an important point today."

"Oh?" Fannar murmured curiously, "what point?"

Hakan paused momentarily, suppressing a smile before he answered, "your study habits are terrible."

"Agh!" Fannar groaned, rolling his head back just as Hakan had earlier in the classroom, "not you too!"

"How am I supposed to appoint you as a council member someday if you're constantly slacking off with

Chapter 2

your academy work?" Hakan asked, his tone and expression serious.

"Don't." Fannar replied dismissively.

"No," Hakan argued, "I know you don't wanna hear it bu–"

"No," Fannar cut him off. "I mean: don't appoint me," he explained.

The words had come out of his brother's mouth as nonchalantly as if he'd told Hakan about the weather. "What?" Hakan asked blankly, hoping he had misunderstood.

Fannar shrugged. "Don't appoint me to the council," he replied evenly.

After a few moments, Fannar noticed he was walking alone. As he spun around, he saw his twin frozen mid-step, looking hurt and lost for words. He walked back and placed a comforting hand on his brother's shoulder. "I do *want* to be on your council," Fannar explained, "I just don't feel like I *need* to be."

"But," Hakan went to argue.

"You're. My. Brother." Fannar continued explaining slowly, punctuating each word. "I will always be here for you whenever you need me, and I don't need a title to do that or to know how important I am to you."

Hakan stared back at him, overwhelmed, before being pulled into a hug. "*I* need you on the council, though," he half-croaked as he brother held on tightly to him.

Fannar closed his eyes and sighed. "Alright, this fall I'll start working as hard as you and Shammoth... okay?"

"Really?" Hakan asked skeptically.

"I promise..." Fannar said sincerely, letting go of Hakan, "now, we'd better get home. I don't want mom and dad to find out we went sparring before chores and get stuck detailing the state dining hall as punishment again."

Hakan cringed at the memory of scrubbing and scraping every inch of the large, intricately carved table with tiny cleaning tools, and the two raced the rest of the way back to the Royal Manor.

Chapter 3

THE GIFTING CEREMONY

The night dragged on and on for Fannar. He was so excited that he barely slept, and as soon as he saw the first rays of sun slip through the cracks of the curtain, he sprang up and went to wake his brother. Hakan, however, was far less excited, and groaned as Fannar insistently shook him back and forth.

"C'mon Hakan, get up already!" Fannar urged after a few fruitless shakes.

Hakan rolled over to face his brother and opened his eyes a fraction. "It's barely sunrise!" he huffed.

"So?" Fannar asked, undeterred.

"So the ceremony isn't for hours!" he grumbled, swatting a hand at Fannar, "Go back to sleep."

Fannar grabbed Hakan's hand and pulled, determined to drag him out of bed. "I can't sleep!" he told him as he tugged, "C'mon, let's go eat and head down early!"

Hakan squinted up at him. "You go, I'll sleep," he replied, shaking his arm free, rolling back over and covering his head with his blanket.

"Ugh!" Fannar groaned before he resumed shaking his brother. "Everyone always gets there early, though! We can go and hang out with the others before the ceremony starts," he excitedly told his brother, who merely grunted another refusal at him from beneath the covers.

"Pleeeeeeaaaaassseeeee," Fannar whined, now climbing on top of his brother, "Haaaaakkaaaaaaannnn, pleeeeaaassseee get up!" he begged as he crushed his twin.

"Fine!" Hakan muffly exclaimed before flipping the blankets off to reveal his irritated face.

While his brother jumped up and ran to the wardrobe to begin rummaging for clothes, Hakan gave a deep stretch, purposefully taking his time getting out of bed. By the time the older prince finally stood, his twin was already dressed in his best white button-down shirt with a tan loose-knit sweater over it.

Fannar was in the process of fastening a black belt around the waistband of his fitted black jeans when Hakan finally shuffled over to the wardrobe, pulling out a snug, black sweater for himself, along with his dark blue jeans and his favorite oversized white button down.

While his brother dressed, Fannar quickly put on his shoes and hurried over to the mirror to fix the delicate diadem he always wore for kingdom ceremonies across his forehead. After double-checking that the twisted golden wires were centered properly, he turned to impatiently stare at his sluggish brother. He was sure it took Hakan an *actual* eternity to finish getting ready and put on the silver, diamond-covered double-banded diadem that signified him as the successor.

No sooner had Hakan turned away from the mirror, than his brother had grabbed him by the arm and began dragging him out the door and downstairs to the manor's kitchen. They greeted and thanked the cook as he happily filled their plates with all of the princes' favorite foods. As Fannar and Hakan cheerfully carried their spoils into the

Chapter 3

dining room, they found their father already seated at the table.

King Eero lifted his slender face from his breakfast, and teasingly questioned them, "What are you two doing up so early?"

Fannar laughed sheepishly as they set their food down. "Uhhh," he sputtered, too embarrassed to share his eagerness for the ceremony with his father.

"He wants to go out to the Falls early," Hakan said, a satisfied look on his face as he took a bite from one of the large strawberries on his plate.

"I see." Eero said, smiling, "well, I hope you two have a good time with your friends."

Fannar's embarrassment instantly melted, and he turned to triumphantly beam at his brother, who rolled his eyes in return as he continued eating his strawberries.

"Uh, Fannar," Eero continued, a mischievous look in his round, blue eyes as he stared at his younger son, "since you seem to know how to wake up early for things now, I expect this same enthusiasm for timeliness when it comes to the Academy going forward," he said, the corners of his mouth creeping into a grin.

Fannar's mouth fell open slightly as he suddenly realized the trap he had accidentally created for himself. "Yes, sir," he replied, scrunching his face and poking disappointedly at his food while Eero chuckled sympathetically and Hakan smirked.

Fannar's disappointment only lasted a few bites, however, as the fluffy pancakes that had been piled onto his plate quickly reinvigorated his good mood and rushed pace. Hakan, on the other hand, dragged out their meal until he could no longer stand Fannar's insistent and repeated inquiries of 'are you finished yet'.

After cleaning their places, they left the Royal Manor, and made their way westward through the market district and the closest Underground Tram station.

Hakan and Fannar walked through the busy streets, ignoring the out-of-towners who gawked when they realized who the twins were. On their way, they passed several families leaving one of the city's nearby inns with their own impatient teenagers–all insisting, like Fannar, their families needed to move faster. Shortly after, the brothers joined the throng of people turning down a packed stairway to a bustling underground platform where an electric tram was filling with people to transport to the other side of the capital.

"Looks like City Guard's got their hands full this year," Hakan remarked, looking around at the uniformed men and women directing foot traffic around the platform.

"Mhm" Fannar agreed, standing on his tiptoes to see over the surrounding people.

He was able to spot five City Guards, all in their standard black cargo pants, fitted black shirts, and royal blue vests.

Despite how crowded the platform was, both Fannar and Hakan were able to make it onto the first tram and were quickly transported to the station on the far side of the city. They plodded along with the other passengers up and out to the city streets and continued their trek westward. As Fannar and Hakan reached the edge of the city, they waved their greetings to the Guards flanking the broad dirt road before breaking into a run.

They darted across the large field that sat between the capital perimeter and the forest that surrounded the waterfall site of the ceremony, avoiding the other groups of people who had been walking leisurely on the road ahead of them. Hakan and Fannar slowed their sprint as they entered the tree line, winding along the road that twisted and snaked through the trunks and roots until they reached the meadow clearing of the Gifting Falls, where they began searching through the faces of the other early-arrivers.

"Finally!" they heard Joule shout off to their left, standing with his mother, father, and brother at the edge of the clearing. "What took you so long?" he asked incredulously.

"Hakan took forever to eat breakfast!" Fannar complained, shooting an annoyed glance at his brother.

"I was savoring my food," Hakan haughtily replied, still searching through the people gathered in the meadow.

"You couldn't've savored faster?" Fannar exclaimed, his voice thick with playful annoyance.

"Is anyone else here yet?" Hakan asked, ignoring his brother.

"No, not yet," Councilman Leal answered, shaking his head sleepily.

"Moritz and Bror won't be here until closer to the ceremony," Chasan reminded, "they're part of the King and Queen's guard detail today."

"Ah!" Fannar exclaimed in disappointment, smacking his hand to his forehead, "I forgot they'd be working."

"Who's working?" Shammoth asked as he calmly walked up behind them.

"Bror and Moritz," Hakan sighed. "What're *you* doing here so early?" He inquired, raising an eyebrow at Shammoth and filling with disappointment as it now seemed that another of the prince's friends had succumbed to the anticipation of the ceremony.

"My parents help run the capital's broadcast system, remember? We had to get here early for them to run all the checks with the equipment," Shammoth explained snippishly, guessing the reason behind Hakan's disapproving tone. "Mom said there hasn't been a single issue with the live-stream to the other cities and villages since she got involved and she plans to keep it that way."

"Oh yeah," Hakan acknowledged with a hint of embarrassment.

"No Iz yet?" Shammoth asked them, as he searched the crowd.

"Not yet," Fannar answered glumly, glancing around at the steadily growing number of families. "Oh!" he said abruptly, turning back to the group, "Did you all see that Avol City beat Cerra Town in the game last night?"

"Yeah," Shammoth replied, "so disappointing."

"I thought after Measham switched to Cerra's team that they were finally going to have a shot at going to the tournament this year," Hakan said, dispirited.

"It was just a pre-game," Chasan pointed out, jumping into the conversation.

"Don't forget, several of the top teams had a bunch of their best players retire last season," Councilman Leal added, "there's no telling how their replacements will affect the team dynamics."

"Yeah," Joule said thoughtfully, "but Thuin was the top recruit this year, and he joined Lynna City."

"Mhm," Fannar grunted in agreement, "an addition like him pretty much guarantees that Lynna will at the very least make it to the finals; honestly, I won't be surprised if they win the tournament again this fall."

Over the next two hours, the six of them debated and speculated what the sport's new season would bring as

Chapter 3

more families arrived, creating a sea of people that filled the meadow well into the tree line. Finally, with little more than twenty minutes left until the ceremony, Ismat arrived.

"Where have you been?" Joule demanded with an insulted expression.

Ismat looked around guiltily at his friends. "Sorry," he sighed sheepishly, "I overslept."

"Must've been nice," Hakan quipped, glancing at his brother, "*Fannar* made sure *I* couldn't sleep-in this morning."

Fannar groaned and threw his head back as he spoke. "You can sleep in next year!" he exasperatedly exclaimed.

"I think we should *all* sleep in next year," Shammoth added with a sly expression. "Since it'll be Ismat's gifting, I think we should all only get here *right before the ceremony starts*... just like Ismat did for us," he explained, placing a hand on his friend's shoulder as others replied their ardent agreement.

"Ha ha," Ismat said in a sarcastic, sing-song voice. "The important thing is that I'm here, and in plenty of time to see you all go through the falls."

"Someone giving you a hard time, Iz?" Bror suddenly said from directly behind Fannar, causing the prince to jump in surprise.

Moritz stretched his arms threateningly beside Bror as he asked, "which one of you was it?"

The two were an imposing sight clad in the uniform of the Ladothite Royal Guard; with black boots, burgundy fitted pants with a leather holster strapped on one leg, and a fitted shirt with asymmetrical color-blocks of burgundy and black. As they stared harshly at their younger friends, Joule, Shammoth, and Hakan hastily pointed to Fannar.

Moritz lunged forward and effortlessly caught the younger twin in a headlock.

"Hey!" Fannar yelped. "You're supposed to *protect* the royal family!" he spluttered as Moritz carefully pulled his arm tighter around the prince.

"I am," Moritz said calmly, looking down at the top of Fannar's head. "I'm protecting you from your own foolishness," he told the prince as he lifted his face up to smirk at the rest of his friends.

The others sniggered as Fannar struggled in vain against the guard's strong hold, and Bror turned from the spectacle, a bright grin on his face. "How long have you all been waiting here?" he asked as his laughter subsided.

"You don't want to know," Leal remarked with a pained expression, looking over at Joule who turned pink.

"We were the first ones here," Chasan informed them, enjoying the embarrassment that outing his brother caused.

"Oh no!" Bror cried sympathetically, "why am I not surprised?"

Moritz let out a breathy chuckle. "Because it's Joule," he teased, finally releasing Fannar as Joule scrunched his mouth into a pout at the continued jokes over his eagerness.

As they exhausted their jabs at him, Moritz' eyes unfocused, and he turned an ear in the direction of the main path. "You all should start heading to the front," he said, turning back to them, "The King and Queen are coming across the field now."

Everyone nodded, and Joule's mom gave him and his father a hug, before she and Chasan said their 'good lucks' to the four friends who'd be partaking in the ceremony. Hakan, Joule, Fannar and Shammoth started

Chapter 3

making their way with Councilman Leal through the crowd of families towards the river opposite the tree line, while Bror and Moritz left to take up their guard positions along the path through the meadow.

As the twins and their friends wove their way between the onlookers, Hakan noticed several of the council members were already inside the large cave carved into the mountainside behind the waterfall.

Nearest the entrance was Councilman Kesavan, a tall man with long, black hair and an elegant manner, talking with Councilman Sythe, who stood almost a full head shorter than him. Scythe's tan, scruffy face filled with delight as they spoke, and they could hear Kesavan's distinct laughter over the crowd several times. Beside Kesavan and Sythe stood Councilwoman Damra and Councilwoman Haldis who represented extreme opposites among the advisors. While Damra, the youngest member of the council, smiled and waved with a palpable warmth and kindness at the younger generation, Haldis–the eldest council member– sternly scrutinized the teenagers packed around the river's edge.

The four friends stopped when they reached the crowd of peers who would be receiving gifts, however Councilman Leal continued slowly working his way through the sea of youngsters towards the cave entrance, where The Royal Guard protecting it gave him a small bow and stepped aside. Leal had barely greeted Kesavan and Sythe when the people at the back of the meadow began to cheer.

They all turned to see Councilwoman Basilah, Leader of the Royal Guard, leading King Eero and Queen Irina through the excited throng and towards the cave, with Councilman Naukaron, Deputy Chief of the City Guard, following closely behind them. The King and Queen smiled kindly at the crowd as they passed, their grins broadening when they reached Bror and Moritz.

The expression of affection for the two guards was nothing compared to the way Irina's face lit up when she finally spotted her sons, who were jumping up and down and fervently waving at her from among the sea of teenagers. Her eyes glistened as her gaze lingered on the boys, her heart overflowing as she took in their father's blonde hair and blue irises, the sole features they had inherited from him.

Once Irina, Naukaron, and Basilah were inside the cave, Eero turned to the waiting crowd and, with a warm smile, raised a hand for quiet.

"Welcome," Eero said cheerfully, his voice amplified through the well-camouflaged speakers placed throughout the meadow, "Welcome Ladothite to the Annual Gifting Ceremony!" As the teenagers gathered around the riverbank broke into shouts and cheers once again, Eero grinned at them all, and patiently gestured for them to settle. "I can see everyone is excited and ready to get started, so I promise we'll keep the speech as brief as possible." He assured them before taking a step back and motioning to Irina.

The queen stepped forward, beaming at all the young faces along the river as she spoke. "For over two thousand years, this waterfall has, on the first day of spring, given the people of our kingdom extraordinary abilities. It has become a right of passage for the young men and women of Ladothite to pass through and receive a special talent to help them better serve their communities."

She turned and nodded to Councilman Sythe, who began moving his hands and arms in a smooth, flowing

Chapter 3

pattern. As he moved, a beautiful bridge made of strong, woven vines grew from the mouth of the cave, and passed through the waterfall, before curving back over to the riverbank.

"In a few moments, we will begin calling the names of those who will walk through the Gifting Falls. You will join us in here," she said, gesturing to the cave, "then walk through the falls and return to the riverbank. At this point, you will demonstrate the ability you've been given. Now, we always have at least one of you who will go through the falls and come out without a new ability. Remember, while we call these 'the Gifting Falls', it cannot give the gift that Ladothite values above all else: The gift of a good heart. The ability to show compassion and make good choices makes someone a gift to Ladothite, and this is not something the falls can give you. For those who do possess a good heart, you have always been, and will continue to be, a gift to this kingdom."

As the queen finished, the crowd erupted with applause and Eero re-joined her at the cave entrance, both turning their gaze on Hakan.

While the families filling the meadow all cheered at her words, Fannar wrapped an arm around his brother and squeezed.

Hakan's eyes glistened. While their mother may have started her speech off speaking to everyone, he and his brother knew she had said the last part especially for her anxious son. "Did you say something to her?" he asked, glancing suspiciously at his brother.

"It's mom…" Fannar replied, his voice full of admiration as he rested his chin on his twin's shoulder, "I didn't have to."

"And with that," King Eero shouted over the noise, "let's begin!"

The swell of applause in the meadow was deafening as Eero and Irina moved back into the cave to join the semi-circle the council members had formed leading to the waterfall. Haldis then stepped forward and began reading the names in birth order.

People had come from all over the kingdom, and despite not knowing most of them, it was still a thrill to see what ability everyone received. The boys clapped politely for each of the unknown teenagers, however—when those from their Academy showed what they had been gifted—Fannar, Hakan, and Joule absolutely roared with enthusiasm.

Over two dozen classmates went through the falls before them. One came out as a speed-gifted, another became a water-gifted, while two who passed through turned out to be wind-gifteds. Everyone in the crowd gasped in amazement when a classmate revealed they had been given the uncommon gift of intangibility, while others became either healers, animal communicators, or received either heightened sight, smell, taste, hearing or touch.

"Joule Bedraget," Haldis announced.

Joule excitedly maneuvered his way through the thinned-out group of teenagers and up to the cave, returning his father's beaming smile as he quickly walked past the council. After taking a deep breath, he stepped timidly forward through the water pouring from the rocks above. He paused momentarily to push his soaking wet bangs out of his face with a shiver, before crossing the remainder of the bridge back to the riverbank. The anxious crowd waited as he closed his eyes and focused.

Chapter 3

After a few moments, Joule's eyes flew open and he whirled around to smile at his father, then back at his friends. He held both hands in front of him, palms facing each other, and within moments, surges of electricity began shooting back and forth between them. Shammoth gave a whoop, while Hakan and Fannar screamed, jumping up and down with uncontainable elation; their friend had received one of the most hoped-for of the common gifts.

As Joule began making his way back through the crowd, Haldis called the next name. "Hakan Aimakos."

The older twin froze at the sound of his name before snapping his head from Joule to where Haldis stood. Shammoth gave him a shove, and he stumbled forward a few steps, hearing his heart pounding in his ears as it raced in his chest. Panicked, he looked back at his brother, who was smiling encouragingly at him.

"Go on," Fannar mouthed as he waved him forward. However, his twin didn't move towards the cave.

Instead, Hakan walked back over to his brother, his expression pleading. "Together?" he asked, his voice shaking nervously.

"Together," Fannar replied reassuringly, giving Hakan a gentle pat on the shoulder.

Hakan turned back around, and he and Fannar walked through the excitedly whispering crowd. As they approached the entrance of the cave, they expected Haldis to look upset that they were breaking with tradition and going in together. Instead, the normally stone-faced Academy Headmistress had a soft, understanding expression, and said nothing as they stepped past her and into the cave. Irina rubbed each of their arms lovingly as they passed, while their father and the other council members nodded at them in turn.

Stopping in front of the waterfall, Fannar leaned over to his brother. "I'll just be one step behind you," he whispered.

Hakan swallowed hard, took a deep breath, and tilted his head down as he stepped through the falls. As he came out the other side, he understood why Joule and the others had shivered – The water was like ice as it landed on Hakan, soaking his hair and clothes. Just a step behind him, as promised, his sopping wet brother emerged from the falls as well.

Fannar pushed his drenched hair out of his face and grinned from ear to ear at his brother. Hakan paused, puzzled by Fannar's reaction (or rather lack of reaction) to the freezing water, until his brother motioned for him to keep moving. Unlike Hakan and the others, Fannar wasn't shivering at all. In fact, he looked like he'd just taken a refreshing swim, and the thought continued to distract Hakan as he stepped off the bridge.

"Together?" Fannar asked brightly, bringing Hakan back to the present.

"Together," Hakan replied quietly, the corners of his mouth lifting in a small smile.

They closed their eyes and concentrated. The moment the water had touched them, they had felt a change in their bodies. A surge of energy had woken deep inside and swept through them. They focused on that energy, gathering it, as they held their hands out, palms skyward. Both could feel it swirling down their arms, and as they opened their eyes, they released it, extending the still spiraling energy beyond their hands.

Instead of the cheers and applause that everyone else had received, however, the twin's display was met with gasps and anxious muttering.

Chapter 3

Fannar's initial excitement from seeing the swirl of snow flurries twisting up from his hands was rapidly destroyed as he realized what had come from his brother.

Beside Fannar, Hakan had instantly gone numb. He stood, paralyzed, arm still extended, staring at his open hand. All his senses had shut down. He no longer heard the whispers or saw the pointing from the crowd, and no longer felt the cold of his still dripping clothes. He felt hollow. All he could do was replay the moment over and over in his mind: A plume of fire bursting from his hand and swirling towards the sky like a phoenix.

Hakan was now a fire-gifted.

Chapter 4
CHOICES

Two days later, Hakan sat in his usual spot at the back corner of the classroom beside his brother, trying his best to take his typical, detailed notes as he followed along on his digi-pad. However, he couldn't shake the constant feeling that there were several sets of eyes boring into him as he scribbled. To his left, his brother was making a concerted effort to pay attention and had even taken several notes – although at least one said "ask Hakan to explain" with an arrow pointing to a circled paragraph. As he attempted to refocus on the instructor's droning economics lesson, his brother's stomach gave an audible growl, and they exchanged amused glances as they suppressed a much-needed laugh.

Afraid of the kingdom's reaction to his fire gift, Hakan had shut himself away in the manor since the ceremony, hoping to avoid the unpleasant repercussions that came with having such a despised gift. Unfortunately, he couldn't escape the enmity it spurred in others entirely, since the manor always had people coming and going from it. Staff, guards, council members, and other officials were constantly filtering through, and every interaction the prince had with them following the gifting ended the same– with a saddened Hakan.

Chapter 4

It didn't help that, since the ceremony had been broadcast across the kingdom, additional village and city leaders who rarely visited the capital were coming to speak to the king with abnormally high frequency – and all now hurried uneasily away if they spotted Hakan nearby.

The most heartbreaking incident Hakan endured was when he and his brother bumped into Councilman Sythe leaving a meeting with their father. Instead of the lengthy and jovial conversation he normally struck up with the twins, Sythe had been tense and near monosyllabic as he hastily bid them farewell before rushing out of the manor.

The end-of-period chimes sounded, and the boys began closing down their digi-pads. As he packed his things back into his bag, Hakan raised his head to look for his friends, but instead of spotting them had his earlier suspicions confirmed. No less than three teenagers had nervously, and hurriedly, looked away from him.

Grrroooowwwwwwwlll.

"Is that *your* stomach, Fannar?" Joule called, still a row away, as he pushed through the other students.

"Maybe," Fannar replied, his cheeks going pink.

"Overslept again?" Shammoth asked with an amused smile as he joined them.

Fannar pushed his cheek out with his tongue, fighting a smile, which Shammoth took as a silent confirmation.

"C'mon, we better get Fannar some lunch before someone mistakes his stomach for a bear running loose through the academy," Joule said jokingly.

"Ha ha," Fannar replied gruffly, grabbing his bag and following everyone from the room.

As they made their way down to the cafeteria, people behaved exactly how the Royal Guard and council members had when they spotted Hakan. Students and staff alike scurried away and avoided eye-contact with him, or suddenly remembered they needed to be anywhere else but in his vicinity. And when the prince and his friends ordered their food, the small, older woman behind the serving counter trembled as she filled his tray.

None of this went unnoticed by Fannar and the others either, and the younger twin quickly suggested they find Ismat and all take their food outside on the pretense of enjoying the nice spring weather. Everyone eagerly agreed, and soon they were settled around the trunk of a large sprawling oak in front of the Academy and attempting to convince Hakan – and themselves – that they were overthinking people's behavior.

"They've probably always been weird around you two because you're the princes and we just never paid attention to it," Shammoth offered, trying to excuse the behavior.

"Yeah!" Joule agreed enthusiastically, "we're probably reading too much into it."

"Maybe," Hakan mumbled, sounding unconvinced.

As the five of them finished their meal, Joule noticed several students starting up a derbala game in a grassy area across from the academy.

"Oh!" Joule exclaimed after counting the students. "They're short players," He said excitedly, tapping Hakan, "let's go play!"

"You go," Hakan sulked, "I'll stay here and watch."

"No way!" Joule told him, grabbing both his and Fannar's arms and dragging them along.

Chapter 4

As they walked over, the players quickly huddled together, shifting their weight uncomfortably as Joule and his friends stopped a few feet from them.

"Can we join?" Joule asked cheerfully. "I saw you're short a few people."

The nervous teens exchanged glances with each other.

Finally, a tall boy with curly brown hair that they recognized from Chasan's year answered, "You two can," he said cautiously, indicating Joule and Fannar before he pointed at Hakan, "but not him."

"Why not?" Fannar asked apprehensively.

"You know why not," the boy darkly replied.

"No, I don't," Fannar answered, feigning ignorance, "Hakan's a good player, there's no reason not to..."

"He's too dangerous." a girl at the back of the group squeaked, immediately regretting the attention it brought to herself.

"That's ridiculous," Joule said dismissively.

"Fannar and Joule could do just as much damage with their gifts," Shammoth said as he and Ismat joined the conversation, "that's what this is about, right? *Hakan's* gift? If you think Hakan's too dangerous, then you must think Joule and Fannar are dangerous too, right?"

"It's different with them," another boy declared.

"How?" Fannar demanded, anger creeping into his voice.

"It's different," the tall boy coolly explained, "because most electric and ice-gifteds don't turn into torturers and killers; and every fire-gifted has. In fact," he continued, now looking Hakan up and down, "the fire-gifteds have all been the worst of them."

"You're all being stupid," the normally non-confrontational Ismat said boldly, surprising them all. "Hakan's not some sort of power-hungry maniac who's going to abuse his gift."

"We don't know that," the tall boy said haughtily, "for all we know he's going to massacre another city someday, just like the last fire-gifted did."

"Hakan would never do anything like that!" Joule argued furiously.

The tall boy gave him a smug look, "of course you'd feel that way," he reasoned, "you're one of the few people deemed worthy of precious prince Hakan's time, unlike the rest of us who aren't even good enough for him to say hello to most days."

"You–" Fannar began furiously, taking a threatening step forward, but Hakan grabbed him by the shoulder.

"Adrig!" Chasan shouted fiercely at the tall boy from the top of the Academy steps.

The two stared at each other for several long, tense moments before the chimes signaling the end of the lunch break sounded, and the fearful teenagers hurried in a wide circle around the princes and their friends. Adrig was the last to leave, giving them all a look of deep contempt as he passed, a look which Chasan unflinchingly returned before following him into the building.

As Hakan watched the scared students leave, he felt a sudden chill at his side. When he looked down, he saw that Fannar's hands were clenched in tight fists and covered with a layer of frost. He looked at the others and found varying degrees of the same anger and frustration etched into each of their expressions as they stared after Adrig.

Chapter 4

"Let's go," Hakan said, trying not to show his own disappointment and frustration, "or we'll be late for the next lesson."

The rest of their classes were a slow-moving blur. None of them could focus on what was being taught, only the interaction with their peers. Mixed feelings of anger and incredulity continued to bubble up in everyone but Hakan, who kept swinging between guilt and hopelessness. Not only was he being treated differently now because of his gift, but his friends were being affected by it too.

The final class chimes rang, and the four boys hurriedly packed before rushing out of the classroom and directly into Chasan, who was waiting just outside the door.

"What's up?" Joule asked his brother, suspiciously.

Chasan's expression was unreadable as he spoke. "You going over to the Royal Manor?" He asked his brother evenly.

"Yes. We always go over to Fannar and Hakan's the first day of the week," Joule replied firmly, "we're not gonna change that just because Ha–"

"Good." Chasan interjected, a slight smirk touching the corner of his mouth, "Go pick up Ismat and get going," he told them with a short nod before briskly walking away.

"What was that about?" Fannar asked as he watched Chasan quickly stride down the hall, completely perplexed by the strange interaction.

Joule turned around, his face a mirror of Fannar's confusion, "no idea," he muttered, looking back the way Chasan had left, "c'mon, let's go find Iz."

They found their younger friend in the crowd of students making their way from the various classrooms and recounted the exchange with Chasan as the five of them trudged their way back to the manor.

"He probably just wanted to make sure we weren't going to let Adrig get to us," Ismat offered thoughtfully.

"Chasan should know that nothing any idiot says would have any effect on us," Shammoth huffed, a hint of disappointment in his voice.

"Exactly," Joule agreed, throwing one arm around Hakan's shoulder and the other around Fannar's, eliciting appreciative smiles from them both.

Once they entered the walls of the Royal Manor, their nerves quickly eased as they fell into their familiar afternoon routine. Ismat prompted a race to the boys' room where they all cheerfully piled their bags onto Hakan's bed before heading down to the kitchen for a snack. They walked down the halls carrying their handfuls of food, leisurely making their way to the open-air courtyard at the center of the manor. As they reached the courtyard steps, though, their blissful bubble was burst by the sight of Bror, Moritz and Chasan waiting for them at the center of the lush, foliage-filled space.

"What, none for us?" Moritz said jokingly, as the stunned group reached them.

"What're you all doing here?" Fannar asked, confused.

Bror smiled warmly at them. "Well, Moritz doesn't start his shift for a few hours, and I had the day off from guard duty, so Chasan thought it might be fun for the three of us to train you all with your new gifts."

"Fun?" Hakan repeated skeptically.

"Yeah, fun," Moritz said cheekily, "you've only had your powers a couple of days, so I imagine as soon as you start trying to use them, there's going to be some entertaining results... especially you," he said, smirking at Shammoth, "I can't wait to see you half-transformed."

Chapter 4

"I'm looking forward to seeing Joule shock himself," Chasan added, rubbing his hands together gleefully.

Bror chuckled. "C'mon, be nice guys."

"Ugh, alright," Moritz pouted, "let's get started, then...you first," he told Fannar.

"Huh?" Fannar grunted, mouth full from shoveling down his food, "Why me?"

Moritz tilted his head to the side, gave Fannar an intense glare and said, "because I said so."

Fannar whimpered and gloomily handed the rest of his food to Ismat, who went back with Hakan, Shammoth and Joule to sit on the steps.

"Now," Bror said, clapping his hands together, "all of you already know how to sense and gather the energy generated by your gift, obviously, since that's how you displayed them at the ceremony. The first thing we need to do today is see just how much of that energy each of you is starting with."

Fannar looked apprehensively at him, "so... you want me to..."

"Gather every last drop of that energy and release it all at once, yes." Bror nonchalantly finished.

"O-okay," Fannar stuttered, as Bror took him by his shoulders and positioned him in front of a small tree nearby, giving him an encouraging pat as he released him.

Everyone watched as Fannar took slow, deliberate breaths. As he breathed, he brought his hands up to chest height, one hovering over the other. He opened his eyes, extended his arms towards the small tree and a blast like a concentrated blizzard rained from his hands, encasing the trunk and several lower branches in ice.

Ismat, Joule and Hakan applauded Fannar's display, while Shammoth nodded encouragingly.

"Not bad!" Bror praised, smiling broadly and giving Fannar a gentle shake and another pat on the back before sending him off towards the steps.

"Joule," Moritz called, "you next!"

Joule rushed forward excitedly.

"Hey, I don't want to have to regrow everything in the courtyard," Chasan announced as his little brother joined them, "so can you all try to only destroy the one tree?"

"Yeah, yeah, yeah," Joule said, waving a dismissive hand at his brother. He positioned himself in front of the now ice-covered tree, taking deep, controlled breaths, just like Fannar. After a few moments, Joule brought both arms up and released two powerful bolts of lightning. One made contact with a frozen tree branch, shattering it on impact, while the other bolt missed the tree entirely and instead struck the roof of the manor. The four seated on the steps gaped first at the roof, then at Joule, stunned by how strong he was. Once the shock faded, they broke into enthusiastic cheers.

"Woah," Joule breathed.

"Wow," Bror said, surprised.

"Regrowing the entire courtyard doesn't seem so bad now," Chasan joked, stepping forward to ruffle his brother's hair.

"Hey, you better watch yourself with him, Chasan," Moritz advised. "If his gift is this strong now, he's going to be a powerhouse in a year or two," he said, giving Joule an impressed nod.

Joule looked apologetically at Bror, who was still staring at the roof. "Sorry... I really did *try*."

Chapter 4

"Yeah, we definitely need to work on your control first," Bror said with an awkward chuckle, squinting at the hole the lightning had made, and rubbing his temple, "anyway... moving on!" He called, turning back towards the steps, "Shammoth! let's see yours now."

Joule and Shammoth switched out, and everyone watched and waited. Shammoth kept his eyes closed tight as he concentrated on the image in his mind. Slowly, his facial features began to change; first his jawline, then his mouth, nose and eyes, and finally his hair, which shortened and lightened from black to a light brown. When he finished, he opened his eyes, and smirked at Bror – who's face he had perfectly mimicked.

"Impressive!" Chasan remarked.

"Yeah," Bror said, echoing Chasan's amazement, "it's like looking in a mirror."

"A taller mirror maybe," Moritz teased.

Since Shammoth had only shape-shifted his head, he still stood a few inches taller than Bror, who was now pursing his lips at the comment and Chasan and Shammoth's laughter.

"Hey!" Fannar called from the steps, "what did he do?"

Shammoth turned to show the rest of his friends and was greeted with similarly impressed compliments.

"How long do you think you can hold that transformation for?" Bror asked.

"Not long," Shammoth said in his own voice.

"Ugh!" Moritz exclaimed. "Don't ask him any more questions until he's back to himself," he told Bror with a shudder, "it's too creepy hearing Shammoth's voice come out of your mouth."

Bror chuckled and they all waited until their friend reverted to his own form.

"Not bad, that was what, like six minutes all together?" Bror wondered aloud.

"Something like that, yeah," Chasan answered.

Bror gave a satisfied nod, and looked over at Hakan, "Your turn."

Hakan reluctantly rose from the steps and took Shammoth's place in front of the older three.

"No holding back," Chasan loudly warned with a sly smile.

"Yeah!" Joule and Fannar called in unison before bursting with laughter at themselves.

Hakan clenched his jaw and rocked his knee back and forth a couple times before nodding his acceptance of their demand and closed his eyes.

Everything was still and quiet as the seven friends watched Hakan with anxious anticipation, noticing every flinch and twitch he made as he gathered the energy in his body, several small flickers escaping his fingers as he did so. Finally, he brought his right-hand level with his face, the tiny flames rapidly licking along his skin increasing in speed and intensity. He opened his eyes, shooting his arm upward, and released a broad column of fire harmlessly into the sky above the courtyard.

The friends seated on the steps all wore identical, astonished expressions; each mouth sat gaping, eyes wide and fixed on the place Hakan had released the fire. Bror, Chasan and Moritz weren't immune to the sight either. None of them had expected Hakan's gift to start off so strong, and the surprise was clear as their heads lowered to face him.

Chapter 4

Hakan stood, ghostly pale, panting from the effort and staring at the place where the scorching column had been seconds before.

"Hakan," Bror said concerned, "what's wrong?"

Hakan moved his mouth to speak, but the burning lump in his throat prevented any sound from coming out. He closed his mouth, eyes welling with tears as his thoughts raced, and he dropped to his knees.

"Hakan?" Moritz cried as he and Bror both grabbed an arm to steady their friend while the four on the steps jumped from their seats and sprinted towards them.

A tear slipped down Hakan's face as he stared off into the distance, unfocused. "Why," he croaked.

"Why what?" Bror asked him, as Joule, Fannar, Shammoth and Ismat reached them.

"Why did I have to get fire?" Hakan's voice cracked, and his face twisted in pain as he said the words.

Bror's heart broke as he looked at the prince. "No one knows why any of us gets the gifts we get," he said, trying his best to console him.

Hakan sniffled and let out a chuckle. "It's not even a weak gift," he lamented, marveling at the cruel irony, "and if anyone else saw that..." he breathed, trailing off as another wave of fear washed over him, seizing his voice.

"So what if they saw?" Moritz said.

Hakan looked up at him, desperation tainting all of his features. "People were already terrified that I had a fire gift, now..." he trailed off again, the tears now streaming down his cheeks.

"People probably also saw Joule blast a hole in the roof. I'd say you're both about even strength-wise. Should we all cower from him too?" Moritz asked coolly.

"It's different for him and you know it!" Hakan cried angrily, frustrated that none of them seemed to understand.

Chasan sighed and took a step back from the group. Extending his arm, he waved his hand in circular motions towards Hakan. As he moved, vines began to grow from the ground, encircling the prince and forcing everyone else several feet back from him.

Hakan looked in confusion from his plant-gifted friend to Bror, who was growing steadily more concerned as he glanced back and forth from the prince to Chasan.

"Chasan?" Bror questioned anxiously as he watched the vines twist into a cage around their friend.

"Pay attention, Hakan," Chasan told him, his voice kind but firm. "*Every* gift, no matter how strong or weak, can be used in one of two ways. To help," he paused, and the vines stopped moving, "...or to hurt."

At this, Chasan flicked his wrist, and a thick vine shot away from the rest, aimed to pierce directly through the prince's heart.

"Chasan!" Bror roared, but as he and Moritz lurched towards the vine-cage, Chasan flicked his wrist again, and a second vine shot through the first like a spear, halting the attacking plant less than a foot from Hakan's now heaving chest. Bror's whole body slumped as he exhaled with relief, and both he and Moritz gave their friend scathing looks.

Chasan waved his hands again, and the vines began to retreat back into the ground. "The difference..." he continued calmly, never taking his eyes off Hakan, "...is a choice."

"You couldn't have just said that?" Joule screamed at his brother.

Chapter 4

"No," Chasan said patiently, "he needed to see it." Finally turning his attention away from the prince, he gave the others a look of unapologetic determination.

"That was too far, Chasan!" Ismat scolded.

"But he's not wrong," Bror reluctantly admitted with a heavy sigh.

Everyone gawked at the eldest friend, whom they had expected to admonish Chasan's behavior.

"He could have killed him!" Fannar shouted.

"That's his whole point," Bror explained, shooting Chasan a disapproving look, "that any gift can be dangerous."

"Precisely," Chasan said with satisfaction. "Take Moritz' gift: he could have been a deadly assassin with his heightened senses if he had chosen that path…"

"…but instead, he *chose* to be an indispensable asset to the Royal Guard and protect people," Bror finished, glancing admiringly at the sensory-gifted.

"Same with Bror," Moritz added, "everyone always underestimates his ability to alter the emotions of others. If he *chose* to, though, he could push people beyond their emotional breaking point and end just as many lives as Afi did."

The heads of the younger five snapped anxiously to stare at Bror.

"The fire-gifted who…" Ismat timidly began to ask.

"Turned into a serial killer, yeah," Bror confirmed uneasily.

"But Bror chooses to use his gift to help. You have the same choice as the rest of us, Hakan," Chasan told him.

"It doesn't feel like I do," Hakan argued, "you saw them today; they're all convinced I'm going to be just like all the other fire-gifteds."

"You're nothing like them, though," Fannar said, kneeling down behind Hakan and grabbing onto his shoulders.

"Exactly, 'you, Hakan, have a good heart' remember?" Joule said, in an admirable impression of James, "good hearts would never choose to do anything like what all those other fire-gifteds did."

"Hakan," Ismat said, kneeling down beside Fannar, "eventually people won't be afraid and will treat your fire just like they do every other gift," Ismat assured him.

"Honestly," Bror said, "I'm pretty sure, right now, you're more scared of your gift than anyone else."

"Just keep on not killing people – that should convince everyone you're not a psycho sooner or later," Shammoth added cheerfully with a smirk.

They all smiled, and Fannar gave Hakan a gentle shake.

"I don't know." Hakan whispered, still doubtful.

Moritz studied the prince for a moment. "I take it back, you're right, Hakan," he suddenly announced.

"What?" Bror and Hakan both asked, confused.

Moritz gave Bror a knowing smile as he spoke, "he's right, he doesn't have the same choice as us."

"Yes he does," Bror argued, frowning at Moritz' abrupt change of mind.

"No," Moritz said, looking back at Hakan with a serious expression "his choice is different; He has to choose whether he is going to give in to fear, hide from the world and hand the crown over to Fannar…"

"What?" Fannar blurted in panic.

Moritz, ignoring Fannar's outburst, continued, "or accept his gift and do what he's always done: work hard to serve the kingdom."

Chapter 4

Bror's frown was replaced with a smile, and he and the other five all turned their attention back to Hakan, who was staring blankly at Moritz.

"You can't expect the rest of the kingdom to stop fearing and hating your gift as long as *you* still fear and hate it," Moritz said, his voice firm, but his eyes full of compassion.

"So what's it gonna be, Hakan?" Chasan asked kindly, "are you going to get out of your own way, or are you going to stick us with him as king?"

Fannar clicked his tongue at Chasan, slightly irritated by the joke that he'd be a detrimental alternative ruler before he and the others laughed.

Hakan studied each of their faces one at a time, searching for a trace of fear or doubt. Every one of them, however, had the same expression as Moritz; each was filled with understanding and resolve. Another tear slipped down his face, though this one was not out of fear or pain, but rather from appreciation. Hakan took a deep breath and nodded.

"Alright, then." Bror said, helping his friend back up to his feet, "let's get back to work!"

They spent the rest of the afternoon and evening practicing with their new gifts, and by the time Hakan's head rested on his pillow that night, his hopes of becoming a good leader had been restored.

Chapter 5
OUR TEAM

Over the next week, they tried their best to go about life as usual and ignore how skittishly people continued to behave around Hakan. In an effort to keep everyone's minds busy, the older friends had made it their mission to assist the newly gifted ones in honing their new abilities.

Every afternoon Joule, Fannar, Hakan, and Shammoth would exercise their gifts in the courtyard of the Royal Manor under Chasan's instruction, with Moritz joining him whenever he was off duty. The most dedicated of the older friend-teachers, though, was Bror, who wouldn't even let work stop him from helping as he offered his experienced advice from the sidelines whenever one of his guard assignments put him in the vicinity.

Everything was going well until Fannar accidentally sent an icicle flying through one of the council room windows like a spear, barely missing Kesavan's head before it sank firmly into the wall behind him.

Fannar stood, hands covering his mouth, as he stared at the broken glass until his father appeared on the other side. "Sorry, dad!" he called.

Eero sighed as he surveyed the web-like cracks emanating from the plum-sized hole in the window and gestured for Bror to join him to the meeting room.

Chapter 5

"Bror I..." Fannar's voice trailed off as he turned his apologetic face to his friend, who gave him a reassuring smile and gentle pat on the shoulder before sprinting off.

A minute later, Bror entered the council room and found King Eero, along with the seven council members, seated around the long, glass-touch-screen table, everyone wearing serious expressions except Kesavan, who instead looked rather amused.

Bror bowed towards the king, seated on the far side of the table. "Your majesty," he greeted, but it wasn't Eero who replied.

"You should tell Fannar, if I've offended him in some way, I will happily apologize. No need to throw ice spears at my head," Councilman Kesavan said playfully, fighting a smile.

"I'm sorry, Councilman," Bror said, apologetically inclining his head, "I should have had Chasan make the barrier wall behind the target wider."

"Bror," Eero interjected, without a trace of Kesavan's levity, "I think we need to find the boys a safer place to practice."

Bror studied the king for a moment. "That's going to be difficult, your majesty," Bror replied anxiously, concerned that the king was about to put a stop to the activity they had found to distract Hakan from his stressful reality as a fire-gifted, "there aren't many open spaces in the capital, and none of them are a controlled enough environment for Fannar, Joule and Hakan to practice using their gifts."

"Yes, I'm aware," Eero acknowledged. There was a pensive pause before he asked, "what do you think about taking them to the Falls? It's much larger than the courtyard, and no one really ever goes there except for the Gifting Ceremony."

"And the only thing out there they could break are trees," Kesavan pointed out, still brimming with amusement.

"Which Chasan could easily repair." Eero added, shooting a baffled look at the councilman, disconcerted that his advisor was taking the near-impalement so lightly.

"That would work," Bror answered, inclining his head in an attempt to hide his own amusement at the interaction between the king and Kesavan.

"Excellent!" Eero said loudly, turning away from the councilman and back to Bror, "you can take them there tomorrow," he told the young guard as he returned to scrolling through the digital documents displayed on the table.

"Me?" Bror questioned, "I'm assigned to her majesty's detail tomorrow."

"I want someone from the Royal Guard to go with them," Eero explained, still looking over the documents, "and I think the boys would be less reluctant if it were you or Moritz. Basilah, who would be easier to pull from their assignment tomorrow?" He asked, turning his attention to the woman seated to his left.

Basilah, squinted as she considered the question. "Probably Moritz. He's currently assigned to the Manor tomorrow, it will be easier to fill that spot than Her Majesty's detail since she will be traveling," Basilah replied.

Eero nodded. "Alright. So tomorrow Moritz will take them. Basilah, I'm gonna need you to adjust their assignments going forward so that the two of them can trade off at the Falls."

Chapter 5

"Yes, sir," Basilah replied with a slight nod.

"I can also assign a few City guards to keep other civilians out of the area if you would like," Bror's father, Councilman Tanlan Naukaron, added.

"All due respect, councilman, I don't think that will be necessary," Bror politely interjected, keenly aware that other guards were still exceedingly averse to being anywhere near Hakan–especially while he was actively exercising his fire-gift–and having them around would defeat the kings implied intention to keep the reinstatement of the princes' guard detail discreet. His father, thankfully, didn't press the issue.

"Alright, well that's settled then. Bror, why don't you go tell the boys practice is done for the day and let them know about the change of venue for tomorrow," Eero instructed, returning once again to the document on the table-screen as the young guard bowed once again and left the room.

Despite everyone's initial hesitations over practicing at the site where their friend's life had been irrevocably altered, the new location had a positive impact on Hakan. Without the added stress caused by the wary guards, staff and council, the prince relaxed enough for his cheerful, expressive self to return. That relief, combined with his friends' consistency in treating Hakan's gift no differently than anyone else's, allowed him to make steady progress along with Shammoth, who worked on increasing both the extent and duration of his shapeshifting gift.

The older twin wasn't the only one the seclusion had a significant effect on, either. Everyone had been so focused on Hakan the first week that no one realized his brother had also been struggling with self-consciousness over his own nearly-as-rare gift. Unlike his twin, though,

Fannar began making rapid improvements at the Falls, and was the first one to achieve what Bror and Moritz felt was a sufficient level of control to start strengthening his gift. By the end of the fifth week, Joule and Hakan had reached the same level of control, and Chasan and Moritz felt comfortable letting all of them begin sparring with the new abilities.

"Yeow!" Fannar yelped one afternoon as Joule's hand made contact with his thigh, and a jolt of electricity seized the muscles, causing the prince to lose his footing and fall to the ground.

"Haha!" Joule exclaimed triumphantly, winning the spar.

"Excellent!" Chasan called, as Hakan and Moritz whooped from the sidelines.

Joule helped Fannar to his feet, and they made their way over to where the others sat on the grassy riverbank.

As they approached, they noticed Moritz looking and listening intently past them, towards the path out of the clearing. They looked over their shoulders just in time to see Bror bolting through the tree line, smiling broadly when he saw them all gathered at the river.

"What's up?" Fannar asked as their ecstatic friend reached them.

Bror, out of breath from running all the way from the tram station, looked at them all excitedly, "I just came from the Manor and I overheard dad talking with Councilwoman Basilah and General Utara..."

"Should you be telling us what you heard?" Moritz asked with a scrutinous expression.

"It's nothing like that," Bror assured him, waving a dismissive hand, "guys, they're planning on holding a

Chapter 5

derbala tournament for all the Ladothite guard divisions at the end of the summer!"

"Nice!" Moritz, Hakan, Joule and Ismat exclaimed.

"Oh sweet!" Fannar said brightly.

"Yeeeesssss!" Chasan shouted, his face as bright and delighted as Bror's.

"Yeah!" Bror said, excitedly clapping his hands.

"I can't wait to see your team play!" Hakan declared, smiling enthusiastically at Bror, Moritz and Chasan.

"*Our* team," Bror corrected, raising a cheeky eyebrow at the fire-prince.

"What do you mean 'our'?" Hakan asked, uneasy.

"Well, the tournament isn't until the *end* of the summer," Bror explained, "and tryouts for the Honor Guard are at the *beginning* of summer, and since Honor Guard is one of the Ladothite guard divisions…"

"You want us to try out for the Honor Guard?" Fannar asked, wide-eyed with surprise.

"Yes!" Bror answered eagerly.

Hakan's expression was incredulous, "are you crazy?" he exclaimed.

"Yes," Ismat answered impishly, eliciting several sniggers from the others.

"You expect us to *all* make Honor Guard?" Joule asked, stupefied. "There's only ten slots, Bror, and they always have at least twice that try out every year!"

"I know, I know, but hear me out," Bror argued, sounding as though he'd already given this an excessive amount of thought, "As good as Hakan is, there's no way he won't get a spot, and, if Moritz, Chasan and I work with you two and Shammoth, I think you could all make the guard."

"Sounds good to me," Chasan said lazily, "it'll help me get ready for City Guard tryouts too." He told them as he cracked his knuckles, looking enthusiastically at the others.

"Wait, City Guard?" Bror asked, a bit crestfallen, "I thought your dad said you were trying out for Royal?"

Chasan shrugged, "because I may not have mentioned it to him yet."

"Why aren't you trying out for the royal division anymore?" Bror asked, his voice tinged with disappointment.

Chasan started to poke at the grass in front of him, making it grow and shrink as he spoke, "you want to take over as head of the Royal Guard someday when Basilah steps down, right?" he asked, his demeanor unusually shy.

"Yeah, so?" Bror responded, confused.

"So..." Chasan continued sounding a bit more confident as he returned the grass to its original state, "maybe, I want to lead a guard division someday too." He looked up to meet Bror's inquisitive gaze and gave a somewhat embarrassed shrug "Royal Guard was my dad's idea, and as great as it would be to serve under you, I have big dreams of my own."

Bror took a deep breath, eyes brimming with pride over Chasan's decision, "Either way, you'll be on a Ladothite Guard and eligible for the tournament."

Chasan chuckled at Bror's response, thoroughly entertained by his friend's obsessive focus.

"You guys are really okay giving up all your free time to get us ready for tryouts?" Joule asked, looking hopefully from Chasan to Bror to Moritz.

"Fine with me," Moritz answered without hesitation.

Chapter 5

"Does that mean you'll do it?" Bror asked hopefully.

"Yeah, I'll do it," Joule said, nodding his head as both Bror and Moritz whooped.

"Shammoth?" Chasan asked, nudging him in the arm.

Shammoth looked at Bror as he thought it over. "I don't know," he said doubtfully, "Honor Guard is supposed to be for the people who want a career in one of the guard divisions after the academy. I don't have any interest in a career with any of the guards. I like the idea of taking over my parent's tech shop someday."

"Actually, that's not entirely true," Bror corrected. "No one is ever compelled to advance to another division after being on Honor Guard. It's just that most members *usually* decide to pursue a Guard career, but it's always their choice. You can't get in trouble or anything for being on Honor and not joining another division after the academy," he explained, smiling broadly at the end.

Shammoth was silent for several long seconds as he considered Bror's argument. "I don't like the idea of taking a spot away from someone who wants it for their future, though."

"Well, being on Honor Guard definitely helps with getting into the Royal or City divisions, but it's not a requirement to join any of them. If they really want that as a career, not getting on Honor Guard won't stop them," Bror told him, solidifying everyone's conviction that he had indeed spent his run from the tram thinking of solutions to any excuses they might come up with. "So, wha'd'ya say, Shammoth? Will you try out too?" he inquired.

"Okay, I'll try out," Shammoth agreed, making Bror shout victoriously. "But I'm not going to sacrifice my academy work for training," he quickly added.

"Fair enough," Bror replied, his grin managing to grow even broader as he bounced on the balls of his feet, his jubilation slowly becoming uncontainable as friend after friend acquiesced to his request.

"Wait," Fannar interjected, his expression concerned, "what about Iz?" he said, looking at the youngest of the friends.

"What about me?" Ismat said, giggling as he watched Bror slowly losing control of himself.

"Well," Fannar said with a shy expression, "you're not old enough to be on any of the guards," he said, a hint of guilt in his voice.

"I'm aware," Ismat said indifferently, still watching Bror.

"Well... if we... I don't want you to get left out," Fannar awkwardly explained.

Ismat turned his attention away from Bror and gave Fannar an appreciative smile. "It'll be fine. It's not like me being on Honor Guard would give us more time to hang out; everyone is given different assignments. Besides, if you all make the Honor Guard, the seven of you make a full derbala team – even if I was old enough to be on a guard, one of us would still have to sit out as an alternate for the tournament."

"You're sure?" Fannar asked.

"Positive." Ismat assured him, instantly melting Fannar's apprehension.

"So..." Bror prodded, "does this mean you'll try out too, Fannar?"

"Yeah," Fannar agreed with a bright smile, "yeah, I'll do it too."

Bror now turned his attention to Hakan, who had remained silent the entire conversation. "That just leaves you," He prompted.

"No." Hakan replied flatly.

Bror dropped his head with a sigh, while Moritz threw his head back and gave an exasperated groan.

"C'mon Hakan," Chasan pressed, "your sparring skills are better than almost the entire current honor guard. You can hold your own with the three of us–" indicating himself, Moritz and Bror.

"You'll probably end up being one of the top fighters of the entire tournament!" Bror interjected exuberantly.

Hakan furrowed his eyebrows, frustrated. "That's exactly why I don't think I should try out for Honor Guard," he argued. "It's been over a month and people are still avoiding me. If I go out for the guard and everyone sees me fight…" he shook his head as he pictured the looks that would fill his classmates faces, "I don't need to give them another reason to be afraid of me."

Chasan crossed his arms thoughtfully. "I think you're better off having all of your skills out in the open sooner rather than later."

Shammoth nodded his head. "I agree. People will find out how good you are eventually, Hakan," he contended, "if you wait – if you try to hide it…"

"It would damage people's trust," Moritz said, completing Shammoth's thought. "It could be considered dishonest and make it even harder to get them to think of you differently than the other fire-gifteds."

"In the long run, it's better that people know everything now, all at once," Ismat concurred.

Hakan looked expectantly from Fannar to Joule, waiting for their opinions.

Joule's eyebrows disappeared behind his bangs. "Don't look at me!" he told Hakan tenaciously, "I agree with everything they said."

"Me too," Fannar added firmly, his expression as unshakeable as Joule's.

Hakan stared unfocused at the empty cave behind the falls, brooding over his friend's arguments.

"Well, your highness," Moritz quipped in a dramatically professional voice that made Hakan roll his eyes, "your council seems to have reached a consensus," he said with a smirk, gesturing to the others who chuckled at being referred to as a council.

Hakan couldn't help but smile weakly at Moritz' comment, a sense of comfort seeping into his heart. Though he hadn't told his friends, Hakan had decided years ago to appoint all of them to his Royal Council someday. However, it seemed that 'someday' had come and gone as the prince realized he was now relying on their advice in the same way his father relied on the current Royal Council. Moritz–still waiting for an answer–made an inquisitive noise, drawing Hakan out of his ruminations, and he sighed in defeat. "Okay, okay," he said, surrendering, "I'll try out."

"Yes!" Bror roared, punching the air with a victorious fist as he jumped up and down before driving them all into an intense practice session.

After another hour, though, Shammoth, Ismat, and Hakan insisted they call it a day, citing the majority of the group's need to study for the upcoming academy finals at the end of the month. Bror reluctantly agreed, but as they dragged him back into the capital, he continued offering excuses for them to keep practicing despite the finals. It wasn't until Shammoth threatened to not try out at all that Bror was finally silenced on the matter, much to the delight of the others.

Chapter 6
TROUBLE

The following week, the announcement went out to the different guard divisions, and by lunch everyone in the academy was buzzing about the tournament. As the boys walked through the cafeteria, it quickly became clear that Fannar and the others weren't the only ones looking to try out for the Honor Guard in order to take part in the competition. Making their way through the bustling room towards the exit with their lunches, they overheard several conversations between students discussing which guard member they were going to approach about preparing them for the tryouts.

"Still feel bad about trying out?" Fannar asked Shammoth as they settled under the oak tree outside the academy.

"No," Shammoth scoffed.

"There's going to be more people than ever trying out this year," Joule said, dismayed.

"Mhm," Hakan grunted in agreement as he chewed his mouthful of sandwich.

"Uh oh," Fannar said softly, his body stiffening.

Hakan wrinkled his face. "What?" he asked, following his brother's gaze.

Chapter 6

They rest followed suit with him, tracking Fannar's stare to the front steps of the academy, where they saw Adrig marching towards them, eyes locked on Hakan.

"Oh great," Joule sighed.

"What do you want, Adrig?" Shammoth demanded.

Adrig stopped several feet from where the group of friends sat and turned his attention to Joule. "Your brother has turned down everyone in the guard who's asked him to join their team for the tournament."

"So?" Joule snapped impatiently.

"He's also turned down everyone from your year who's asked him to train them for tryouts–even the ones willing to pay him," Adrig continued incredulously, "no matter how much they offered."

"Again, so?" Joule asked, his tone dripping with annoyance.

Adrig tilted his head to the side, leering at the impetuous student. "*So,* I want you to tell me why," he answered coolly.

"Go ask him yourself!" Joule bit back, making a rude gesture at the older teen.

"I did," Adrig sneered, "everyone did actually, but he wouldn't give anyone an answer."

"I'm an electric-gifted, Adrig, not a telepath. How should I know why Chasan said no?" Joule retorted, trying to resist the growing urge to punch his obnoxiously smug face.

"You don't have to be," Adrig told him silkily, as his eyes passed one-by-one over them, finally resting on Hakan with a look of deep contempt. "See, I'm pretty sure Chasan's reason involves the four of you."

"Get lost," Fannar snapped.

"Is he helping you get on the guard?" Adrig asked, sounding simultaneously convinced and disbelieving that this was Chasan's reason.

"Whether or not he's helping any of us is no one's business," Shammoth replied, matching Adrig's cool tone and manner.

"So, yes then," Adrig said, sounding disgusted as he eyed Hakan up and down. "You really think the guard leadership is going to risk putting someone like you in the ranks?"

"We're losing brain cells listening to this stupidity. Let's get out of here," Shammoth taunted as he began gathering his things.

Joule and Ismat sniggered and they, Fannar and Hakan followed suit with their friend, feeling it would be better to head to class early than to listen to Adrig.

"Just because they let you keep coming to the academy doesn't mean they trust you, your *highness*." Adrig sneered, disdain filling the emphasis of the last word.

Hakan clenched his jaw, trying to ignore the provocation, but as he tried to walk around the bullying schoolmate, Adrig seized him by the arm. After having spent so much time sparring Bror and Chasan over the last few days, the prince reacted instinctively–swiftly twisted out and away from Adrig's grasp, surprising his attacker with the natural and smooth reflex.

"I guess Chasan already taught you a few tricks," Adrig spat.

"Maybe," Hakan taunted in reply.

The prince's unshakable confidence infuriated Adrig. "Why wait for tryouts?" he said, curling his fingers into a fist, "let's see what you can do now."

Chapter 6

Adrig lunged to attack Hakan, but Joule jumped between them, shocking Adrig's shoulder and making him stumble backward, growling in pain.

"How 'bout I show you what I can do instead?" Joule offered, extending his arms warningly towards the older student as he planted himself protectively in front of Hakan and Fannar. As he spoke, Shammoth and Ismat quickly moved to stand just behind him, reinforcing the buffer between the princes and Adrig.

Adrig smirked maliciously at the group of friends. "Right, I forgot, can't let the prince fight his own battles, that's what you minions are for."

"Sounds like someone's afraid of getting their strength-gifted ass kicked around by a newbie-electric-gifted," Shammoth goaded.

At this, Joule threateningly released crackles of electricity around his outstretched arms, and Adrig smirked, cracking his neck as he drew back his arm to take an unnaturally hard swing.

"Joule! Adrig!" Councilwoman Haldis, Headmistress of the Academy, called from the top of the stone academy stairs, her expression severe. "My office! Now!"

The two looked up at the headmistress, then back to glare at each other a final time before making their way towards the steps.

"And you four," Haldis continued as the two walked tensely up the stairs and past the stone-faced woman, "I suggest you all head to your classrooms now," She raised an eyebrow at them before turning on her heels and marching off after Joule and Adrig through the heavy wooden door.

The remaining four friends exchanged worried looks before silently making their way into the building, and upstairs to their classrooms. The minutes dragged on as they waited anxiously for Joule to join the class, but by the end of the period it became clear that they wouldn't be seeing him in any more lessons that day. Headmistress Haldis had a low tolerance for student's violating academy rules... rules which included a ban on fighting and resulted in immediate suspension.

"Do you think we should call him?" Ismat asked after the final class period as they walked down the hall.

"No," Fannar replied, dismally, "we can just ask Chasan about it when we get... to..." his voice trailed off halfway down the staircase.

"Fannar?" Hakan asked, his chest reflexively tightening, as for the second time that afternoon he followed his brother's gaze.

Fannar had been the first to notice Moritz waiting, in uniform and on duty, just inside the entrance to the academy.

"This can't be good," Hakan remarked as the four of them made their way down the rest of the steps and along the crowded main hall towards him.

As they got closer, Moritz jerked his head towards the door before turning to lead his younger friends out of the building. They trailed silently behind him down the front steps, but instead of turning left towards the underground tram station, which they took to get to the Falls, he turned right – towards the Royal Manor.

Hakan cursed under his breath.

"I heard that," Moritz said, half-heartedly scolding the prince, who then rolled his eyes.

Chapter 6

"I take it we're not practicing today, then?" Fannar asked tensely.

Moritz smiled slightly and looked over his shoulder at them, "good guess."

"Should Shammoth and I head home, too?" Ismat inquired cautiously.

"When Basilah called me in, I was only instructed to bring Fannar and Hakan home, nothing more; As far as I'm concerned, there's no reason you two can't walk with us to the manor, but I'm pretty sure both of you are gonna be sent home when we get there... besides, by now your parents would have heard about what happened at the academy."

"You guys should just head home," Hakan urged.

There was a pause as the two friends studied his expression, searching for any hint that the prince was just being kind and would truly rather they stay.

"Okay," Ismat finally replied.

"Call us and let us know what happened as soon as you can," Shammoth said as everyone exchanged their goodbyes before parting.

They walked mutely along for several minutes before Fannar's anxious curiosity got the better of him. "Are we in trouble?" he asked as they trudged beside Moritz.

"Like I said, Basilah only instructed me to bring you home," Moritz reminded Fannar.

Hakan looked at him, puzzled. "How do you know about the academy stuff then?"

"Joule told me. He stopped by mine and Bror's place when they sent him home to give me a heads up. He was worried it might turn into a big thing and wanted me to meet you guys after classes to tell you he had been sent home and that he wasn't sure if he'd be able to call later or not... a few minutes after he left, Basilah called."

"Looks like he was right." Hakan lamented, wondering what had happened in the headmistress's office that had made Joule so concerned. He glanced over at Fannar, who, judging by the worry etched into his features, was wondering the same thing. As they continued their walk in silence, the princes struggled with a growing sense of guilt. Joule had been suspended and possibly faced additional punishment at home because he had put himself between Adrig and the twins.

Hakan continued to ruminate on all the dreadful possibilities until they arrived at the manor, where they were directly escorted to the Council Room.

Their father sat at the head of the table, looking up from the reports on the screen as they entered. "Thank you, Moritz, you can wait outside." Eero said, dismissing him with a nod.

Moritz gave a short bow and left the room while the boys looked apprehensively at their father, waiting for him to speak.

Eero's expression was unreadable as he turned his attention to his wary sons. "So, who wants to go first?" he asked calmly.

"Go first for what?" Hakan said, stalling; afraid to say anything without knowing what or how much his father had been told.

"I got a call from Haldis. She said there was an incident at the school today," he told them evenly, "you wanna tell me about it?"

"Adrig started it," Fannar answered bluntly.

"Started the fight?" Eero pressed, his expression still passive.

Chapter 6

"There wasn't a fight," Hakan corrected, a bit annoyed.

"Adrig tried to start one, though," Fannar explained, "he tried to have a go at Hakan."

Eero's eyes narrowed slightly as he looked at Fannar. "Is that when Joule attacked Adrig with his gift?" he questioned.

"It was a tiny zap to stop him attacking Hakan for no reason!" Fannar exclaimed incredulously, his temper starting to rise.

"Joule was just trying to help," Hakan added instantly, "Councilwoman Haldis got involved before anything really happened."

Eero looked thoughtfully from one son to the other. "Adrig claimed that Joule started the fight."

"He's lying!" Hakan cried, his eyes burning with outrage.

"He says he came to wish Joule and the rest of you luck with Honor Guard tryouts this summer, but Joule started throwing around insults and instigated a fight," Eero continued in the same calm tone, his scrutinizing gaze continuing to shift between the twins.

"Lies!" Fannar yelled, furious, "Adrig was trying to provoke Hakan over the tryouts but Hakan wouldn't take the bait, so he took a swing at him and Joule stopped him! Joule was just protecting Hakan!"

"So that part was true then," Eero said, nodding thoughtfully. He turned to Hakan as he continued, "you *are* planning to try out for Honor Guard."

Dawning realization stunned the brothers into silence as Fannar and Hakan exchanged uncomfortable looks.

"So… so you already knew Adrig lied about Joule starting the fight?" Fannar asked, somewhat embarrassed.

"I know Joule well enough to know he's far more likely to get into a fight to protect one of his friends – which is what he claimed happened – than he is just for the sake of starting trouble." Eero explained, "Councilwoman Haldis felt the same way, but she said when she questioned him about the Honor Guard tryouts, he was very careful with his words, especially when the two of you got brought up," He finished, his tone laced with frustration.

"So, is Joule not in trouble then?" Fannar asked hopefully.

"I haven't talked with his dad," he told Fannar, shaking his head, "we don't have a council meeting today, but Councilwoman Haldis was going to pass along her assessment that Joule's actions didn't warrant any further punishments; that he only needed to be sent home for the remaining periods as required by the academy's policy."

There was a pause as relief swept over Fannar and Hakan. It was short-lived, however, as their father continued.

"When were you going to tell me about the tryouts?" Eero asked, locking his eyes on the elder twin.

"I don't know," Hakan answered softly, looking away.

"And you?" Eero pressed his other son, displeasure spreading through his features.

Fannar hung his head guiltily. If he were honest with himself, he probably wouldn't have told his father until the day of tryouts, if at all.

"What were you thinking?" Eero scolded, staring with astonishment at Hakan. "What in the world made you think this was a good idea?"

Chapter 6

"It wasn't Hakan's idea," Fannar said forcefully. His brother quickly gave him a 'shut up now' look, which Fannar determinedly ignored. "We're all trying out for Honor Guard so we can play in the derbala tournament. Hakan was against it for every reason I'm sure you're thinking of too, but we all convinced him to do it."

Hakan, stunned by his twin's confident candor, stood speechless as he gaped at his brother.

"You think you know my reasons, Fannar?" Eero demanded, his voice raising harshly.

"Is Hakan trying out a problem because he's your successor or because of his gift?" Fannar asked heatedly, his boldness successfully shocking his father into silence. "If it's because of his gift, then yes, I think I do," he brazenly added.

For several long seconds, Eero stared blankly at his son, and as the initial shock subsided, his expression reflected the internal struggle he had as he thought about Fannar's words. When their father finally spoke, instead of sounding angry at how his son had spoken to him, he sounded almost mournful.

"Hakan, I'm sorry," Eero apologized, his expression filled with compassion, "your gift complicates things. As much as I wish it didn't, that's just the reality we have to deal with. Every day since the gifting, I've received calls and messages from all over the kingdom – messages full of demands that no father should have to read or hear people make about his son."

"Isn't that more of a reason to have him try out for the guard though?" Fannar argued.

"When they see how strong he is – how he's already more than a match for every freshman guard in any division – It c... don't look at me like that," their father said in response to the startled looks on their faces, "Leal called that day he saw you spar Chasan at their place."

They glanced at each other, and Hakan saw an almost imperceptible note of triumph in Fannar's eyes. He and the others were right: Hakan wasn't going to be able to conceal his fighting capabilities indefinitely.

"He's going to have to spar in the tryouts and people seeing him fight could make things worse," Eero told them, his voice almost pleading.

At that moment, the door creaked open, and Moritz entered. "I'm sorry, sir, I couldn't help overhearing."

"Oh I'm sure," Eero said with amused exasperation, well aware that Moritz *could* technically help it, but that he kept his heightened hearing active while on duty.

"Sir, we all feel that people learning about Hakan's level of combat skills is no worse than leaving everyone to their imaginations," Moritz explained, making Fannar and Hakan gawk at him, unused to the professional-royal-guard side of their friend, "on Honor Guard he'd be serving the kingdom; he'd be helping people. He'd be doing something directly contradicting the selfish evil everyone expects from a fire-gifted."

Eero leaned back in his chair, considering Moritz' argument. "You're being awfully quiet about this," Eero eventually pointed out, turning his gaze back to Hakan.

"I agree with them," Hakan answered, quiet but firm. "I can't expect to earn trust from the people in the kingdom if I'm not honest with them about what I can do."

Eero sighed. "If you do this," he began, his tone making it clear that he didn't like the idea one bit, "you need to realize that you are going to be scrutinized far more than anyone else, both at the tryouts and on the Guard if you're selected. Everything you do and say will not only be

Chapter 6

put under a microscope because you're my son, but many, *many* people will be looking for any excuse to believe that the fire-gifted legacy will be continued with you."

Hakan's mouth dropped a little. "Does that mean you're going to let me try out?" he asked, surprised.

Eero sighed again, and Fannar, Hakan and Moritz waited anxiously for his answer.

"Yes," he finally replied, "you *both* have permission to try out."

The three of them smiled at each other, the tension rapidly evaporating.

"So can Moritz take us to the falls now?" Fannar pleaded, his eyes growing wide.

"Don't you have finals coming up in a couple of weeks?" Eero said knowingly, "I think it would be better for you to spend the rest of the day studying. Going to the falls can wait until tomorrow."

"Okay," Fannar agreed, disappointedly pursing his lips for a moment. "Ooh! let's go tell mom about the tryouts first, though!" he exclaimed, grabbing Hakan by the arm, and bolting for the door before their father could say another word.

Chapter 7

EXPECTATIONS VERSUS DREAMS

"Freedom!" Fannar howled as he raced down the front steps of the academy, jumping over the last few to the ground. He lifted his head to the sky, soaking up the bright rays of sunshine for a few moments before jogging over to the oak tree where Shammoth and Ismat sat – thoroughly entertained by his excitement. As he settled himself among the roots next to them to wait for his brother and friends, Fannar let out a sigh of relief that exams were finally over for the year.

"How did you do?" Shammoth asked casually.

"Pretty well," Fannar optimistically answered, "I'm not gonna be top of the year or anything, but I definitely did better than usual."

"Actually, putting in some effort to study will do that," Shammoth teased, making Ismat chuckle.

"Yeah, yeah, yeah," Fannar said, smiling as he waved a hand at them. With all the stress his brother was under because of his fire-gift, Fannar had decided to start early on his promise of studying harder; putting in nearly as much effort as his twin and Shammoth over the past two weeks.

"What's so funny?" Bror asked, startling his relaxed friends who hadn't heard or seen him arrive.

Chapter 7

"Nothing," Fannar quickly replied, leaning up to survey Bror, who still stood like a guard at attention even though he was in his street clothes. "Moritz working today?" he asked with a small frown.

"Yeah," Bror told him with a sigh, looking nostalgically up at the academy, "he asked me to bring him home a couple of the cookies for later, though."

"But he doesn't like sweets," Ismat commented, with an inquisitive expression.

Bror, who had no explanation for him, simply pursed his lips and raised his shoulders.

"Chasan's done," Shammoth suddenly announced, and they all turned their attention to the academy and watched their exhausted friend plodding his way down the steps and over towards them.

"Uh oh," Bror said as Chasan staggered closer, "exams not go well?"

"No it went fine, it was just... So. Many. Questions." Chasan told him, collapsing against the tree beside Fannar and closing his eyes. "I see we're still waiting on my brother and Hakan?"

"Yep," Bror answered, looking back up at the building.

Chasan rubbed his stomach pitifully as it gave a loud growl. "Agh! How much longer do they have? I'm hungry!"

"You're always hungry," Fannar replied smartly, as he grinned from ear-to-ear.

Chasan flicked his finger, causing the root the prince was leaning on to abruptly roll in a wave-like motion, which sent Fannar tumbling onto the grass several feet away.

83

"They only have fifteen more minutes," Ismat said through a snicker, answering Chasan's question as he watched the disgruntled prince clamber back to his resting place.

Ten minutes – and many other students and Chasan complaints – later, Hakan and Joule finally emerged together from the academy, both looking as exhausted and relieved as everyone else they had seen depart. Unlike the rest of their friends, though, Joule and Hakan weren't afforded the luxury of resting beneath the sprawling green canopy. Before the two had reached the bottom step, the other five were up and ushering them off to their next destination: James' Bakery.

Chasan eagerly led the way, his schoolmates dragging their feet behind him and Bror, their mental fatigue from the week-long marathon of exams finally manifesting as physical weariness. As they lumbered along, they discussed their predictions of how they all did until Bror inevitably shifted the conversation to the tournament, tryouts and his plans for their future practices. His monologue, which they were only somewhat listening to anyway, came to an abrupt halt once Chasan threw the Bakery door open and the smell of fresh-baked goods wafted enticingly through the air.

Everyone filed inside the shop just in time to see James carrying out a tray of assorted cookies from the kitchen, which he made every year on the last day of exams. The baker began handing the warm aromatic discs out to the small group of young students lined along the counter, who cheerfully thanked him before turning around to leave.

They spotted Hakan and froze in fear at the sight of the fire-gifted prince.

Chapter 7

After a moment of anxious gulps from the three youngsters, one of them decided the best course of action would be to bolt out the door and run as far away from Hakan as possible, the rest quickly following behind.

The prince sighed, a small ache growing in his heart as he stared woefully after the fleeing children. Two months had gone by, and people were still running from him.

Shammoth and Fannar on the other hand, rolled their eyes and said "idiots" in unison, lightening the soured mood a fraction.

"Oho!" James exclaimed, realizing who had entered. "Look who's come to see me!"

"Hello, Mr. James," they all greeted quietly.

"Haven't seen much of you boys recently. 'Specially you and Moritz!" James disappointedly scolded, pointing an accusatory finger at Bror. "I know you boys have important jobs, but that's no excuse to not stop by and see this old-timer once in a while!"

Bror flushed, and tilted his head forward in a little bow, "I'm sorry, Mr. James. I'm afraid it's my fault no one's been to the shop lately."

"Oh?" James questioned, eyes full of curiosity.

"Well, I sort of talked everyone into forming a team for the Guard Derbala Tournament, but that means we have to get everyone on a Capital Guard Division, so we've all been taking every chance we can get to prepare for tryouts next month," Bror explained sheepishly.

"Is that so!" James exclaimed, grinning broadly, "you're all going to be on Honor Guard, are you?"

"Well, everyone but Ismat," Chasan corrected.

"Mmm," James grunted, nodding his head, "not old enough if I remember right."

"Yes, sir." Ismat confirmed, politely.

"Ah well, next year then?" The baker asked expectantly.

"Hopefully, sir," he answered shyly, setting Bror's face alight.

"You even talked this one into it?" James asked Bror, jabbing a scarred thumb in Hakan's direction.

"Mhm," Bror murmured proudly.

"Good for you!" James praised as he beamed at Hakan, who tried to suppress a small smile. "Now, Chasan, you're already on Honor Guard, right?"

"You remembered," Chasan remarked, impressed.

"Nothing wrong with my memory, son," James said sternly, quickly making Chasan's ears turn bright pink. "So, does this mean you'll be trying out for another division this summer, then?" he inquired.

"I'm trying out for City Guard," Chasan answered, ignoring the suppressed giggles of the others who had noticed his embarrassment.

James nodded approvingly. "You've been helping them all get ready?" he questioned, looking back at Bror. However, it wasn't Bror that replied.

"Yes, sir," Hakan told James, smiling at his eldest friend, whose flushed cheeks were beginning to rival Chasan's ears.

"Him and Moritz have been working with us every day since the Gifting Ceremony," Joule added, his voice full of appreciation.

James' expression became wistful. "Ah...his parents would've been so proud of him," he remarked, his eyes glazing over pensively. "First ever Ladothine recorded with five heightened senses, a Royal Guard, and a good boy to boot," the old baker marveled.

Chapter 7

"His mom was a professional derbala player, wasn't she?" Fannar asked, squinting his eyes as he strained to think back several years.

"Mhmm," James mumbled, slowly coming out of his reminiscence. "Moritz gonna play in the tournament too?" he asked, which resulted in a chorus of confirmations. James smiled and dropped his head in amusement. "Oh! Here, help yourselves!" He offered, remembering the sheet of cookies in his hand, and setting it down on the counter as he sniffed the air. "I've gotta go grab the next batch from the oven–I'll wrap some from that one for you to take back for Moritz," he told them merrily, and shuffled off to the kitchen as everyone grabbed a cookie.

Treats in hand, they ambled over to the circular tables inside the shop where Chasan, Bror, and Fannar began pushing two together while the others gathered seats.

As Hakan pulled one of the chairs out from an adjacent table, he found James' ferret curled up on the paint-chipped surface, sound asleep. He smiled as he stuck the still-warm cookie in his mouth before carefully scooping the animal up with one hand and moving the chair with the other. After situating himself among his friends, he gingerly placed the lanky creature on his lap, where it curled back up, unbothered by the commotion.

Fannar, who had settled into a seat opposite his twin, noticed Ismat staring wistfully off into space beside him, "You okay?" he quietly asked.

"Yeah," Ismat lied, hurriedly trying to mask the grief that had unexpectedly surfaced.

Bror, seated on Ismat's other side, overheard them, and studied the youngest's expression carefully. "How're you and your mom doing, Iz?" he asked.

Ismat sighed, trying to decide what to say. "Better," he finally answered, though it sounded half-hearted.

Bror wrapped an arm around Ismat's shoulder and leaned his head against his friend's. "Moritz said the first year was the hardest," he told Ismat gently, giving his friend a comforting squeeze as the five other sets of eyes focused their concerned attention on them.

Ismat swallowed hard, his eyes filling with tears. "I told mom I want to try out for the Honor Guard next year like you guys," he said in a cracky-whisper, "she was really excited; she said my dad would be proud…"

Joule smiled warmly at him. "Mr. Pyaara'd be the proudest of all our parents," he told Ismat confidently. "Not like my dad," he whispered tartly, taking another bite of his cookie, and eliciting a chorus of confused 'huhs" from the group.

"You didn't tell them?" Chasan criticized, scowling at his little brother, who shook his head gloomily. He turned back to the dumbfounded faces of their friends with an exasperated expression as he explained, "our dad thinks it's a waste of time."

"How?" Bror questioned with a puzzled frown, "he was all for *you* joining. What's different now?"

Chasan sighed. "The difference is it's Joule. Our dad has certain expectations of us–"

"–Chasan's supposed to join the Royal Guard," Joule interjected, "and I'm supposed to take over his business," he added despondently.

"I can't see either of you taking over your dad's business," Shammoth said with an amused grin.

"Right?! And neither of us really wants to take it over," Joule replied, his face screwing up with frustration the more he thought about it.

Chapter 7

"What do *you* want to do?" Bror asked.

Joule shrugged. "I just know I want to do something to help people; managing properties really won't be helping anyone." He paused, turning the last bite of his cookie over between his fingers, "Honestly, I wish I had gotten the healing gift. I really wanted to join the capital's Healer Corps."

"Well, why don't you join the City Guard like Chasan?" Fannar suggested.

"No!" Chasan moaned. "I already spend enough time with him at home and with you all! I don't need him at my work too!" he jokingly grumbled.

"Actually," Bror interjected, his expression thoughtful, "your gift is perfect for guard work... *and* it's a job where you'd be helping people."

Joule paused again as he considered Bror's point. "I don't know," he finally said, "I mean it's one thing joining Honor with you all for the tournament, but–"

"You should join the Royal Guard," Hakan interrupted, staring thoughtfully at the tabletop.

"Yeah right!" Joule laughed, assuming the prince was joking.

"I'm serious," Hakan told him, his expression sincere as he looked up at his friend.

Joule gawked at him. "They're the most elite of the guards!" he exclaimed looking at the prince as if he'd gone mad, "they only take people like Chasan and Bror."

"You could be as good as them if you worked at it; you'd actually make a really good Royal Guard." Ismat argued encouragingly.

"You definitely acted like a Royal Guard the way you jumped in front of Hakan that day Adrig started causing trouble," Shammoth added, smirking at his friend.

"That's different," Joule said, dismissing the example.

"Not really," Chasan told him, his expression as serious as Hakan's.

Joule turned to the older twin and gave him a pleading look.

"Not fun being on that end of things, is it?" Hakan smirked, making everyone chuckle.

Joule rolled his eyes. "You all really think I could do it?" he asked, his face full of doubt as he looked around the table.

"You may not have spectacular hand-to-hand skills yet," Bror began, Joule's heart sinking a little from the brutal honesty, "but the power-level of your gift might make up for it. I personally think you'd have a good shot… especially if you make Honor Guard," he finished, giving his friend a sly smile.

Joule, ears now bright red, turned to Shammoth and Fannar and asked, "what about you guys? What are you gonna do after we're done at the academy?"

"I already told you," Shammoth said in a bored tone, "I want to take over my parents' tech-shop. What about you, Fannar?"

"Well," Fannar paused, thinking hard, "I'm not sure; I've never really thought about it, actually."

"You'd be more than welcome to come work here." James offered, as he walked up to them, a small paper bag clutched in his hand.

"Really?" Fannar asked brightly.

"Sure!" James exclaimed with a broad grin, "I'm not getting any younger, and since I was never lucky enough to have any youngsters of my own, I need to find

Chapter 7

someone to take over the shop some day when these old bones get too achy to run things anymore."

Chasan's eyebrows creased as he stared at the younger twin, "Have you ever baked anything before?"

Fannar's face fell as he realized the answer. "No," he admitted sadly.

"Tell you what," James said, passing the brown bag to Bror, "once tryouts are done, and Bror and Moritz give you your free-time back, come on by and we can see about teaching you a few things."

"Alright!" Fannar excitedly agreed, his eyes sparkling with joy.

James laughed heartily, "well, now, as always, you boys feel free to hang around as long as you'd like and help yourselves to anything in the shop – no charge," he told them as he made his way back behind the counter and out of sight.

"I don't know how he stays in business with all of the food he gives away," Shammoth wondered quietly as he listened to James rattling around in the back.

Fannar gave his brother a knowing look, and Hakan gave him the tiniest smirk in reply.

Chapter 8
HOLD NOTHING BACK

Over the next month, Bror worked with Shammoth to improve his hand-to-hand combat, Moritz focused on strengthening Fannar's gift, and Chasan helped Hakan and Joule improve the fluidity with which they switched between physical and gift-fighting. Everyone was thoroughly impressed by Joule's progress during the first two weeks given the fact that he had missed the bulk of their practices due to an unforeseen conflict. Shortly after finals, Councilman Leal had demanded that his younger son spend the summer working at the business he was to inherit, much to Joule's annoyed protests. Despite the impressive accomplishment of keeping pace with his friends, Fannar and the others couldn't help but worry for him as they noticed dark circles slowly materializing under his eyes.

Finally, outraged by Joule's increasingly pale and sickly appearance, Moritz demanded to know what was going on and – although the electric-gifted attempted to dismiss the concern – Joule could only hold off the relentless interrogations for so long. Eventually he was forced to admit that he had been sacrificing sleep to practice on his own every morning before his father woke; something his friends insisted he stop immediately.

Chapter 8

Their demand ended up being unnecessary though, as the day following this revelation Joule was mysteriously granted a reprieve from work until after the tryouts. After a great deal of suspicious prodding, Moritz confirmed that he had gone to confront the councilman and convince him to cut Joule some slack.

Exhilarated by Moritz' triumph, the boys became even more devoted to their training during the remaining practices. Before they knew it, the first day of summer, and the day of the Honor Guard tryouts, arrived.

Hakan and Fannar's alarms sounded on their mini-tabs as the first rays of morning light crept between the curtains. The two, brimming with nervous energy, quickly dressed, ate, and headed out for the tryouts at the Capital Guard Headquarters. Traveling to the city's center, they jogged to a stop outside the imposing stone and steel building of the headquarters as they looked around for Joule, Chasan, and Shammoth.

"Are we the first ones here?" Hakan wondered aloud.

Fannar pulled out his mini-tab and began rapidly tapping out messages to the absent members of their group, the device giving several little 'badoops' as the replies came in.

"Shammoth's waiting on the tram, says the station's packed," Fannar told his brother, pausing as he flicked his thumb on the screen.

"And the others?" Hakan prodded, anxiously staring at the small rectangular device in his twin's hands.

"Nothing from Chasan or Joule yet," Fannar answered, locking the device, and replacing it in his pocket. "Should we head in or wait for everyone else?"

Hakan thought for a minute, wringing his hands, and staring at the large, glass doors. "Let's wait a few minutes," he answered tensely, "Chasan will know where we need to go, and I'd rather he shows us than waste time wandering around trying to find the right room."

"Okay," Fannar replied, bouncing anxiously on his heels.

Hakan leaned on Fannar's shoulder. "You're going to do fine," he said, giving his brother a reassuring shake.

Fannar pursed his lips and exhaled deeply through his nose. "I just keep imagining Bror's face if one of us doesn't make it," he told his brother somberly.

Hakan let out a matching sigh as he righted himself again. He was afraid to let their friend down as well, but unlike everyone else, Hakan was convinced that his gift would prevent him from being chosen for the guard no matter how good his tryouts went. So, in his mind at least, Bror's disappointment was going to be unavoidable.

"We're here!" They heard Joule call as he and Chasan ran towards them. "Do we know how close Shammoth is?" Joule asked, breathing hard as they halted beside the twins.

"Checking again now," Fannar replied, his mini-tab already in-hand as he sent Shammoth another message.

"If he's not right behind us, I won't be able to wait," Chasan said, "the current Honor Guard are all supposed to be here at least fifteen minutes before the start, I'm already cutting it close."

"I don't think any of us should wait if he's not right behind you guys," Hakan added.

"Mhm," Joule grunted as he nodded his agreement.

"He says he's another five to ten minutes out, depending on if he can get on the next tram or if he has to

Chapter 8

wait for the one after," Fannar informed them, his tone echoing their collective feelings of frustration.

"Okay, tell him we're heading in now so Chasan can show us how to get to the tryout room," Hakan told him, "and to call if he has trouble finding it once he gets here."

Fannar grunted an acknowledgement as he relayed the message to their friend. Once he had again re-pocketed his mini-tab, they followed Chasan inside, checking in with a member of the city guard at a thick, wooden desk before proceeding deeper into the headquarters.

Chasan took them down a wide, concrete-walled corridor covered with small groupings of little metallic plates, which, Hakan noticed, bore neatly engraved names. As they walked along the polished stone floors, the sound of their footsteps echoed ominously against the masonry, increasing the feeling of apprehension that was already weighing on them.

Chasan led them to the end of the corridor, turning right at the last hallway and stopping half-way down in front of a set of glass double-doors that read 'Sparring Gym' in faded white lettering. He opened one of the doors and gestured for the others to go ahead of him, sniggering as they halted several steps inside after being hit by the strong scents of sweat and cleaners that filled the imposing room.

The younger three stood frozen, overwhelmed by the sight that had met them: Rows of smoothed-concrete step-like seating lined the walls of the large, well-lit space. At the center lay two square, thickly-padded areas, which, combined with the raised seating, made the room feel more like a crude arena than a training gym. Along the right wall, a few dozen academy students dotted the step-seating, and on the top row opposite the door sat several members of the current Honor Guard, dressed in their earthy-green accented uniforms.

Chasan slipped in around his awe-struck friends and darted up the step-seats to join the rest of the guards, briefly bowing his head to the Guard Leadership as he passed them. Councilwoman Basilah, Councilman Naukaron, and General Utara stood on the padded-area closer to the academy students, so deep in conversation that they barely acknowledged Chasan's arrival as he hurried by.

"What's Mr. Tanlan doing here? Joule asked, spotting Bror's councilman father.

"Yeah, isn't Chief Satna supposed to be here?" Fannar asked, feeling a bit relieved to see his friend's dad instead.

"Technically, yeah she should be," Bror brusquely replied from behind them.

They spun around in surprise to find him looking as anxious as they all felt.

"Where's Shammoth?" Bror asked, noticing his absence as he glanced around the gym.

"On his way," Fannar quickly reassured him.

Bror nodded stiffly. "Okay," he replied, checking the time.

"Hey," Hakan said, eyeing his clearly uneasy friend. "What're you doing here?" he questioned suspiciously, noticing Bror was wearing his Royal Guard uniform.

Bror clenched his jaw ever so slightly. "Long story," he said, sounding agitated, and giving Hakan an expression which the prince took to mean 'don't ask because I'm not going to be able to tell you'.

"Hey, why's your dad here and not Chief Satna?" Fannar asked, looking puzzled.

Chapter 8

"City Guard tryouts got moved up to tomorrow, and Satna's busy getting things ready for that, so she asked dad if he could fill-in for her today," Bror explained, as several more academy students entered the door behind him. "You guys should go get seats," he told them, pulling out his mini-tab, "I'm gonna check how close Shammoth is," he added, quickly stepping back out into the hallway.

Not wanting to add to their friend's obviously excessive amount of stress, they did as he suggested, and headed over to the empty wall of seating opposite the Honor Guard. Minute after minute ticked by, and more teenagers trickled in... but none of them Shammoth. This didn't deter them from turning hopefully to the door every time it opened, though. Even when – much to their annoyance – one of those times it was Adrig who walked in dressed in his Honor Guard uniform.

"I forgot he'd be here too." Joule grumbled as he glared after Adrig making his way up the steps to join the rest of the Honor Guard.

"Me too," Fannar agreed, his nervousness instantly replaced with annoyance.

As the two fumed over Adrig's arrival, the doors swung open again, and a girl with long, curly, chocolate-brown hair entered, calmly surveying the room. When she noticed Hakan looking her way, she waved and gave him a tiny, polite smile.

Hakan returned the gestures, a sense of relief trickling through him from the knowledge that at least one person from their class, outside of his brother and friends, didn't seem fazed that he had become a fire-gifted.

"Who's that?" Fannar asked, a hint of playful curiosity in his voice.

Hakan raised his eyebrows at him, "that's Amehllie. she's been in our class for like four years."

"She's the other brainiac like him and Shammoth," Joule added, nodding coyly at her.

Fannar's face screwed up in thought as he tried to remember her. "Ooooooh yeaaaahhh," he eventually sighed, "she was the one at the desk in front of us who raised her hand to answer the instructor's question the day before the gifting, right?"

"Yes," Hakan sourly confirmed, rolling his eyes at which memory had stuck with his brother.

"Well, that's why I didn't recognize her–I've only seen the back of her head!" Fannar explained indignantly.

Hakan rolled his eyes again and slumped forward, dropping his head into his hands. It was only there for a moment, however, as he heard the door open yet again. Their three heads snapped up in time to see Shammoth walk hesitantly into the gym, a slightly more relaxed Bror following right behind him.

"About time!" Joule scolded as the late comer joined them.

"Yeah, I know, I already heard it from Bror the whole walk through the building," Shammoth huffed as he took a seat beside Fannar, "but It's not my fault! The station was over-packed, and I couldn't get on until the third tram."

"The important thing is you made it," Fannar said, patting him on the shoulder.

"Exactly!" Shammoth exclaimed, shooting a frustrated glance behind them at Bror, before taking in sight of the gym. "Woah. There's like fifty people here," he nervously marveled.

Chapter 8

"Yeah," Joule agreed from the other side of Hakan, glancing around again, "I knew there were a lot of us at the gifting, but I didn't realize we had so many people from the capital."

"I don't think we did," Shammoth said slowly, scrutinizing the crowd, "I'm pretty sure a couple of the ones on the third row are too young to be here."

Fannar followed Shammoth's gaze to two girls who seemed a bit green in the face as they continually glanced from the crowd of candidates to the guard leadership. "Aren't those two from Iz's class?"

"Well, I don't know about them," Bror began from behind Hakan, his eyes following a skittish-looking boy who had just entered, "but I know I've seen *that* one hanging out with my little sister a bunch."

"I always forget you have a little sister. She's what... two years behind Ismat?" Shammoth asked.

"One year," Bror corrected, fighting a smile as he watched the jumpy boy take his seat.

"Alright everyone!" General Utara's gravelly voice suddenly boomed through the gym, "Welcome to the annual Capital Honor Guard tryouts!"

"He doesn't seem very welcoming," Fannar whispered cheekily to Hakan, who suppressed a giggle.

His brother wasn't wrong. Utara's voice and demeanor reminded Hakan of a large, fierce black bear; Strong, solid, and imposing. Perfect for his position as the head of the kingdom's Battle Guard Division, but far from being a welcoming presence.

"As I'm sure you are all aware," Utara continued, "there are only ten spots on the Capital Honor Guard, which means that most of you in this room will get disappointing news after Leader Basilah, Deputy Naukaron, and myself make our final decisions, which will be based on your performance in a one-on-one spar with an outgoing member of the current Honor Guard," he explained, motioning to wear Chasan and the others were perched on the top row, smirking down at the hopeful candidates.

"It's a very simple process. You will be called on one at a time down to this sparring mat to fight…" Utara told them, gesturing to the padded area he, Basilah and Tanlan were standing on, "and once your match is over, you will leave the gym. After we've seen all of the candidates spar, we will decide who will comprise the next Capital Honor Guard, and notifications will be sent to the families of those who have been accepted."

"Now," Tanlan called, smiling warmly at the teenagers, "hopefully all of you here have remembered that only those entering their final year at the academy are eligible to try out."

"Thank you, councilman, that is correct," Utara replied, giving Tanlan a respectful bow of his head, "and to be sure that no one under, or over, the appropriate age attempts to break this rule, Headmistress Haldis has once again provided us with a list of all the students who are eligible for this year's guard."

"So, if you are too young to be here," Councilwoman Basilah interjected, scanning her dark, cool eyes down the rows of candidates, "it would be far less embarrassing for you to leave now, rather than when you are called and your name does not check out."

Apparently Bror had been right about the skittish boy, because no sooner had Basilah finished speaking than he had bolted for the door, with another boy and one of the green-faced girls caving to the Royal Guard Leader's stare mere seconds after him.

Chapter 8

Basilah's mouth curved into a satisfied smile as she watched them scurry out. "Anyone else?" She asked coolly, turning back to the remaining candidates, but no one moved. "Very well. Let's begin," she announced, and she and Utara moved to stand on the other sparring mat, while Tanlan called the first candidate down.

Match after match, Fannar's confidence would shrink and grow. While some students clearly were not going to make the cut, many seemed to do as well, if not better than both himself and Joule felt they would perform. The only thing Fannar was certain of was that Bror had been right: Hakan *should* be guaranteed a spot... assuming the Guard Leadership remained unbiased towards his brother's gift.

Shammoth's estimation of how many students had come to tryout hadn't been far off either. They had started with forty-eight candidates in the gym at the beginning of the first spar, and by the end of the second round of matches, they had weeded out two more under-aged students.

Throughout the whole process, Hakan, Shammoth, Joule, and Fannar's favorite matches were the two with Chasan. He had dominated both of his fights, ending them in under five minutes compared to the eight to twelve the other spars took. When they called his opponent for the third round, their excitement piqued; Amehllie was going to be next to face him.

Hakan and Shammoth leaned forward with curious anticipation as she made her way down and squared off against him.

"No way she wins," Joule murmured confidently.

"Obviously," Shammoth scoffed in reply.

The fight began and Chasan, just like in his previous matches, went all in right from the start. To their surprise, though, Amehllie was more than capable of keeping up with him physically. They were even more shocked when instead of catching her off guard with an attacking vine, she vanished from Chasan's view. In the next instant, Amehllie reappeared just behind him, quickly wrapping an arm around his neck, and squeezing firmly.

"Ooooh," Joule said, impressed, "she's the one that got teleportation."

Chasan tried to throw her off, but the attempt only resulted in her locking her legs around his waist, adding to her leverage as she continued restricting his airway. He then jumped backwards, trying to slam her onto the ground beneath him, but she vanished once again just before they hit the surface. She reappeared mid-air over him and spun into a strong strike at his chest, but Chasan quickly rolled away and sprang back to his feet, sending several vines in her direction as he moved.

"Woah," Fannar and Hakan breathed as they watched.

"I think she might last longer than others." Shammoth remarked, a little in awe.

"Mhm," Joule grunted in agreement, still engrossed in the fight which lasted for several more intense minutes before Chasan finally bested her, sending the remaining candidates into an enthusiastic bout of applause.

"That was definitely the best one so far," Shammoth declared as everyone settled down.

"Definitely," Fannar echoed, still stunned.

"See?" Joule snapped, pointing a stern finger at Shammoth as the next teenager made their way down to the

Chapter 8

mat, "brainiacs can fight too! You've got no excuse to not make the guard!"

Bror and Hakan chuckled at Joule as they turned their attention back to the next fight. It was between a tall, lean, red-haired boy from their class and...

Fannar looked sourly at the pair facing off, "I hope he kicks Adrig's a–"

"Shh," Bror hushed firmly from behind him, trying not to smile as Fannar pursed his lips, and fell silent.

The prince's unfinished wish, sadly, didn't come true. Even Shammoth, the weakest of their group, would have been able to beat the red head sulking his way out of the gym. The princes and their friends watched with disgust as Adrig strode victoriously over to the watercooler placed on the front row of step-seats beside the guard leaders who immediately called for the next candidate.

The next spar began, and nearly everyone focused on the action in the center of the gym; everyone except Bror. He had continued to watch Adrig, who had lingered a little too long at the cooler and was now talking with an urgent expression to the guard leaders. Basilah turned to Adrig as he spoke and gave him a stern glare, while Bror's father continued to impassively watch the fight taking place on the mat. Adrig's mannerisms became more insistent with every breath, until Utara finally replied, the general's words satisfying the persistent guard enough that he returned to his spot looking exceptionally pleased.

The match finished, and as the glass door closed, Basilah called for the next candidate, "Joule Bedraget!"

Joule, the first one to be called by name instead of his physical description, swallowed hard.

As his friend made his way down the steps, Bror shifted uncomfortably in his seat and glanced back up at Adrig to find the guard leering down at their group.

Joule walked to the center of the mat and took a ready stance opposite his opponent. Their fight began and, though the guard was smaller than him, she outmatched Joule in hand-to-hand combat. Luckily, Moritz had helped him develop his gift to the point where he could keep a charge going steadily throughout his body during a fight. This meant that any time she was able to land a strike on Joule, she would injure herself as well, and was quickly forced to shift her tactics and rely more on her wind gift to fight him.

After several minutes of her sending gusts to knock him off-balance–and him retaliating with uncomfortably accurate lightning strikes–she created a tornado inside the gym, encircling Joule in the rushing air. Disoriented by the hair whipping at his eyes, Joule fell to his knees inside the whirlwind.

The guard smirked as she watched him struggle against the furious air current, convinced she was about to win the match, and took three confident steps forward. However, before the fourth footfall could hit the floor, Joule swiped his hair out of his face and extended his arm, sending a shock of electricity straight into her shoulder.

The swirling wind ceased, and Joule rushed forward, dropping to his knees, and sliding under a desperate kick she had made at his head. He grabbed firmly onto her calf, and sent a jolt through her leg, making her collapse as he sprang to land a finishing strike at her, stopping his crackling hand inches from her chest.

Joule stood up, breathing hard, and looked to the top row of seats, searching for his brother. Chasan was

Chapter 8

beaming with pride down at him, giving an impressed nod as he applauded along with the others in the gym, and Joule smiled shyly back before turning to shake hands with the guard. As he turned and headed for the exit, he glanced over at his friends who were all smiling and clapping excitedly–especially Bror, who gave him a thrilled thumbs-up as he passed.

Once the door had closed behind Joule, Basilah called another name. "Shammoth Adimena!"

After taking a deep breath, Shammoth made his way down to where the next guard stood waiting. Their friend put in a good effort, but as everyone watched, their hearts sank little by little. Even with all the time and training, Shammoth's skills were on the lower end of the talent scale, and his defeat came quickly without a single use of the guard's speed gift.

As Shammoth walked out, he glanced apologetically over at Bror, who mouthed "it's all good," and smiled warmly at his friend.

"Fannar Aimakos!" Basilah bellowed, as Shammoth's hand reached for the door handle.

Both Bror and Hakan gave him an encouraging pat on the back as he stood and made his way down for his spar with the much larger guard already cracking his knuckles on the mat.

Right from the start, it was clear Fannar's match was going to be nothing like Shammoth's. There was no hesitation as Fannar made the first move, sending a forceful blast of ice crystals at the guard to disorient him before rushing in for a physical strike. The guard countered by lashing a thick vine the prince's way before Fannar could land the hit. The ice-gifted prince quickly changed directions, reacting as gracefully as if it had been a well-rehearsed dance. Several of the onlookers 'ooh-ed' when he then created an ice wall, encircling himself and the guard and blocking them from view. As everyone in the gym raced for the top row of the stands for a better vantage point, they heard several loud *thwunk-crunch* noises from the ice wall, quickly followed by excited howls from the Honor Guard. Fannar, learning from the incident at the manor, had created the ice-wall to protect the people in the gym from the four ice-spears he had hurled at his opponent.

A second round of cheers sounded as the other candidates reached the top and could once again see Fannar, who was standing behind a thick pane of ice with half a dozen vines penetrating it. The excitement-filled match continued, and Fannar became the first candidate to pass the twelve-minute mark, his graceful reflexes convincing everyone that he was eventually going to be the victor of the match. This led to palpable disappointment when the guard suddenly outmaneuvered him, bringing the fight to an abrupt end. As the crowd groaned and cheered, the guard stood and offered his hand to the appreciative prince.

"Thanks," Fannar gasped, breathing hard as he shook his opponent's hand.

The guard glanced around at the ice-wall and back at Fannar. "Good job," he complimented, thoroughly impressed.

Before Fannar could respond, he heard a familiar whoop, and looked up to find Chasan proudly grinning ear to ear at him. He smiled back and began dissipating the ice wall. Then, just like Joule and Shammoth, he looked over to where Bror and Hakan sat with broad grins and excited expressions. While they watched Fannar head towards the exit, a hum of anticipation grew in the gym as everyone

Chapter 8

realized Hakan would likely be the next one called. Fannar locked eyes with his brother and gave him an encouraging nod before walking through the door and out of sight.

Basilah's voice rang out once again, calling the other twin's name, and everything fell silent.

Hakan's footsteps echoed eerily as they fell on the concrete seats. He reached the edge of the mat and glanced up at Chasan who raised an eyebrow, tapping his nose to remind Hakan of his agreement to hold nothing back, and the prince nodded in reply. Taking a deep breath as he met the anxious guard at the center of the sparring area, he inclined his head in a respectful bow.

The prince and the guard took their ready stances, Tanlan yelled "start" and Hakan waited. For a moment, a trace of fear crossed the hesitant guard's face before he lunged at the prince, who spun away with ease and immediately moved into an attack. Hakan landed his strike, sending the guard stumbling and the spectators' mouths falling open. The guard attacked again, but once more the prince evaded and landed another hit of his own. There was a pause as Hakan let the guard get his bearings, a look of mingled shock and fear on the latter's face as he realized *this* prince wasn't just going to do as well as his brother – he was going to be *much* better.

The guard took two large steps back and swung his arms in a wide circle, a glistening, snake-like mass forming as he did so. Hakan waited and watched as the form swirled and grew and was suddenly sent hurtling towards him. The prince quickly leaned left, dodging the rushing column of water that had shot at his chest, and rushed at the guard before the water-snake could get turned back around, drawing back his arm for another strike.

Hakan heard a splash behind him as the guard abandoned the water-snake, spinning out of the path of his fist. Reversing his direction, the prince turned into a kick, which he landed firmly on the guard's ribcage and knocked the wind out of his opponent long enough to drop into a spinning kick at the guard's legs. It connected, but his opponent was getting over the shock and fear of facing the fire-prince, and the guard rolled with deliberation into the fall, narrowly avoiding the next punch Hakan had thrown.

In another minute the guard was fighting at his peak capacity, but Hakan had barely begun to sweat, despite the rapid increase in speed and intensity. If an outsider had walked in on the fight, they would have assumed the guard was the candidate trying out rather than the prince. In a few more minutes, Hakan won the fight, beating the guard almost as quickly as Chasan had defeated the first two academy students. The whispered murmurs that had grown over the course of the spar were instantly silenced, as everyone in the room gaped at him in either impressed awe or horror.

Hakan stood and extended his hand to the guard, who looked blankly from it to his face. Hakan sighed, dropping his arm to his side, and took a discouraged step back as the guard scrambled anxiously to his feet.

"Thank you Hakan, you may go," Basilah said evenly.

Hakan nodded, relieved it was all over, and turned towards the door.

"What?!" one of the guards suddenly exclaimed.

"Is there a problem, Chorn?" Basilah asked calmly.

"He didn't use his gift!" Chorn howled, his face incredulous.

Chapter 8

"Gifts aren't a requirement to join any of the guard Divisions, Chorn," Tanlan reminded him, "If it was, I wouldn't be Deputy now," he added with a chuckle.

"With all due respect, sir, it's different for you," Chorn argued, "You didn't get a gift, he did."

"All the other candidates who have combat-useful gifts demonstrated them," Adrig added adamantly, "why does he get special treatment?"

"If he wants to be considered solely on the basis of his hand-to-hand combat skills, that's Hakan's choice," Tanlan said with a dismissive shrug, "the other candidates *chose* to utilize their gifts in their fights. They could have chosen not to, just like he did."

"That may be true, Tanlan," Basilah spoke up, as she stared pensively at an empty section of concrete seating, "but Adrig is right also; Hakan has a gift – one that can be used in combat – and he needs to be tested with it just like all the other candidates," she said, turning to face Hakan.

"How?" Utara asked incredulously. "We can't have any of the Honor Guard fight his fire-gift."

"I'll do it!" Chasan volunteered, already descending the step-seats.

"No!" Utara replied forcefully.

"Why?" Chasan questioned as he joined them. "I'm the best fighter in the guard, and his gift doesn't make any difference to me," Chasan insisted.

"That may be, Chasan, but you're not of age yet, and as a member of the Honor Guard, you are still our – the Guard Leadership's – responsibility," Utara explained with an almost pleading tone, "we cannot allow you to endanger yourself like this."

"I won't be in any more danger than I was in my other matches," Chasan argued, fixing the general with a determined expression.

"I'll do it!" Bror offered as he raced over to stand beside Hakan.

"No," Basilah said flatly, "I appreciate the offer, Bror, but you do not have the right kind of gift for this. It would not be an accurate test of Hakan's abilities to fight you."

"We've done it plenty of times," Bror persisted, "It'll be fine–"

"Do I need to repeat myself?" Basilah interjected curtly, and he fell silent.

"Forgive me, Councilwoman, but who do you suggest he fight, then?" Tanlan asked with polite curiosity.

Basilah turned to Hakan with a sly smile, stepping towards him on the mat. "Me," she said coolly, taking a ready position and motioning for Hakan to do the same.

Utara shook his head in disbelief and sighed as he and Tanlan backed away from the mat, the General both concerned and frustrated that his fellow leaders were going to permit the prince to use his fire-gift.

Hakan looked to his friend, eyes full of worry.

"Just treat it like another practice," Bror told him firmly, giving the prince a reassuring squeeze on the arm before joining his father and Utara beside the mat.

Hakan bowed to Basilah before mirroring her stance and waited.

"Whenever you are ready, Tanlan." Basilah chided as she smirked at Hakan.

"Alright, then," Tanlan said, an intrigued smile playing at the corners of his mouth. "Start!" he bellowed.

Chapter 8

Basilah instantly became a blur, using her speed gift to run in an endless circle around Hakan. He glanced over at Bror, fear creeping into every muscle at the thought of using his gift with so many classmates still in the gym, worried for their safety. His friend gave him a single, resolute nod, and Hakan closed his eyes, taking a slow, shaky breath.

When he reopened them, flames began flickering off of his hand, growing with his next breath before he lashed his arm out like a whip, and a long tail of fire extended from his palm towards Basilah's path. She halted a foot from the fire-whip and turned, running alongside it straight for Hakan. He quickly abandoned the whip and sent a large fireball barreling towards her, forcing her to again change direction.

This went on for several minutes; Basilah would run for Hakan, and he would in turn use his fire to repel her. Eventually, though, he failed to keep her at bay. As they exchanged physical blows, Basilah began slowly drawing on her gift, her movements picking up to an unnatural speed.

"C'mon Hakan, use your fire; force her back," Bror pleaded under his breath.

The next second, as if Hakan had heard him, the prince released a controlled explosion of fire from his arms, burning away the sleeves of his shirt and forcing Basilah to retreat. They returned to the prod-and-repel pattern and several more minutes passed, with Hakan displaying the full strength and mastery of his fire-gift.

Sixteen minutes into the fight, the prince dripping in sweat and almost gasping for breath, Basilah decided to end the match. Taking an opportunity as Hakan sent another fire-whip her way, she rushed in and knocked him to the ground. In an instant, Hakan was lying flat on his back, the Royal Guard Leader's knee on his chest, her fist hovering over his face.

"Hm," Basilah grunted approvingly before standing up, extending a hand to the prince, and helping him to his feet. She nodded, and turned to the leadership, casually interlacing her fingers. "I do believe that should be a satisfactory exhibition of Hakan's gift abilities for his tryout," She said, looking pointedly at Adrig and the other Honor Guard as she made her way to join Utara, Tanlan and Bror.

"Thank you, Hakan," Tanlan said, his expression thoughtful, "that will be all."

Hakan nodded, chest heaving, and gave the Deputy and General a small bow before heading for the glass door as quickly as his exhausted body would carry him, internally begging that no more objections be made before he reached the door.

Bror stared lost in thought at his exhausted friend as Hakan exited the gym.

"Bror, shouldn't you be going as well," Basilah quietly asked him as she reached the group beside the mat.

Bror ground his teeth for a moment, gave her a short nod, and hurried after the prince. His irritation that the councilwoman had pushed Hakan so much harder than anyone else at the tryouts evaporated as he caught up with his staggering friend in the main corridor.

"Thanks for making me practice with my gift," Hakan mumbled feebly as his friend wrapped an arm around the prince's shoulders.

"Any time," Bror replied quietly, glancing sideways at him.

Chapter 8

They stepped out into the bright afternoon sun and found Shammoth, Joule and Fannar waiting anxiously outside for Hakan's match to finish.

"What happened?" Joule demanded, eyes popping as he looked Hakan up and down, "Fannar came out like half an hour ago!"

"Long story," Hakan said weakly, trying to brush the long, sweat-soaked hair out of his face "let's get something to eat first."

"No offense, but you look like you need a shower more," Shammoth said with an amused smile, eying Hakan's damp, singed clothes.

Hakan chuckled. "No, definitely food," he replied, sighing, and lifting his face towards the sun.

"You good?" Fannar asked, concerned.

Hakan thought for a moment. Nearly two dozen students, the entire Honor Guard and the guard leadership had just witnessed a full exhibition of what Hakan was capable of... and so had he. His friends had been right to push him into joining the tryouts; in honoring his promise to them to use his full strength, he had been forced to see that he had complete control over his fire and truly was no more dangerous than anyone else. Regardless of the fact that he was probably about to face an onslaught of negative reactions to his display, it couldn't diminish the peace Hakan had found in overcoming his own fear of his gift.

"Yeah," Hakan answered as he smiled at his brother, "I'm good."

Chapter 9

GOOD NEWS AND BAD NEWS

Flump.

Hakan was abruptly awoken by Joule excitedly jumping on top of him, and loudly whispering, "wake up, Hakan!"

"What the…" he mumbled, his brain trying to catch up with his racing heart as his friend awkwardly climbed off his bed and bounded over to Fannar's, unceremoniously flopping down on top of him next.

"Fannar!" Joule said in the same yell-whisper, giving the other twin a shake.

"What time is it?" Hakan asked, rolling over and fumbling for his mini-tab.

"Almost eleven o'clock," Joule answered brightly, scrambling up to perch on the edge of Fannar's bed while his friend rolled onto his side and curled up in a ball beside him. "Guys, guys, guys!" Joule almost shouted.

"Joule! Joule! " Hakan replied hoarsely from across the room, pressing his palms to his face.

Joule jumped to his feet and Hakan reflexively tucked his legs to his chest, holding his arms out defensively, afraid Joule was about to jump on him again.

"Guys," Joule said once more, standing in the middle of the room, looking excitedly back and forth between the twins, "I made the Honor Guard!"

Chapter 9

"Congrats!" Fannar said through a yawn before smiling up at his friend, and sleepily clapping his hands through his blankets.

"That's great," Hakan said as he sat up and extended his arm, grasping his friend's hand and pulling him into a hug.

"I've been trying to call you two for hours, but you weren't answering, and I couldn't wait to tell you any longer," Joule explained as he pulled away from Hakan's hug.

"You're not the only one who tried calling," Fannar told him with a chuckle as he went through the notifications on his mini-tab, "I have just as many messages and calls from Bror."

Hakan began scanning his own notifications, smiling in amusement. "Me too," he announced as he scrolled.

Joule pursed his lips. "He was probably calling to ask if you two made it or not," he said sheepishly, "I called everyone as soon as my dad told me I'd been accepted."

"What'd he say about you making the guard?" Fannar asked hesitantly.

"He was actually really proud," Joule replied, sounding relieved. "He said I still have to work the rest of the summer like he agreed with Moritz, but he seemed really happy I made the guard like Chasan."

Fannar smiled sweetly at Joule as he nestled further under his blanket mound, "I'm really glad to hear that."

"I told Bror we just got up and we haven't talked to dad yet," Hakan announced through a stretch before standing up. "Has Shammoth heard anything?" he asked as he walked over and began rummaging through the wardrobe.

Joule shook his head, "Nothing. So far I'm the only one." A 'ping' sounded from his mini-tab as he finished his sentence, and he let out a short laugh after quickly reading the message. "Bror wants me to make you guys move faster," he told them, holding up the device with a little wiggle.

Fannar's mini-tab then 'badooped', and he let out a deep groan as he stretched out on his bed. "We better go ask Dad if he's heard anything before Bror loses his mind."

Hakan and Joule laughed and continued to poke fun at their friend's excessive investment in their honor guard results while the twins dressed. A few minutes and messages later, they headed down the corridor towards the stairwell that led down to the residence wing's living areas.

"Good morning boys," a gentle voice greeted from the sofa as they stepped off the stairs into the sitting room.

"Morning mom," Fannar said, striding over to give her a hug, Hakan following right behind.

Irina turned her warm smile to Joule. "Were they still asleep?" she asked, as her younger son settled himself on the arm of the sofa.

"Yes, ma'am." Joule said, returning her kind smile.

"Well, thank you for saving me the trouble of having to go up and wake them," Irina said with an appreciative nod, "I was beginning to worry they would sleep the day away."

"I'd've liked to," Fannar complained, scrunching up his face in a pout, "it's the first day in months we haven't had to do anything."

"Mhm," Hakan grunted in agreement, plopping down beside his mother, and resting his head on her shoulder as he closed his eyes.

Chapter 9

"Poor babies," she said, giving them both little pats, instantly changing their sour expressions to content smiles. "You should go get something to eat."

"We will once we talk to dad," Fannar replied.

"Ah," Irina said, nodding her head, "well, unfortunately, your father is not here right now."

"Where'd he go?" Fannar exclaimed, his eyebrows disappearing under his bangs.

"Snow Valley," Irina answered calmly, the corners of her mouth twitching as she tried not to smile, "He and Utara are on their way to inspect the village's Battle Guard Reservists and meet with the village leaders about some problems they've been having."

"Can we call him?" Hakan pleaded, tugging at her arm.

"Why?" she asked with a knowing smile.

"We need to ask him if he's heard anything about yesterday's tryouts," Fannar explained.

"You do realize you have two parents Utara could have talked to, yes?" Irina chided, giving them a mildly hurt expression.

"So…" Hakan slowly asked, looking at her with anxious eyes, "did he tell you if either of us made the guard or not?"

"Well, you know how your father and I feel about you boys being treated any differently than your peers," She reminded calmly, "and they were only notifying the families of the ten students selected."

"Mom?" Fannar asked hesitantly, disappointment in his voice as worry grew on his face.

The corners of her mouth slowly crept into a smile as she gave his arm a loving squeeze. "Congratulations, sweetheart!" she said proudly, her eyes glistening as she stared back at her son.

Fannar's jaw dropped as his eyes widened with joyful surprise, while Hakan sprang up to wrap his brother in a hug. Joule threw his arms around his friends and squeezed with all of his might, as both he and Hakan shouted their enthusiastic congratulations.

"Hakan," Irina said loudly, interrupting their celebration, "he's not the only one I need to congratulate," she announced as her eyes sparkled.

Hakan stared dumbstruck at his mother, while Fannar spun around in his grip to hug him back.

"I knew it!" Joule proclaimed loudly, jumping up and down as he thumped Hakan on the back, "Chasan said you were the best one at tryouts! No way they weren't going to put you on the guard!"

Hakan smiled in disbelief; the leadership had chosen him.

A new wave of elation washed over them, and the brothers pulled Joule into their hug as the three resumed jumping up and down with uncontrollable excitement at their accomplishment.

"Ah! Mom!" Fannar exclaimed, breaking the circle to turn back to her. "Can we go over to Shammoth's?"

Irina sighed as she considered his request. "I suppose your chores can wait until after you find out if he made it or not."

"Yes!" the boys exclaimed in unison before bolting for the door leading out to the courtyard.

"Wait! Eat something before you go!" Irina shouted after them.

Hakan paused at the door. "We'll stop at Mr. James's on the way and get something there," he assured

Chapter 9

her, grinning broadly before he raced off across the courtyard after his brother and friend.

"Well, well!" James exuberantly shouted, peeking his head out from the back room of his shop, "I'll be out in just a minute boys!"

"No rush!" Hakan called, taking in the smell of fresh bread. As they waited, he noticed his brother peering over the tables as if he had lost something. "What are you doing?" Hakan asked, his face screwed up in confusion as he watched his brother.

Fannar frowned as he continued his search. "Where's the ferret?" he wondered aloud, noticeable disappointment in his voice, stirring the other two to join him but the little animal was nowhere to be seen.

A few minutes later, James emerged from the back room, wiping his hands on a towel. "Now, what can I do for you boys today?" He asked jovially, beaming at them.

"What happened to the ferret?" Fannar questioned sadly, frowning at the baker.

"Oh nothing," James assured the prince, sounding a little sad himself, "someone just complained about him being in the shop, so I have to keep him up in the office with the rabbit now."

Fannar stuck his bottom lip out at this. "I thought it was nice getting to play with it when we visited."

"You and about a hundred other people!" James exclaimed, shaking his head in frustration, "but apparently all it takes is one person complaining about it being unsanitary blah, blah, blah," he waved a dismiss hand at this, "honestly, you'd think I had had the little guy in the back mixing the dough the way the sanitation minister was acting."

"Well, it's not like he was in a cage," Hakan pointed out, "an animal possibly being around the food they're buying is a reasonable concern for someone to have."

James sighed, "yeah I know, I know," he muttered, shuffling over to grab a basket of cookies from the counter and offering the treats to the boys. "I guess you're wearing your 'responsible-future-king' hat today," he teased with a wink as Hakan grabbed a cookie.

"Akchewawee, heev warring hib ahber gah ha," Fannar mumbled through the large bite he had taken, inciting a round of giggles from everyone. He rolled his eyes as he quickly chewed and swallowed. "*Actually*," he began again, giving his brother a sideways glance, "he's wearing his Honor Guard hat."

"Ho, ho! Well done, Hakan!" James praised, extending a hand to shake the prince's.

"Thank you, sir" Hakan replied shyly, a slight smile tugging at the corners of his mouth.

"And what about you two?" James inquired eagerly.

Joule and Fannar beamed as they confirmed that they too had been selected for the Honor Guard.

"Congratulations," James boomed, "Shammoth too?" he asked.

"He hasn't heard anything yet," Fannar explained, his smile fading.

"Hmmm," James pursed his lips and looked at the floor, "and I take it you all think that means he's not going to?" he asked, and they all nodded woefully, "well, if one of you isn't gonna make the cut, I'm glad it's him–at least he won't be heartbroken by it."

Chapter 9

"I'm sure Bror will be heartbroken enough for the both of them," Hakan said dully as he pictured what Bror's reaction was going to look like.

"Probably," James agreed with a chuckle as the front door swung open. "Afternoon, missy, be with you shortly!" he called.

Amehllie had entered the bakery, eyes as bright as the broad grin on her face. "Okay," she replied sweetly to the baker, and walked up to check the display case full of bread and sweets.

"Fannar, you gonna start coming by now that guard tryouts are over?" James prodded, a hopeful expression on his face.

"Yes, sir!" Fannar answered enthusiastically.

"Excellent!" James replied, clapping his hands together, "Well, I'm afraid you boys will have to excuse me now," he said, stepping over to Amehllie. "What can I get for you my dear?"

"Can I order a cheesecake, please?" Amehllie asked through her immovable smile.

"Of course! When would you like it for?" James asked, as he began scrawling a note on a piece of paper.

"Tomorrow morning, please," she answered, lacing her fingers together and holding her hands under her chin.

James nodded and added the information to his note. "Is this for a special occasion?"

"I made the Honor Guard," Amehllie told him, her face flushing a little as she beamed with pride.

"Congratulations!" James exclaimed in his most grandfatherly voice.

"Congratulations, Amehllie!" Fannar echoed.

"Thanks!" Amehllie replied, "did any of you make the guard?"

"All three of us did," Joule said, standing a little taller as he pointed to himself and the twins.

"We're still waiting to see if Shammoth makes it," Hakan added.

"Well, congrats to you guys!" Amehllie said, gently clapping her hands, "and good luck to Shammoth! I think that makes 6 spots I know are filled now."

"Oh," Fannar uttered, disheartened, "really?"

"Yeah. Me, you three," she said as she began counting on her fingers, "and a friend's classmate who said he and his friend made the guard."

"When did you find out?" Joule asked, his hopes for Shammoth rapidly fading.

"Um," There was a pause as Amehllie checked the time, "a few hours ago."

They exchanged worried looks as they realized how slim Shammoth's chances probably were if he still hadn't heard anything.

"Well, Ms. Amehllie," James said, interrupting their disparaged thoughts "would you like a cookie? On the house to all new Honor Guard members!"

"Oh, yes!" Amehllie squeaked appreciatively, picking up one of the large treats. "Thank you, Mister James!"

"Don't mention it," the baker said, replacing the basket on top of the display case and giving the air a quick sniff. "Is there anything else I can get you before I go grab my next batch from the oven?"

"Mhm" Amehlie grunted as she rushed to swallow her bite, "can I get two slices of the lemon pound cake to go, please?"

"Sure can," James said, grabbing the slices, and placing them into a paper bag, "here you go."

Chapter 9

Amehllie thanked James again and paid for her food before turning to Hakan and the others. "See you guys at orientation!" she said with a wave as she left.

"See ya," Fannar replied as he waved back.

"Bye" the other two called after her.

Hakan sighed at the floor while Fannar pursed his lips and Joule fidgeted anxiously with his hands.

"Now there you boys go again," James scolded, shaking his head. "Remember what I told you before the gifting?" He inquired as they quietly stared back at him. "You'll get what you get, and there's no sense lettin' yourselves fret." He paused, giving each of them a warm smile before he continued. "Now, I have to go grab the next round of goods from the oven. Help yourselves to whatever you like... Oh, and Hakan... don't even think about it!" he said, stopping in the doorway and pointing a knowing finger at him.

Joule whipped his head around to look at his friend, "think about what?" he asked, perplexed

"Nothing," Hakan told him, smiling at the now empty doorway.

They grabbed a few things each, called their goodbyes back to James as they left the bakery and trudged the rest of the way to the tech shop that Shammoth's family owned.

"Good morning boys," their friend's mother energetically greeted as they entered. "Shammoth is in the back working on a repair order," she said pointing to a door with a sign that read 'staff only' before returning her attention to the customer she was helping.

They thanked her and made their way through the rows of devices and accessories to the room she had indicated, which doubled as both an office and workshop.

Shammoth sat with his back to them at a desk covered in parts and tools – undoubtedly from the baskets and buckets that filled the numerous shelves above him – working on a disassembled digi-tab.

"Hey," Hakan said, giving Shammoth a gentle poke on the back of his shoulder.

"Hey yourself," Shammoth said, setting the device down and turning to greet his friends. "Did you bring me anything?" He asked, noticing the bakery bags clutched in their hands.

Fannar and Joule exchanged guilty looks, realizing they hadn't thought to bring anything for their friend, but Hakan immediately reached into his bag and withdrew a muffin.

"Ah," Shammoth sighed gratefully as he took the puffy, fruit-filled treat, "At least *one* of you still cares about me," he reprimanded, clicking his tongue as he shook his head at Fannar and Joule in mock disappointment.

"Mhm. I also have one for Bror when he shows up," Hakan added, joining in Shammoth's teasing, "I thought one of us should make sure you both eat well today."

"Speaking of Bror," Shammoth replied, looking up at Hakan, his expression now serious, "he's been messaging me every fifteen minutes asking if I've heard from any of the leaders."

"Guessing you still haven't?" Fannar asked, disheartened.

Shammoth shook his head, his face surprisingly glum.

"I'm sorry, man," Joule said, "I didn't realize how much you wanted to get on the guard."

"I don't care one way or the other," Shammoth explained, his face still fixed in a frown, "but I feel bad

Chapter 9

every time I have to tell Bror 'no' since *he* wanted so badly for us all to be on the derbala team. Have you two heard anything?"

"Yeah," the twins said together.

"We both made it," Fannar told him as he pursed his lips and furrowed his brows apologetically, but their friend's face broke into a wide smile.

"That's great," Shammoth exclaimed, nudging Hakan, "especially after they made you basically try out twice; you definitely deserved to make the guard!"

"Thanks," Hakan smiled meekly.

"That's not too bad, then," Shammoth said, slumping in relief as he stared thoughtfully at the floor, "Bror will still have you three, Moritz and Chasan – I'm the only one he'll have to replace in his line-up."

"We don't know that for sure yet," Joule interjected, trying to keep them hopeful.

Shammoth cocked his head to the side, and raised an disbelieving eyebrow at him. "They only had to notify nine families at the most, Joule. If I haven't heard from them by now, I'm not going to," he pointed out, making his friend's face fall.

Beep-beep! Badump! Ping!

Fannar pulled his mini-tab from his pocket, scanning the message before looking up at the others.

"Bror?" Shammoth asked, and everyone nodded or grunted their confirmations in turn.

"He wants to know if we can meet up when he gets back from Snow Valley with Dad." Fannar told him, his voice somber.

"Do you think he asked General Utara if Shammoth made it?" Joule asked.

"Knowing Bror, there's at least half a chance he would," Fannar replied

"Better question is would Utara answer," Shammoth wondered.

Hakan chuckled. "Depends on which Bror Utara's stuck in the valley with; the serious guard one, or the derbala-obsessed one."

The others laughed and began discussing the image of two Bror's standing side-by-side, arguing over what was more important – maintaining a professional manner while on duty with the king and head of the battle guard, or finding out if he was going to have his dream derbala team for the tournament.

"Should we message Chasan or Moritz so they can start thinking of someone else for the team?" Shammoth thought aloud, changing the topic, "if either of them can find someone before Bror gets back from the valley, it might soften the blow when we tell him the bad news."

Hakan nodded his head, "that's a good idea."

"Yeah," Joule agreed, and began flicking through his mini-tab, "I'll tell them."

"What about Amehllie?" Fannar offered.

"What about her?" Shammoth asked, confused.

"We ran into her on the way here," Hakan explained, "she said she made the guard too."

"That's perfect!" Shammoth exclaimed.

"No," Hakan interjected. "Perfect would be you getting on the guard," he corrected pointedly.

"*Well*," Shammoth said impatiently, "since it doesn't look like *that's* going to happen, she's the perfect alternative. Think about it – she did really well during tryouts, *and* she doesn't hate our little fire prince!" He explained with a smirk at Hakan, who made a face and rolled his eyes at the comment. "Too soon?" Shammoth asked as the prince glared in reply.

"Great!" Fannar cried with delight. There was a pause as he looked around at the rest of them. "Uh, does anyone have a way to contact her?"

"She's going to James' Bakery tomorrow morning, we could go over really early and just hang out until she comes to pick up her order," Hakan suggested.

"Yeah," Joule said, as he turned to Fannar, a playful smile on his face, "and Fannar can start working on his career as a world-class baker while we wait."

Fannar scrunched up his face in embarrassment, and elbowed Joule in the ribs. "Why don't you ask Chasan and Moritz what they think about having Amehllie on the team," he said, his friend letting out exaggerated groans of pain as he rubbed at his side.

"Hopefully they like the idea of asking her," Shammoth muttered.

"Hopefully Bror likes it," Hakan added.

Chapter 10

THE TOURNAMENT

"Does anyone see Shammoth and Iz?" Fannar asked, looking around the buzzing arena as they took their seats, six other pairs of eyes joining his search through the faces in the stands.

"Over there," Amehllie said, pointing to one of the top sections off to their left.

The others followed her finger and spotted Shammoth and Ismat, jumping and waving their arms in the air to get the friends' attention, broad grins plastered across their faces. As Fannar and the rest of the team returned the enthusiastic gestures, a voice rang over the arena speakers.

"Good morning!" Basilah greeted from one of the referee boxes nestled among the closest rows of seating as the thirty-two teams and thousands of spectators roared with excitement. "Welcome to the Ladothite City Inter-Guard Derbala Tournament. It is the hope of myself and the other guard leaders that this tournament will strengthen the bonds between the guard divisions through a friendly, *annual* competition."

At the word 'annual', almost everyone on their team turned to look at Bror, who swiveled his head around, giving them all a look of exuberant surprise as he clapped his hands with uncontainable joy. The expressions of the others, however, ranged from Chasan's equally excited

Chapter 10

smile to Moritz and Hakan's grimace as they realized they'd have to deal with their friend's newfound level of derbala-mania again... every summer... for the foreseeable future.

"I'm sure I do not speak only for myself when I say it has been exciting these past few months having even more of the sport to look forward to while watching our favorite teams work their way towards the Pro-Tournament this the fall," Basilah said, a rare smile gracing her features as another round of cheers echoed through the stands. "So, players," she called, narrowing her eyes as she glanced to the teams on her left, and then her right, "Are you ready?"

A round of affirmative whoops from the twenty-eight people on the waiting decks overlooking the playing pit answered her, eliciting a satisfied smile. She nodded before taking her seat beside one of the referees, and the four teams raced down the steps of their respective staircases to take their places on the lowered platforms in the divided pit below.

Hakan, Fannar, Moritz, and Joule cheered, gasped, and groaned along with the rest of the crowd as they watched the first set of side-by-side games, chastising the other three who had approached it as an opportunity to study their potential opponents. Half-way through Bror and Chasan's analysis of the second set, though, it was time for them to make their way down to one of the waiting decks themselves. As they stood along the rail, nervousness crept into the younger half of the team, their gazes continually shifting left and right as they fidgeted anxiously between stretches. They watched the teams playing on either side of the heavy net hung to divide the pit for the first half of the tournament, palms sweating as the time ticked closer to when it would be them standing on the one of sets of five platforms. In what simultaneously felt like an eternity and an instant later, it was their turn.

Fannar, who was playing one of the pelter positions, walked left to the closest of the four smaller, circular platforms. He stepped onto the three-foot-wide sheet of metal, looking far more confident than he felt as Amehllie– one of their team's two runners–tossed him a melon-sized ball. Meanwhile, Joule and Moritz had sprinted over to another circular platform in the far-right, the pelter position caddy-corner to Fannar's. The electric-gifted stepped up onto the dull, silver circle, and Moritz gave him a reassuring pat on the back before hurrying off to retrieve another ball.

As Joule and Fannar assessed their counterparts on the remaining corner platforms, Bror, Chasan and Hakan hovered by the stairs, the younger two waiting for Bror to decide which one of them would take the fighter position first on the much larger, rectangular platform in the center of the pit.

Their friend was fruitlessly hoping the other team would send their player out first, when Chasan leaned over to him. "I think they're doing the same thing," he whispered cautiously, "none of them wants to fight–"

"I know," Bror whispered quickly, cutting him off, a hint of concern in his eyes as he watched the anxious expressions on the other side of the pit. He let out a sigh that rapidly turned into a growl, "okay... we'll do Chasan, then me, then Hakan if one of us loses our round," he told them.

The other two nodded their understanding, and Chasan picked up the three-and-a-half foot long wooden staff left on the ground by the previous team before jogging out to the center platform. Once the other team's fighter

Chapter 10

had joined him on the platform, the players were lifted six feet into the air, and Chasan walked forward to cross his staff with his opponent's. Everyone took a deep breath and waited until a horn pierced through the din, and the game began.

Moritz and Amehllie raced to keep Fannar and Joule continually armed as the boys cycled between throwing the balls at the opposing fighter and the other pelters, attempting to either distract or knock them off the platform. In the meantime, Chasan was doing his best to avoid the leathery, black spheres being shot at him as he worked on his main objective: getting the other fighter off the platform without getting thrown off himself. After a twenty-minute round, and Bror's heart briefly ceasing to beat when his friend nearly fell himself, Chasan succeeded.

"YEAH!!!" Joule, Bror and Fannar screamed as they watched the other fighter plummeting to the ground with a muffled thud.

Amehllie whooped, clapping her hands as the center platform lowered. "That's what I'm talkin 'bout!" she said, walking past Chasan and giving him a high-five on his way back towards their other fighters.

"Good job," Bror said, with a quick congratulatory hug as Chasan, face covered in sweat, handed him the staff.

The second round ended quickly as Bror secured the team's first victory, and everyone howled with delight at having passed the first bracket of eliminations. As the other five joined Hakan and Chasan on the sideline, Bror corralled them into a group hug before they made their way up the stairs and back over to the participant seating to hydrate and rest.

"Okay, so next game is us and team eleven," Bror said, thinking out loud.

"We should send Hakan out first next game," Chasan stated firmly, "None of them were at his tryouts and he didn't fight the first round–none of them know what his fighting style is like. It'll give us an advantage."

Bror thought it over and looked at Hakan. "What do you think?"

"You're the captain, I'll go when you say," Hakan replied, returning Bror's scrutinizing stare with confidence.

Bror slowly nodded his head, suppressing a proud smile at Hakan's response, and turned back to the game that had started in front of them. "Okay, then. We'll do Me, then Chasan, then Hakan," he told them.

Chasan's head snapped back and forth between the captain and the prince, confusion etched into his face. "Why are you putting him last again?" he demanded, frowning at his friend.

"Because," Bror said patiently, keeping his eyes on the action below, "as you just pointed out, the other team, along with *most* of the people playing today, have no clue what to expect going up against Hakan; I wanna keep that advantage for one more game," he finished calmly, a sympathetic wince crossing his face as one of the pelters hit her head falling from the platform. Before long, it was time for their second game, and within an hour the seven of them were bounding back up from the pit, exhilarated by their second win of the tournament.

As they reached the waiting deck, they turned to watch the game still playing out on the other side of the net. It was in the third round, and the fighters were unevenly matched. A member of the royal guard who Hakan and Fannar recognized instantly was steadily moving her opponent towards a corner of the platform.

Chapter 10

"Hey, it's–" Fannar and Hakan exclaimed in unison, before turning to each other, broad grins breaking across their faces.

The twins, along with Bror and Moritz, cheered enthusiastically for the guard as she continued to force her opponent to the corner. With a final, determined kick, the guard sent the other fighter flailing over the edge and won the game.

"Wait, that was Adrig's team?" Fannar asked incredulously from beside Hakan, as he spotted the newly minted City Guard skulking up the stairs with the other defeated players.

"What!" Joule blurted, voice full of disbelief, searching through the faces of the losing team. "Oh, I hope he was the other fighter who lost," he scoffed, one of his eyebrows twitching at the satisfying thought.

Fannar let out an evil giggle and Hakan smiled at the idea that Adrig may have contributed to his team's elimination from the tournament.

"That's not very sportsman-like of you, Joule," A familiar, smooth voice said from behind them.

Joule, Fannar, and Hakan spun around to find Councilman Kesavan standing in the waiting deck, gently waving his delicately painted fan, and looking them each over with a critical eye.

Kesavan sighed and began rapidly clicking his tongue at the sight of the players clutching or rubbing different limbs. "Come, let me take a look at you all," he instructed, flicking the fan closed, and stepping up to Bror. He gently rested his fingers-tips on the captain's forehead and closed his eyes. After a few moments, he reopened them with a sigh. "You know, players like you are exactly why we do these mid-tournament health checks," Kesavan grumbled, frowning as he pointed at the ground and ordered Bror to sit.

"Bror?" Hakan asked, his concerned expression mirrored throughout the team.

"I'm fine," Bror insisted, trying to hide a wince as he followed the councilman's command.

Kesavan knelt down beside him and placed both hands on Bror's left shin. "Yes, you're perfectly fine," He said sarcastically, closing his eyes as he took slow, steady breaths, "except for the fracture in your tibia."

"What!" Hakan exclaimed, looking worriedly down at Bror's leg as Kesavan used his gift to begin healing the injury.

Amehllie and Fannar's eyes nearly popped out of their heads at the news, and Chasan's brows shot to his hairline.

"Oops?" Bror chuckled as he looked innocently up at them.

"Oops?" Moritz repeated, a hint of anger in his tone. "Is that from this game, or the first one?" He demanded furiously.

"This one," Kesavan answered, opening his eyes and moving to lay one of his hands on Bror's chest and the other on his back. "The bone would have repaired itself more if it had been from over three hours ago," he explained as he closed his eyes again to begin healing the muscles throughout Bror's body.

"You better start sending Hakan out to fight before you," Moritz grumbled, still upset that his friend had stood around watching the other game instead of tending to his injury. "Clearly you can't take that much of a beating anymore, old man."

Chapter 10

Bror said nothing; he simply pursed his lips and closed his eyes as the rest of the team sniggered at Moritz' teasing.

"If you think Bror's old, then you must find me ancient," Kesavan, who was about fifteen years older than the team captain, teased back with a smirk, making Moritz flush with embarrassment. Kesavan glanced up at him and chuckled. "I'm sorry, I only meant to join the fun, not spoil it," he apologized kindly before sitting back on his heels and fixing bror with a satisfied expression. "Well, that's it for you. Now," the healer grunted, standing and glancing around at the team, "Who's next?"

"Moritz," Bror answered quickly, springing up from the ground, his body fully restored, "after all, you're only a year younger than me, gotta make sure your old bones are all good too," he explained in an affectionately mocking tone as he patted his friend on the back.

Moritz scrunched his face, torn between amusement and annoyance before dropping his head back in defeat.

The councilman placed his hands on Moritz' chest and back as he had done with Bror and began the process of healing the young guard's muscles, repeating this with each team member who had played thus far.

By the time they had said their thanks and goodbyes to Kesavan, the arena had been altered for the second half of the tournament. The ten platforms that had been used for the previous games now sat hidden beneath precisely cut sections of padding that fit seamlessly in with the rest of the floor. The net that had hung in the middle to divide the pit had been retracted up to the ceiling, and the main platforms at the center of the arena had been uncovered.

Hakan and the others remained on their waiting deck as they watched the first semi-final game. The hunger to win immediately became apparent as the players on both teams steadily became more daring, the dauntless behavior leading to almost all the pelters being knocked from their platforms by the end of the second round – one getting hit so hard in the head, the disorientation prevented him from being able to safely break his fall. By the end of the third round, the remaining pelter was able to land a strong blow to the other team's fighter, disrupting the opponent's attention just long enough for her teammate to knock her off the platform.

The stadium erupted in deafening applause, and Fannar and Joule turned to stare apprehensively at their friends.

"Don't try and pull any stupid stunts like them and get yourselves knocked off," Moritz warned, much to their relief.

"We keeping the same line-up?" Chasan pointedly asked Bror.

Bror clenched his jaw, his brow furrowed as he looked across to the other team and considered their fighters. "No," he finally answered, "New line-up: You, Hakan, then me."

Hakan and Chasan nodded, and they all made their way down to the floor of the arena and their respective platforms.

The teams were lifted into the air, and the first round began. Both Amehllie and Moritz got consistently out-paced by the other team's runners, but Joule and Fannar made up for it with their strategic assaults with the pelting-balls. In the end, it was Fannar who won the round for their team. Chasan had knocked the other fighter off-balance, but it was Fannar's hit that had added the force needed to finish the opponent off. The center platform lowered, and Chasan

Chapter 10

bounded back over to where his friends stood waiting for their turns.

"You've got this," Bror said, giving Hakan's shoulder an encouraging shake.

Hakan took a deep breath as he stared at the platform in the middle of the arena, took the staff from Chasan, and began to walk forward. There was an audible, collective gasp as the spectators and opposing team realized that Hakan, and not Bror, would be the next fighter. He stepped onto the thick plane of metal and looked toward the three opposing fighters huddled on the other side of the arena speaking quickly and repeatedly glancing over their shoulders at him.

After a heated deliberation, their second fighter apprehensively made his way towards the center platform. Hakan bowed his head to the opponent before holding his arms out, the staff gripped firmly in his hands. The opposing fighter mirrored Hakan's stance, jaw set as he stared at the prince.

The horn bellowed and Hakan lunged. The other fighter evaded his attack, swinging his own staff at the prince in the process and missing. As Hakan twisted away, he saw motion from the corner of his eye; one of the other team's pelters had caught a ball from their runner and immediately thrown it, with all the force he could muster, at the fire-gifted fighter.

Sorry, Bror, Hakan thought to himself as he took a step away from his opponent and towards the incoming ball.

Over and over, Bror had drilled into him and Chasan to ignore the pelters and let Joule and Fannar worry about knocking them out. Bror wanted Chasan and Hakan to focus only on the other fighter–their job was to avoid the ball or brace for the impact.

Hakan, however, decided to do neither. He spun, kicking the black sphere hard and sending it flying back at the pelter, who barely ducked in time to avoid it. As soon as the ball had changed direction, so had Hakan. He continued the momentum of the kick to turn back to the confused fighter who now looked both mildly frightened and impressed.

The look didn't last long, though, as Joule landed a solid hit on the fighter's back, which Hakan took advantage of, rushing forwards to slice his staff low at the fighter's leg. The fighter, realizing what was happening, jumped forward into a somersault on the cool metal. He rolled back onto his feet, quickly rising and spinning around just in time to block another fierce strike from the prince. Suddenly, there was an all too familiar thump of a body hitting the padded floor, and Hakan fought the urge to check who's pelter had fallen. For what felt like hours, he kept swinging, spinning, kicking, and dodging. Beads of sweat grew and slid down his face in a continuous stream as he pressed on, both fighters taking hit after hit from the respective pelters.

There was another thump followed by loud screams, but Hakan couldn't tell which team they were for.

Don't think about it, he told himself, *just get the fighter off the platform.*

Thwack!

Fannar had thrown a ball at the back of the fighter's knee, causing it to buckle, and Hakan abandoned his staff as the fighter stumbled to the right. Grabbing onto the flailing player's arm with both hands, the prince pulled as hard as he could. The muscles in his right arm burned in

Chapter 10

protest as he yanked on the other fighter, who quickly lost his footing–and staff–and rolled towards the edge of the platform. Hakan thought it was all over, that he was about to win the round, when the fighter twisted, bringing his feet under him and sprang back upright. Groaning in frustration and pain, Hakan rushed forward as another ball suddenly struck the other fighter, this time in the head. The prince slammed into the disoriented fighter, and a moment later there was a third and final thump on the pliable surface below as he won the round.

The deafening roar of screams was overwhelming as Hakan looked around. It had been the other team's pelters he had heard fall during the game and the prince couldn't help but beam as he watched his brother and Joule screaming and jumping uncontrollably on the small circles in the air. The platforms began to lower, and Hakan sat down on the edge of his own, breathing hard and glancing around for the others who were running towards him, yelling indiscernible words as they raced across the padded floor. His feet had barely reached the ground when Bror and the other three reached the center platform and excitedly tackled him. Shouts of "you did it!" and "we're in the finals!" wailed in Hakan's ears as Joule and Fannar joined, piling on top of the heap of teammates crushing the victorious prince.

The fervor in the arena faded, and Moritz and the others began pulling one another back to their feet while the final team made their way down the stairs.

Hakan took Bror's hand, wincing as a sharp pain shot through his shoulder when the captain brought him to his feet.

"What's up?" Bror asked, his eyes filling with concern.

"It's nothing, I'm fine," Hakan lied, as all eyes on the team turned to him, and Bror raised his eyebrows disbelievingly. "My shoulder's just a little sore, but it's nothing serious," he insisted, waving his hands dismissively. The motion sent another throb of pain through the joint, which Hakan unsuccessfully attempted to cover.

"Okay," Bror said, more to himself than anyone else, quickly looking around. "Okay, okay, okay... final game we do me, then Chasan, then Hakan."

"You don't have to put me last because of my shoulder," Hakan protested, fixing Bror with a defiant expression.

"We're doing Me, Chasan, *then* you," Bror said firmly, "I don't want you to make whatever's going on worse. The healers aren't allowed to treat again until after the final game unless we forfeit because they'd have to restore fourteen players to keep the game fair, and the Corps. doesn't have enough level-ten healers for that."

Hakan's eyes glistened as he welled up with frustration and disappointment. He wanted to help his team, his friends, win; wanted to take the opportunity to push himself to be more open with the kingdom. Most of all though, he had wanted to prove to the other players that it was no different facing him than any other fighter in the tournament–none of which he could do if he didn't play. Eventually, he nodded his reluctant agreement to Bror's line-up, and made to head back to the sideline when a hand gently closed on his good shoulder.

"Hey," Bror said softly, turning the prince back to face him. "You did really, really well last game. By the end, a bunch of the people in the crowd were rooting for you." he told his friend, his eyes full of pride and warmth.

Chapter 10

"Really?" Hakan asked, surprised.

"Really." Bror said with a reassuring smile.

The tension in Hakan's body dispelled, and he hurried off to the sideline with Chasan while the others took their places for the final game.

After being instrumental in helping both Chasan and Hakan win the semi-finals, Fannar was immediately targeted by both pelters as the final game began. Again and Again, the prince was forced to dodge incoming fire, leaving few openings for him to retaliate. This required Joule to focus all his attention on the pelters as well, trying to knock one out in order to ease the fire his friend was taking. Luckily, Fannar drawing all the pelters' attention left Bror uninhibited on the center platform with the Battle Guard fighter that had been sent to face him. Their captain had another advantage: he hadn't fought since Kesavan had restored his strength and stamina. After ten minutes, Bror sent the battle guard flying off the side of the platform, ending the first round.

The fighters switched out, the starting horn blew for the second time, and the pelters once again focused all their energy on trying to knock Fannar off his platform. One of the fervent attacks eventually hit the prince's leg out from under him, and he fell forward over the edge of his platform, managing to grab onto the curved metal on the way down.

"C'mon Fannar," Hakan said under his breath as his brother dangled precariously from his fingertips, "pull yourself back up."

Bror stood beside Hakan, biting his fist as he repeated the same thought in his head.

"You got this Fannar!" Amehllie called from the ground as she and Moritz raced to bring Joule more ammunition to throw against the pelters still gunning for their swaying friend.

Fannar swung his legs back and forth, building momentum and letting out a yell as he heaved himself back onto his platform, swatting away another ball that had come at his head.

Hakan and Bror let out a relieved sigh, and Amehllie tossed Fannar a ball, which he quickly fired at the nearest pelter with renewed vigor.

Meanwhile, on the center platform, Chasan wasn't fairing well. He had lost his staff and was being inched closer and closer to the edge; it seemed that the other team's strategy of keeping Fannar busy was working to their advantage this round. While Joule had the same power behind his throws, he couldn't get the accuracy Fannar could, and now that Chasan had been forced to side furthest from his brother, Joule was no help to him. Bror stood frozen beside Hakan, watching in shock as Chasan fumbled and fell from the platform while the arena erupted into a mixture of cheers and boos.

Bror jumped in front of Hakan and clutched the prince's face. "I don't care about winning this tournament, do you hear me?" he cried over the noise of the crowd, his voice urgent and eyes wide with concern. "I *do not care*," he shouted again.

Hakan gave Brors arms a gentle squeeze and met his eyes with confidence. "I know," he yelled, releasing himself from his friend's grip and stepping around him. Hakan had only taken two steps towards Chasan before he called loudly over his shoulder at the still concerned captain, "but I *do*."

Chapter 10

The prince walked up to Chasan, who handed over the staff before grabbing onto Hakan's arm. "Be careful," he said, the same look of deep concern as Bror.

Hakan nodded appreciatively and continued on to the center platform. He stepped up to the waiting fighter, inclined his head, and took a ready stance. The horn sounded and around the edges of the pit, the other team resumed their strategy of 'keep Fannar out of play'.

Joule noticed, from the corner of his eye, the pelter closest to him slip ever-so-slightly from the effort to lob another ball at the ice-prince, and as Moritz re-armed him, he quickly hurled the sphere at the unsteady pelter. The speeding orb connected, and the opponent went tumbling from his platform. "Wooo!" Joule cried, causing Moritz to scream triumphantly below him, raising an excited thumb as the rest of his team realized they had finally eliminated one of the pelters from the game.

Fannar gave an appreciative whoop, and he and Joule sent another set of spheres flying – Fannar's for the pelter closest to himself, and Joule's for the center platform.

Hakan watched as Joule's shot headed for his opponent's right arm, and he fought to keep him in place. The sphere connected, temporarily weakening the fighter's grip. Hakan quickly slid his staff around and behind his opponent's and tore the wooden pole out of the fighter's grasp. As his opponent dove for the fallen staff at the prince's feet, Hakan gave it a hard flick with the toe of his boot, sending it speeding for the edge of the platform.

Amehllie called to Fannar, heaving a ball to him from across the arena. Fannar's fingers latched onto it, and he turned back to the main platform. He saw his brother send the other fighter's staff rolling towards the edge, and took aim, waiting for the opponent to follow his weapon. The fighter, however, decided it was too risky to follow the staff and instead lunged for Hakan. Fannar quickly changed tactics and shot the ball in his hands to intercept the one zooming towards his brother.

Hakan heard the thump of the two orbs colliding behind him as his brother's shot successfully interfered with the attack on him, and ducked as his opponent flung a kick at his head. Spinning as he dropped, Hakan sent a swipe of his own at the fighter's legs, but missed, leaving an opening for the fighter to strike him hard on his right shoulder; the pain that shot through Hakan's arm and chest was blinding. The fighter, realizing the prince's right arm was hurt, seized it and began dragging Hakan toward the edge. In a moment of desperation, Hakan rolled backwards, kicking his leg up as he went, hoping for it to connect somewhere on his assailant. A groan of relief escaped his lips as the fighter released his arm to block his kick.

As Hakan brought his legs back, he twisted, flipping himself over to his stomach and quickly sprang back upright. The fighter sent another jab towards Hakan's injured shoulder, but the prince spun out of the way, whipping his body parallel along his opponent's to strike hard on the fighter's back. Hakan could barely make out the noises of the crowd through the throbbing in his ears, an unfortunate side effect from the agony in his shoulder.

Slowly... steadily... Hakan began moving himself and the fighter closer to the edge of the platform while his brother and Joule kept the remaining pelter busy. Everyone in the arena held their breath as the players drew dangerously close to the edge; both fighting hard and fast. And then...

Thwump.

Chapter 10

Hakan collapsed on the cool metal, an almost unbearable pain shooting through his shoulder as he felt the platform begin to lower.

"Amehllie, there!" Moritz shouted.

Hakan heard the muffled cry of his friend from the floor below as he curled into a heap. A few moments later, both Amehllie and Councilman Kesavan were kneeling at his side, the healer's smooth fingertips gently resting on his forehead.

As Kesavan attempted to pinpoint Hakan's injury, the players from the final game rushed onto the center platform.

"Hakan, can you hear me?" Kesavan asked.

"Yeah," Hakan groaned through the pain.

"You've got a dislocated shoulder," Kesavan explained calmly, "healing it is going to hurt until it's back in place."

Hakan simply nodded, worried that he may vomit if he tried to speak.

"I told you not to make it worse," Bror scolded, his voice thick with worry.

"He went into the round injured?" a new voice asked.

"It feels like he suffered a moderate tear in his shoulder during the semi-final game," Kesavan told them disapprovingly.

Bror, wracked with guilt, looked sorrowfully down at his friend. "I didn't think we would need him to play the final game," he told the healer somberly.

There was an audible *'pop'* as Hakan's shoulder finally snapped into place, the pain instantly dulling. Hakan opened his eyes and saw the faces of not only his friends, but also the seven players on the opposing team.

"He was injured and still went almost twenty minutes?" another unfamiliar guard wondered aloud. "Impressive," he mumbled and several of his teammates nodded their heads in agreement.

A minute later, Kesavan let out a sigh as he released Hakan's shoulder. "There we go, good as new."

Hakan sat up and gingerly rotated his right arm. "Thank you, councilman," he said, giving the healer a grateful smile as Bror and Fannar cautiously helped him to his feet.

Just then, Basilah, Setna, and Utara arrived on the platform, the latter two carrying medallions in their hands.

"Congratulations to our winners," Basilah said, her voice amplified by the almost imperceptible microphone she wore, "team four, well done."

Setna and Utara stepped forward and handed out the medallions to Bror and the rest of the team as Basilah and the spectators broke into applause. Amehllie, Fannar and Joule waved happily at the crowd, while Bror, Moritz and Chasan simply beamed around at their friends.

Basilah motioned to let the winners exit the platform first when someone spoke.

"Hakan," yet another unfamiliar voice called from across the platform.

The prince turned; It was the player he had fought in the final game.

The fighter stood at attention before leaning forward into a bow, his face filled with admiration as he rose.

Hakan's eyes sparkled, surprise and gratitude touching every feature of his face. The prince made to return the gesture, but before he could the rest of the second-place team had joined the fighter at attention, and–

Chapter 10

as one–bent forward. Dazed, Hakan bowed back, an appreciative tear slowly rolling down his face as he stood upright. The crowd erupted once again after witnessing the interaction, and he looked around in disbelief. His brother and friends gathered around him, each wearing a proud smile as they ushered Hakan off the platform and out of the arena.

Chapter 11

SURPRISES

"Ismat Pyaara," Councilwoman Haldis called, her voice magnified through the speakers placed around the Gifting Falls.

The seven friends bobbed on tiptoes at the back of the crowd as they watched the now sixteen-year-old Ismat with excited anticipation.

It had been six months since the tournament, and much to the royal family's relief, Moritz and the others' support of Hakan joining the Honor Guard and subsequently playing in the tournament had been vindicated. Not only had the prince been open about what he could do physically, but he had also shown what his heart was capable of. The spectators and guards had watched Hakan's every move throughout the tournament; they had seen his concern for his brother's fall, his joy for Bror and Chasan's wins, and his humble respect for his opponents.

Most importantly, as hard as people had tried to search for it, they did not find a single moment in which Hakan betrayed any hint of malice towards anyone. In a matter of weeks, the entire Royal Guard was once again relaxed when they entered the prince's vicinity, and over the next three months of fulfilling his duties on the Honor Guard, most of the capital had warmed to the idea that he

Chapter 11

would be different from the previous fire-gifteds. This meant, as Hakan stood among the other families at the Gifting Falls, they paid him no more attention than they had at the previous ceremonies.

Everyone waited, anxiously fidgeting as they watched Ismat walk through the crystal-clear stream of water cascading from the rocks overhead. Their sopping friend then shivered his way along the remainder of the new vine-bridge and stepped back onto the bank, wrapping his arms around himself as he closed his eyes in concentration. Several long moments passed as Ismat shakily inhaled and exhaled, before his eyes snapped open, a pained expression filling his features.

"Oh no," Hakan breathed, crestfallen.

"Iz," Fannar whispered, a lump forming in his throat.

Ismat turned numbly back to the cave and shook his head, the crowd sighing sympathetically as he began weaving his way through the sea of teenagers. As he reached his friends, Fannar immediately pulled him into a hug, the other six wrapping their arms around the pair one-by-one as the next name was called.

"I'm so sorry, sweetie," Ismat's mother said softly to her son as she joined the group of friends huddled together.

Ismat stepped out of the massive hug only to be enveloped by his mother's arms, a small tear falling from her eyes as she pulled him close.

"Don't cry, mom. It's okay," Ismat reassured her, smiling as he stood back upright.

"Iz–" Joule began, his face screwed up with pity.

"Why do you all look so miserable?" Ismat asked, glancing around at all their despondent faces, "it's no big deal."

"You sure you're alright?" Hakan asked, scrutinizing his still dripping friend.

"Positive," Ismat said confidently, giving him a bright, grateful smile.

Bror squeezed his young friend's shoulder, and they all returned their attention to the remainder of the ceremony as teenager after teenager was called from Haldis' list, almost all receiving either common or uncommon gifts – the only exception being a girl who, like Ismat, came out of the falls without receiving any new abilities.

"Well, that's that then," Ismat's mother said with a deep sigh as the last teenager returned to her family.

"Hey, I know you probably don't feel much like celebrating," Joule began, looking at Ismat apologetically, "but I kind of talked my mom into buying a bunch of food for us to give you a small party after your gifting. If you don't want to come over, I get it, but we got all your favorites and–"

"That sounds perfect," Ismat said with a broad smile.

"Who says we can't still celebrate?" Fannar interjected indignantly.

"Yeah, Iz doesn't need a gift for us to celebrate him!" Bror said, seconding Fannar's sentiment.

"We can celebrate the falls deciding Ismat was already perfect just the way he is," Chasan offered as he thought longingly of the delicious foods he'd been forbidden to touch for the last twenty-four hours.

"You just want an excuse to eat," Shammoth teased, giving Chasan's stomach a poke.

Chapter 11

"Hey! There's nothing wrong with satisfying my hunger while I celebrate my friend!" Chasan retorted playfully, his comment sending his friends into a hearty fit of laughter.

"To the Bedraget's!" Moritz proclaimed through the guffawing, and they set off towards the city.

Once they entered the glass door of Chasan and Joule's home, they were met with a mixture of sweet and savory aromas wafting from the kitchen. Mrs. Bedraget had indeed tracked down almost all of Ismat's favorite foods and was in the process of filling the large marble-topped island with them. The boys enthusiastically dug into the various dishes, the two mothers watching with amusement as they filled plate after plate for the next few hours until even Chasan's bottomless stomach was satiated. As evening approached, Ismat's mother excused herself to return home and the eight friends slipped into the sedate feeling that accompanied fullness, a nagging sense about the ceremony creeping into their thoughts.

"Not many healers this year," Fannar remarked as he slumped onto the sitting room sofa.

"Yeah," Joule mumbled plopping down beside him and laying his head over the back of the seat, "and why were there so many strength-gifteds this time around?"

"It's weird that we got two bioluminescence ones too; usually the uncommon gifts don't repeat in the same ceremony," Bror pointed out from his prone position on the plush rug.

Chasan grunted in agreement as he settled into an armchair across from Fannar and Joule, "the Falls have been so weird the past few years–three rare gifts in the same generation, two in the same year?"

"I still don't think we can count Moritz' gift as rare," Shammoth argued as he sat cross-legged beside Bror, tracing the pattern of the carpet.

"Even without mine, it's still odd that we had two really rare ones gifted in the same ceremony," Moritz remarked thoughtfully from another armchair opposite the sofa.

"I wonder if you two being twins has anything to do with it," Bror said, looking over to the sofa, where Hakan was now laying across Joule and Fannar's legs.

"There've been other twins that went through before, though," Shammoth said, shaking his head, "none of them got rare gifts."

"But maybe they all got the same level of rarity," Bror suggested, "maybe twins always both get common or both get uncommon, and no one ever thought anything of it before because no one really pays much attention to the gifts we see all the time."

"Oh goodie," Hakan said sarcastically, "so not only are we the first twins to get rare gifts, we get two of the rarest ones, and one of them is probably the most hated one."

"No one really seems to mind your gift anymore, though," Ismat reminded him, his voice hopeful.

"Yeah, because he listened to me and didn't go around killing people like a psycho," Shammoth teased, making Hakan send an annoyed kick at his head as everyone else snickered.

As Fannar lifted his head off the back of the sofa, he gazed lazily out the window-wall towards the gate, "Joule, You're Dad's home," he said, prodding his friend with a finger.

Chapter 11

"Huh," Joule said, raising his head and looking across the large yard, "hey, Bror," he said quickly, nudging his eldest friend with his foot, "your dad's here too."

"What?" Bror asked, popping up to his feet and looking through the glass.

"Guess the council meeting's done," Chasan said as he stood from his armchair and stretched, watching his father and Deputy Naukaron approach the house.

"Good evening, boys!" Leal greeted, as Moritz and the others stood upon his entry, a chorus of 'hello sir' greeting him in return. He sighed, noticing the sedate mood of his sons and their friends, remembering the only thing that could cause that phenomenon. "Is it too much to hope that you all left some scraps in the kitchen?" He asked with a bemused smile.

The boys chuckled guiltily, as Chasan rubbed the back of his head, "sorry, dad, I don't think we left much."

"Oh well, c'mon Tanlan," Leal groaned, giving the other councilman a pat on the shoulder, "let's see what we can scrounge up,"

"After you," Bror's father said, extending a hand towards the opening that led to the kitchen. "Oh, and Ismat," he said, turning to the teenager with a bright grin, "I'm glad to see you aren't letting the results of the gifting spoil your day. As nice as having a gift might be, some of us don't need any extra help making a difference in the world." He gave Ismat a wink and turned, following Leal from the room as the young un-gifted smiled shyly at the floor.

"Dad's right, you know," Bror said, gently nudging his friend, "You don't need a gift to make a difference... or to get on Honor Guard," he finished with a mischievous grin.

"Don't worry, Bror, I'm still planning on trying out for Honor Guard," Ismat assured his friend with an amused smile.

"Yes!" Bror whispered, clenching his fists in excitement. "We need to start getting you guys ready for tryouts this summer."

"Thanks again for agreeing to help me train guys," Joule said gratefully to his brother, Moritz and Bror.

"No problem," Moritz replied. "City guard tryouts will be a breeze by the time we're done with you," he said confidently, adopting the mischievous smile Bror had worn moments before.

"And then once someone retires, you'll already have some experience going into Royal tryouts," Chasan added, reminding everyone that the end-goal was for his little brother to *not* be in the same division as him any longer than absolutely necessary.

"Have you thought about who you're going to ask to take my spot in the guard tournament this year?" Hakan asked Bror, "No offense, Iz, but I think you'd be a better replacement for Fannar's position."

"Well, about that," Bror said, his tone reminiscent of the day he convinced everyone to try out for the Honor Guard, "I've been thinking… what if you two joined the Battle Reserves?"

"What?" Hakan asked, his expression and voice incredulous.

"Still crazy," Ismat said, grinning ear-to-ear as he shook his head at his friend.

"I don't see dad letting me join any of the other divisions, let alone Hakan," Fannar told Bror doubtfully.

Chapter 11

"Why not? Reserves just train once a month, and haven't been called into service in centuries," Bror argued, the familiar mania slowly coming to the surface.

"Your parents have always made a big deal about not treating you guys any differently than the rest of the kingdom," Shammoth pointed out, eliciting a 'not you too' face from Fannar. "What? I think he may go for it," Shammoth told him with a shrug.

"It's worth asking," Joule added, "It'd be nice if we could keep the team together from last year."

"We should get in some practice now to work off Iz's celebration meal," Chasan suggested, eagerly rubbing his hands together.

"I'm down," Bror cheerfully agreed.

"Of course you are," Moritz moaned, "You don't have a shift tonight."

Despite the grumbling of their friends, Bror and Chasan eventually convinced everyone to follow them out the glass door, down the steps and onto the grassy area they now often used for practice. The sun had nearly set, giving the trunks of the tall trees around them a warm orange tint as they swayed and creaked in the cool spring breeze. They took turns pairing with Ismat and Joule, working to improve both friends' hand-to-hand skills. Ismat had worked hard over the last year to keep up with his ice and electric gifted friends despite not having a gift himself, and the determination in his expression as he fought now made it clear he intended to exceed them some day.

As the practice progressed, Moritz suggested they start fighting Ismat with their gifts, starting with Chasan, then moving on to Fannar, then Joule. Finally, it was Hakan's turn to spar with their youngest friend. The older twin started off easy, creating a fire-whip which he slowly slung at Ismat, giving him time to learn how to dodge and find a weakness in Hakan's approach. His friend ducked and jumped his way right up to the prince, forcing the fight to switch to physical skills.

"Good job, Iz!" Bror called, stopping the fight, "start again; Hakan, this time make it a little harder for him."

The friends nodded and reset their positions as the last traces of sunlight disappeared from the sky. This time, Hakan encircled his body with three rings of fire–one at shoulder level, one at his waist, and the last around his legs. Ismat rushed forward, and the prince pulled the bottom ring away like a snake, sending it flying directly for his friend. At the last second, Ismat dove down under the torpedo of flames into a roll, standing as the fiery trail dissipated, and immediately resuming his race to reach Hakan. The prince shot another fire-ring at his friend, this one aimed for Ismat's legs, but again missed the target.

Suddenly, Hakan's mind froze. The muscles in his neck and shoulders tensed, and his heart raced as the memory of his first fire-column in the courtyard came rushing to the forefront of his thoughts.

Ismat was almost right on top of him now, getting ready to drop below the final ring of fire suspended in the air around Hakan's shoulders. He gave his head a quick shake, and the third ring pulled away from his body and turned towards Ismat. His friend veered out of the way and off to Hakan's left. Once again, though, his body tensed up as anxious memories flooded his mind's eye.

The fearful moment at his gifting when the fire swirled out of his palm...

The infuriating realization at the manor of how strong his fire gift was...

Chapter 11

The hopeless image of the children running from the bakery...

Hakan dug his palms into his forehead and groaned.

"Iz stop!" Fannar yelled as Ismat made to spin into a kick. His friend halted mid-attack and looked over at him with confusion.

"Iz move!" Bror shouted as he began racing towards the sparring pair.

Hakan had noticed Ismat's movement through the fog of turmoil, but all the painful memories were now blurred with the present, and he'd forgotten about spar.

He reacted, mistaking the friendly fight with Ismat for an attack from a stranger and shot an inferno, as tall and broad as himself, at the perceived danger.

As Ismat stumbled backwards, realizing too late what was happening, Fannar quickly created a protective ice-wall between his brother and stupefied friend.

Bror had almost reached the prince when the fire hit the ice-wall, but Hakan was still stuck in the fog of memory and fear and again lashed out. This time, however, there was no time for Fannar to create a barrier; Bror took the full brunt of Hakan's fireball in his chest, knocking him backward and to the ground.

As soon as he heard the thump of his friend hitting the grassy earth, Hakan's mind cleared, and he gaped in horror at what he had done.

"Bror!" Moritz and Chasan yelled as they rushed forward.

"No," Hakan whimpered softly. "No, no no!" he cried, dropping to his knees beside Bror as his other friends reached them. "Bror, I'm so sorry," Hakan sobbed.

"It's ok, it's not that bad," Bror grunted, trying to mask the pain.

"Get to Chasan and Joule's house, now," Shammoth said as he walked closer, lowering his mini-tab from his ear as he surveyed Bror's injury, Fannar and Joule still gripped with shocked-silence beside him.

A few moments later, Amehllie appeared just inside the gate and Shammoth waved her over.

"What's going on?" She asked as she jogged up to them, "Oh my g–"

"Chasan, you and the others stay here with Hakan until Amehllie gets back," Moritz ordered, helping Bror up to his feet as he spoke, "Amehllie, get us to the Healer Corps."

After his friends had nodded their understanding, Amehllie rested her hands on Bror and Moritz, and the three noiselessly disappeared.

Fannar slowly knelt down beside his distraught brother who was gazing, unfocused, at the place Bror had landed. "Hakan?" he said gently, "Hakan what happened?"

"I... I don't know," his twin whispered, not moving his eyes from the grassy spot.

Ismat joined the twins on the ground and slowly rested a hand on Hakan's arm, saying nothing as his eyes watered with sympathetic tears in the flashes of moonlight filtering through the trees.

Hearing a deep sigh, Hakan finally looked away from the ground, and up at the youngest of his friends. Though he had expected to see fear or anger, neither was present. Every inch of Ismat's face was filled with kindness and compassion as he gave the devastated prince a reassuring smile and tugged at his arm.

As Fannar and Ismat helped Hakan to his feet, Amehllie reappeared. "Bror said for me to take everyone

Chapter 11

home. Starting with you two," she told them, holding a hand out to each twin.

Fannar and Hakan somberly took hold of her, and a second later were teleported just outside the manor.

"Bror also wanted me to tell you to go to your room and let him handle everything," Amehllie added before disappearing once again to the Bedraget's.

The brothers made their way as silently as possible up to their room, where they waited to hear from their friend. Nearly half an hour later, the door slowly swung open, revealing the fully restored Bror.

"How're you feeling?" Fannar asked anxiously.

"I'm fine," Bror assured him, the corners of his mouth turning up slightly as he crossed the threshold and closed the door behind him.

Hakan stared apologetically at his friend, "Bror I–"

"Are you okay?" Bror asked the older twin as he walked over to sit beside him on the bed.

Hakan looked flabbergasted. Bror was the one who had gotten hurt, and Hakan had done the hurting, but here his friend was asking if *he* was okay. "You're not angry?"

"No," Bror told him, his voice patient and kind, "I'm pretty sure you're mad enough at yourself for us both."

"I'm so sorry, Bror" Hakan apologized again, his face full of regret.

Bror reached his arm around the prince and gave him a comforting squeeze. "I know you are," he said sadly, "now, what happened?"

Hakan began explaining the memory flashes, shame welling up inside him with each word. "I don't know what made me think of those things but once I had thought of it, it was like I couldn't stop, and the stress just kept building and I got confused about what was going on."

Bror looked thoughtfully at the floor. "Well, I mean, like you already said, last year's gifting was really stressful, it makes sense that you'd be tense because we had the ceremony today."

"Iz not getting a gift probably didn't help either," Fannar added sympathetically.

"I still shouldn't have let it get to me, though," Hakan grumbled, angry at his failure.

Bror sighed. "You'll get to a point soon enough where you won't. Try not to beat yourself up too much in the meantime, though, okay?" he told him, dismissing the incident.

Hakan nodded, his friend's compassion easing his frustration. "You're sure you're fine?"

"Yeah, it's all good; Moritz got me to the healers so quickly it didn't even leave a scar."

"That's good," Hakan said, relieved.

Satisfied that the prince had calmed down enough, Bror released him, stood and headed for the door. "Now," he said, "you two try and get some rest. I'm gonna head home and figure out a training schedule for us to get Iz and Joule ready for their tryouts."

"Kay," Fannar replied quietly, as he watched his brother.

"Talk to you guys tomorrow," Bror said with a wave as he left.

Several minutes passed as Hakan and Fannar sat on their beds, staring at the floor. "Do you think he's gonna tell dad what happened?" Hakan finally asked, breaking the silence.

Chapter 11

"I don't know," Fannar replied, as he stood and stretched, "but knowing Bror, if he does tell dad, he'll just say there was an accident while we were all training and leave off the part about you having some sort of panic attack."

Hakan pressed his face into his hands, listening as his brother shuffled around the room. Unable to muster the motivation to get up, he buried himself under his blanket, still in his dirt and sweat-stained clothes, and closed his eyes. After a few minutes of rustling fabric and scratching dresser drawers, Hakan heard the creak of his brother lying down on the other bed. He listened as Fannar's breathing slowed, turning into soft snores as he drifted off to sleep, and Hakan sighed, hoping things would seem better in the morning.

Chapter 12
AN ALMOST BEAUTIFUL MOMENT

Sadly, things were no better the following day. Hundreds of people had seen Bror leave the gifting falls with his friends–the fire-gifted prince included–so when Amehllie teleported him to the Healer Corps with a severe burn in the middle of his chest, it wasn't hard for people to guess where the injury had come from. The single bright spot of the whole affair was that Fannar had been right about how Bror was going to describe the incident. Any time someone questioned their friend about what had happened, he would say it was simply a training accident and people were making too big a deal out of it. The more he reiterated this over the coming days, though, the more resistant people were to believe him, and the more frustrated Hakan became with himself.

One afternoon, as he sat sulking on his bed after returning home from the academy, he received a notice that his Honor Guard assignments were being changed, worsening his already dejected mood. Rather than the rotation of City and Royal Guards he had been working with, he was going to be shadowing the Guard Leadership for his remaining months in the Honor division.

"So much for us not being treated any differently than other people," Hakan muttered ruefully as he finished reading the notice to his brother.

Chapter 12

"You're the successor, though. It makes more sense for you to work with Basilah and them," Fannar said, trying to put the change in a positive light, "you don't need to know all the details of an entry-level guard career, it would be more useful for you learn the administrative stuff."

"I guess so," Hakan grumbled, sounding unconvinced.

"Who've you got first?" Fannar asked as he pulled his Honor Guard shirt over his head.

Hakan scanned the notice on his mini-tab again until he found the name. "Councilman Naukaron," he answered.

A smile broke across Fannar's face as it popped through the neck hole of the shirt, "ahh!"

"What?" Hakan asked, confused why this information had made his brother so happy.

"That's smart," Fannar said to the air, consumed in thought as he finished dressing.

"What's smart?" Hakan questioned, annoyance rising in his voice as he waited for his brother to explain.

"All this nonsense with people got started when Bror got hurt," Fannar reminded him.

"So?" Hakan asked, screwing up his face.

"So, your first assignment is with *his dad*," Fannar continued in a tauntingly slow manner, "it's not a punishment, Hakan, it's the leadership's way of showing confidence in you."

Hakan stared at Fannar, his expression still contorted with disbelief.

Fannar growled in frustration. "Think about it. You shadowing Bror's dad will show people that there's no animosity between our families– *and* he doesn't have a gift, so it also shows that the Leadership don't think you're dangerous."

Hakan paused as he considered his brother's argument. "You think so?" he asked hopefully.

"Yeah," Fannar confidently exclaimed, "you had a bad day, nothing more. This'll blow over soon enough and things will go back to normal again."

Hoping his brother was right, Hakan dressed in his own uniform and headed for the Guard Headquarters to meet with the councilman.

"Ah, Hakan! I see you got your updated assignment, good!" Tanlan beamed from behind his deputy's desk.

"Yes, sir," Hakan replied politely as he stepped timidly into the office.

"Well, why don't you grab that chair and join me over here. I want to give you an overview of the sort of things Chief Satna and I handle before we head out for the meeting I have this evening," the councilman said, shifting his chair over to make room for the prince.

Hakan nodded and did as instructed, gently placing the chair down next to the councilman. He listened attentively as Tanlan showed him examples of patrol and training schedules, updates being made to the application for new recruits, and the records system used to track investigations of kingdom-law violations. Much to Hakan's relief, Deputy Naukaron seemed quite at ease having the prince shadow him, smiling patiently as he answered questions. After an hour going through the digital system, it was time for them to head out to Tanlan's meeting in the industrial area nestled between the East and Southern residential districts.

Chapter 12

Hakan stepped out of Councilman Naukaron's electropod and looked up at the small warehouse they had parked in front of. "What is this place?"

"This particular warehouse is used by a small company that imports specialty textiles from other cities to be made into clothes, blankets, you name it," Tanlan explained.

"Who're you meeting with?" Hakan asked curiously.

"The warehouse manager. They had a thief break-in a few months ago, but there wasn't enough evidence left behind for us to catch them. Fortunately, they did it again several days ago." Deputy Naukaron said with a sly smile.

"Doesn't sound very fortunate for the company," Hakan observed, feeling sorry for the unknown people.

Tanlan nodded his head, "no, sadly the thing that helps us is them having more *mis*fortune."

The councilman pulled the steel door open and ushered Hakan ahead of him. Once inside, the space felt unrealistically large compared to how small the structure had seemed from the outside. To Hakan's left were rows of shelves, each one as deep as he was tall, that towered nearly to the metal trusses of the roof. Directly in front of himself and Nuakaron were several tables and chairs situated beside a long, stained, rough-looking counter. Beyond the tables stood a haphazardly erected room, clearly added by the occupying company as an office space.

Tanlan led Hakan across the deserted break-area to the office door and knocked. A disheveled man answered, his already anxious expression worsening as he realized who the Deputy-Chief had brought along with him.

"Oh, Deputy Naukaron, I, uh, didn't realize, wh-when you said you had a student shadowing you I–" The warehouse manager stuttered, wringing his hands nervously, and trying not to let his gaze drift to Hakan.

"Ah yes, introductions," Naukaron said, ignoring the manager's uncomfortable behavior, "This is Hakan Aimakos, one of the ten exceptional students who were selected for this past year's Honor Guard."

"Ye-yes, I'm... I'm aware who he is," the manager said nervously. "Your highness," he said, giving Hakan a little bow with his head.

Hakan returned the gesture, trying as best as he could to not let his disappointment show as his heart sank from the man's fear.

"Now that that's out of the way," Tanlan said boldly with a clap of his hands, "why don't you show us where it is you think the thief broke-in at."

The manager made an affirmative noise before scooting carefully past Naukaron and Hakan. He led them passed row after row filled with bundles of fabric, turning left as he reached the second to last one.

"It's just over here," he told them, pointing to the wall at the end of the row.

Hakan looked around, confused. The only place for a thief to enter was through a window that sat at the top of the wall. However, as far as he could tell at this distance, it didn't look broken.

"And you said this is the only blind spot in the security system?" Tanlan asked, looking around at the shelves, wall and roof.

"That's right," the manager said, his eyes nervously darting Hakan's direction every few seconds, as if the prince were going to explode at any moment.

The Deputy turned back to the man, "and you said the thief didn't show up on the footage of the windows?"

Chapter 12

"Yes, and they only took bolts from this spot here. Like I told to the other guards, the cameras don't pick up this end of these last few rows" he explained, indicating the shelves they had walked between.

"I see why you think it's an intangible-gifted behind the theft; Let's go ahead and take another look at the videos while I'm here," he told the manager before turning to the prince, "Hakan, while we're gone, why don't you put those sharp eyes of yours to work and see if you can find something the other guards missed."

Hakan nodded while the manager looked between the two, appearing as if he wanted to protest the prince being left alone in his warehouse, but ultimately decided it was best not to argue with the councilman. The skittish man led Tanlan back towards the office, and Hakan began looking around for anything that could possibly be out of place. As he searched, he heard the echo of the entrance door opening followed by voices, speaking too softly for him to make out their words. He ignored them and began running his hand along the metal wall checking for any loose panels.

As he pressed his palm against the warm steel, he noticed movement out of the corner of his eye. A little girl had rounded the end of the first set of shelves, stopping when she caught sight of him. They stared at each other for a moment before the child raised her hand and waved, giving Hakan a bright smile. He half-chuckled as he let out the breath he hadn't realized he was holding, and waved back at her.

At this, the child began to skip down the aisle towards him. "Hi," she said brightly, looking up at the prince with curiosity.

"Hi," Hakan replied, bemused by the child's intrepid behavior.

"Whatcha doin'?" She asked sweetly.

"Umm…" Hakan muttered, looking anxiously around the warehouse for her parents.

"You don't look like the guards that were here a few days ago," The precocious child noted as she looked over his uniform.

Hakan looked back down in wonder at her, a small ache piercing his heart as he realized the fearless behavior was probably because she had no idea who he actually was, "those were probably City Guards, I'm part of the Honor Guard."

The girl nodded importantly at his answer before furrowing her brows at him. "So, what does an Honor Guard do?"

"W-we work with members of the other guard division to learn about their jobs," he told her, the corners of his mouth slowly creeping upwards with each inquisitive moment.

"Very nice," the little one said, nodding satisfactorily, "and what are you learning in the warehouse today?"

"Uh," Hakan paused as he wracked his brain, unsure how to describe to the clever child what he was doing, "I'm learning how to help Deputy Naukaron catch the person who's been stealing from here."

"Okay," The girl said, content with his answer as she studied his face.

"Uh, I…I should probably get back to looking around," Hakan mumbled, her penetrating stare making him slightly uncomfortable as he returned to his examination of the wall.

Chapter 12

"You're Prince Hakan, right?" She asked a few seconds later in the same sweet, bold voice.

Hakan pursed his lips for a moment before nodding, not daring to look and ruin the image he had of the happy little girl who had treated him like she probably had all the other guards up to that point.

"I don't get it," she huffed after a few seconds, "you don't seem very dangerous to me."

Hakan's head snapped around in surprise to face the little girl, who's expression hadn't changed a bit after confirming his identity. "Thanks," he said quietly, his appreciation for the spirited child growing as he once again turned to the wall.

"Can I see it?" She asked cheerfully.

"See what?" Hakan replied, confused, as he pressed on another panel.

"Your gift," she squeaked, clasping her hands pleadingly as she bounced in place.

Hesitation gripped Hakan. He had been reassigned to Naukaron because of his gift, and it was probably her parent's opinion of him being dangerous that she had parroted–the parents who were probably only a few yards away in office with the Deputy Chief.

"Pleeeeeaaaasssse," the girl begged, interrupting Hakan's thought and pouting her lip out at him.

Hakan chuckled, her expression reminding him of the face Fannar had often used to get his way as a child. The prince ran his hands over his face as he debated whether or not to give in, finally letting out a deep breath and kneeling down in front of her, his hands grasped together. As he slowly opened them, he revealed a small flickering flame. The girl watched in wonder as it danced in Hakan's palm, looking up briefly to smile at him. He then waved his empty hand over the flame, turning it over to show a second one, making her absolutely beam with delight. Hakan dropped his hands, extinguishing the fire, and the girl frowned.

"Can I see more?" She asked, immediately returning the pout to her face.

Hakan smiled at her. "What's your name?"

"Maritsol," She answered, as she continued her pitiful expression.

"Okay, Maritsol, I'll show you one more thing," Hakan said, with a small smile.

The girl clapped her hands and watched Hakan with excitement.

Once again, he created a flame in each palm, only this time they were noticeably larger. "Alright," he said, his smile gone as he stared at her with a nervous expression, "now, I need you to stay *very* still."

Maritsol nodded seriously and snapped her arms to her sides at attention, standing as motionless as a statue. Hakan exhaled, and the little girl watched with joy as the flames floated up and away from his hands, dividing into tinier flickers as they went until they hung like stars filling the space between them.

"I don't understand why people are scared of your gift– this is so pretty!" she marveled.

Hakan smiled, watery-eyed at her as he soaked in the happiness on her face.

"It's only pretty until someone gets burned," came a familiar, unwelcome voice behind the prince.

Hakan let the fire-stars fade away with his smile as he stared into the distance. "You should probably go back to your parents now, Maritsol," he said, feebly attempting to keep the cheer in his voice.

Chapter 12

"Awe, okay," she sighed, giving him a sudden, quick hug before skipping off down the nearest row.

Hakan stood and clenched his jaw as he turned to face Adrig, dressed in his City Guard uniform.

"What's the matter, your highness? Don't want to tell your new little friend what you did to your old one?" Adrig heckled.

"Get lost," Hakan snapped at the guard.

"Not that it really matters, eventually someone will tell her how Bror had to be flashed to the healers because of your 'pretty' gift." Adrig continued, a smug smirk growing on his face as he eyed the prince.

"Any gift can be used to help or to hurt," Hakan said, remembering Chasan's words, "the thief used their gift to hurt this family; an intangible gift–not fire."

"There's always an exception to the rule," Adrig replied coolly.

The image of Bror lying on the grass, a large, angry burn in the middle of his chest, floated to the forefront of Hakan's mind, and his body tensed as he filled with panic.

No, Hakan thought, *not again.* He shook his head, trying to rid himself of the picture as his breath quickened. Adrig spoke again, but it sounded distant and incoherent.

Have to... get this... under... control. Hakan turned and walked swiftly up the aisle, turning sharply down the last row and racing towards the front door as more memories flashed in his mind:

The looks of fear from the council members in the days following his gifting...

The guards refusing to be posted anywhere near him...

Hakan swung the sheet of metal open, and stumbled out of the warehouse, his frustration with people's treatment of him growing with each memory. Every muscle in his body was demanding he act, that he do something to make people see him differently. His feet kept walking, but Hakan wasn't conscious of anything besides the pounding in his ears as his heart raced. Suddenly a hand clutched aggressively onto his shoulder with crushing force, and Hakan reacted instinctively, twisting away to escape Adrig's painful grip. Hakan tried to get his bearings, but another memory flooded his vision.

Adrig ceaselessly taunting him and his friends at the academy time and again, as onlookers stared spitefully at them...

He couldn't stand it anymore; he had to move. Hakan took off running as hard as he could, his long legs quickly propelling him out of reach of the agressive city guard.

The smug look on Adrig's face at the Honor Guard tryouts...

The memory overtook Hakan's mind, and he tripped, the momentum sending him skidding and rolling several feet down the road. As he made his way back to his feet, he looked back the direction he had come. Adrig was racing towards him with the same look of smug triumph he had worn at the tryouts... a look Hakan was sick of seeing. His neck and shoulders ached, filled with tension as he fought the urge to lash out at the guard.

The venom in Adrig's voice as he ruined the innocent moment with the little girl...

The memory faded but the wrath did not, and Hakan locked his eyes on Adrig, drawing back his arm and covering it with flames. He let out a scream as he threw a large, blazing fireball at the advancing guard, forcing him to stop his pursuit and dive behind a dumpster nearby.

Chapter 12

As the fire faded, Hakan's body trembled from the mental and emotional exhaustion. He closed his eyes, the world sounding as if it was plunging underwater, and let the quiet-calm of unconsciousness over-take him. When Hakan awoke a short while later, it was in the dim lighting of his and Fannar's room with Kesavan kneeling beside his bed, both hands resting on his torso.

"Don't move yet," the kind councilman told him quietly.

Hakan looked around the room, and saw Bror, Fannar and the queen anxiously waiting as Kesavan worked.

"How much longer?" Fannar asked from the foot of the bed, his voice thick with worry.

"A few more minutes," the healer answered.

Bror let out a frustrated sigh beside Fannar, and leaned his head against the wall, his gaze boring into the ceiling.

"Does talking count as moving?" Hakan mumbled, making his brother and friend smirk.

The corners of Kesavan's mouth twitched. "Yes," he answered, sounding mildly amused, "just be patient."

Less than a minute later, Hakan couldn't help himself and opened his mouth to speak again. "What ha–"

"There's nothing wrong with your hearing, Hakan," Kesavan scolded gently, "now, shh."

Hakan sighed and joined Bror's staring contest with the ceiling until the councilman finally permitted him to speak. "What happened?" he asked, looking around at them.

"We were hoping you could tell us, sweetheart," His mother said, "Tanlan said you threw a massive fireball at one of the city guards."

"I didn't mean for it to be that big," Hakan said apologetically, "I just…" he trailed off, quickly glancing at Bror.

"But why were you using your gift against a guard in the first place?" Irina questioned, her voice confused and scared.

Hakan looked away, the muscle in his jaw twitching as he unconsciously clutched at the blanket he was lying on, afraid to tell in his mother and Kesavan the truth.

"Hakan?" Bror prodded, suspecting the reason behind the prince's evasive demeanor.

"There was a little girl. She wanted to see my gift, so I made the fire-stars for her, but Adrig saw it and tried to tell her I was dangerous. When she left he wouldn't stop, and I… I just kept getting more and more upset," Hakan took a shaky breath and closed his eyes, trying to stay calm.

Bror exchanged worried looks with the other twin as he asked, "what happened next?"

"I tried to leave; I wanted to just get away from there, but he followed me," Hakan croaked, his throat tightening, "I ran, but I tripped and fell, and he was right behind me–he just wouldn't leave me alone!" he growled, as the memory reignited his irritation. He tried to take another steadying breath, but as he exhaled, tears formed under the lids of his eyes. "So… so, I…" he stammered, unable to admit the thought aloud: *so I tried to hurt him like he wanted to hurt me.*

Fannar climbed to the back of the bed, laying down beside his silently crying brother as he wrapped a comforting arm around him, and Bror took the younger prince's spot on the bed. The queen and Kesavan gave each other concerned looks before excusing themselves to update King Eero on his older son's condition. As the door

Chapter 12

closed behind them, the question that the prince was most afraid to answer was finally asked.

"Did it happen again?" Bror said gently. "What happened that day at Joule and Chasan's – the memory flashes – did it happen again?"

Hakan nodded, afraid to open his eyes and face his friend. It hadn't been just one bad day like his brother had said. He had been attacked by all his worst memories and again let his emotions get the better of him – even more so this time.

"Had it ever happened before that spar with Iz?" Bror asked, his voice calm but serious.

"No," Hakan replied firmly, "that was the first time." Another tear slipped from the corner of his eye as a fresh wave of guilt washed over him from the memory of burning his friend.

Bror sighed. "And it didn't happen again until today, right?"

"Right," Hakan whispered back, and his friend nodded, lost deep in thought.

"What're you thinking?" Fannar asked from beside his brother.

Bror shook his head, "I'm thinking things just got a whole lot more complicated."

Chapter 13
COMPLICATED DESPERATION

Complicated ended up being an understatement as the next morning Hakan was awoken by a terse call from his father summoning him to the council room. He somberly made his way downstairs and across the courtyard as the sun rose over the roof of the manor, avoiding eye-contact with the handful of Royal Guards that pointedly kept their distance as he passed through the entrance foyer. As he entered the large meeting space of the council room, Hakan timidly approached the end of the long, glossy table, opting to stare down at his reflection on the smooth surface rather than meet his father's piercing gaze.

"You wanna tell me about what happened yesterday?" The king asked from the far side of the table, his voice stern.

"It was an accident," Hakan said quietly, still staring unfocused on the dark glass in front of him.

"An accident?" Eero repeated incredulously. "You attacked one of the city guards!" he bellowed, making son's eyes dart up to meet him.

"He attacked me first!" Hakan shouted back defensively.

"How?" Eero demanded, staring hard at his son.

Chapter 13

"He... he..." Hakan stuttered, realizing from the tone of the question that his father
didn't believe him.

"Look," Eero said, his demeanor growing more severe with every sentence, "I know you and this guard have a rocky history; he's the one who claimed last year that Joule tried to start a fight at school, right?"

Hakan paused, surprised that his father had remembered the quarrel, and silently opened and closed his mouth a few times before finally answering, "yes."

"And he was part of the group who insisted you be re-evaluated with your gift at Honor Guard tryouts?" Eero pressed.

"Yes," Hakan answered again, his voice fading as the too-familiar lump in his throat returned.

"Yes," Eero repeated as he scowled at his son, "so I'm fully aware that the two of you don't get along. But what I'm having trouble understanding here, Hakan, is if this guard really attacked you, why on earth would you use your *fire*? Basilah said you're a highly-skilled fighter – more than a match for this guy – so why would you use your gift when you could have easily defended yourself without it?"

"I..." Hakan began, a torrent of emotions twisting up his insides. "I wasn't thinking clearly when it happened" Hakan explained shakily, "he'd destroyed my shoulder; I was in so much pain, and I just wanted him to leave me alone–"

"Do you have any idea what this has done?" Eero boomed, cutting his son off, "people are beginning to think this is part of a pattern. It was bad enough Bror showing up badly injured by your gift–and don't give me that garbage about it being a training accident!" He said, waving an austere finger as his son who had opened his mouth to speak, "You and your friends have sparred more than enough with your gift over the last year to avoid an 'accident' like that. Do you realize that what happened yesterday not only has the citizens terrified, but the guard leaders as well? Tanlan saw the whole thing, and he didn't say you looked like someone who was afraid and just defending yourself..." Eero's face filled with a cold fear as his eyes bored into his son's, "he said you looked like someone out for blood."

Hakan's stomach dropped at the words as he gaped at his father, horrified at the description. He remembered being furious with Adrig but didn't realize just how bad he must have looked in that moment.

The prince's genuine shock and apparent regret finally softened Eero, and compassion began to ease into his features as he continued. "Satna wants me to strip you of your Honor Guard status and revoke your protections as a member of the royal family so the City Division can press charges for misusing a gift and assaulting a guard."

Hakan swallowed hard. "Are you?" he asked nervously.

"I take the advice of my council, Hakan," Eero said bluntly, fixing his son with a conflicted stare before he sighed, and looked down at his hands. "I'm not going to hand you over to the City Guard," he said calmly.

Hakan's shoulders slumped slightly with relief. "Thank you," he whispered.

"Don't thank me," Eero replied brusquely. "Kesavan said your shoulder injury was consistent with a strength-gifted attack, which led Damra to insist that you were being truthful about defending yourself and the overuse of your fire was probably due to your age and

Chapter 13

inexperience. The two of them were able to persuade the majority of the council in favor of a less severe punishment."

"I'm guessing I'm off the Honor Guard, now," Hakan said sullenly.

"You'd be right. In addition," Eero explained, "You will be restricted to the manor for the next month, no exceptions."

"What?!" Hakan interjected. "But my lessons!" he cried, the prospect of missing so many classes right before exams upsetting him far more than losing his place in the guard had.

"Haldis said half the staff threatened to quit if you showed up at the academy after your 'accident' yesterday," Eero said, his voice raising as he spoke firmly. "You *will* be restricted to the manor, and your brother will bring lessons home for you to complete here."

Hakan rocked his knee back and forth a few times in frustration. It had been hard enough to make good marks with his instructors there to help, and now he was on his own going into his final exams to complete the academy. "Yes, sir," he finally responded through a stiff jaw.

Eero exhaled deeply through his nose, irritated by his son's ignorance of just how little punishment he was walking away with.

"Is there anything else?" Hakan asked shakily, desperate to be dismissed.

"Yes," Eero replied curtly, "you are also forbidden from using your gift until further notice."

Hakan said nothing but nodded his submission to the unnecessary demand. After finding out he had been everyone's exact image of a fire-gifted, he had no intention of ever using his gift again.

Things only continued to deteriorate for the prince in the coming weeks as essentially being put under house-arrest did nothing to quell the outrage of the kingdom. When Hakan was finally permitted to venture outside the manor – just in time to take his final academy exams – everyone he encountered beyond the walls of his home either ran in fear or fixed him with a look of deep loathing. Months of building trust with the kingdom had evaporated in a matter of weeks from something that, like his gifting the previous year, was out of Hakan's control.

It was like reliving the time following the ceremony, only worse, as this time Joule, Shammoth and Ismat's parents had forbidden them all from being in physical proximity to the prince. Councilman Leal had tried to impose the same restriction on his older son, but Chasan refused to be barred from visiting his friend and his disobedience resulted in him leaving his family's home and being taken in by Bror and Moritz.

Between the weight of guilt he felt causing problems for his friends and the daily worry he might have another attack, Hakan found it increasingly more difficult to sleep and eventually his restlessness got the better of him. No longer able to fight the urge to escape from the unbearable hatred he felt was constantly pressing in on him, Hakan dressed as quietly as he could in a dark hooded sweater and pants before creeping softly from the bedroom. He made his way down the stairs, and through the residential and guest wings, being careful to avoid the Royal Guards stationed around the manor on his mission to reach the front door.

"Well, that took longer than I expected," Moritz droned as he leaned against the wall of the entrance foyer.

Chapter 13

"What?" Hakan whispered, a mixture of surprise and confusion in his voice.

"To sneak out," his friend explained as he walked towards the prince with an amused expression, "I was sure you were going to try it the first week of your grounding."

Hakan pursed his lips and turned to head back to his room.

"Giving up so easily?" Moritz teased.

Hakan turned, brows furrowed, to look back at his friend. "You *want* me to sneak out?" he asked disbelievingly.

"What I *want* is to get my friend back. I'm sick of this sulky, defeatist imitation of him," Moritz complained, a hint of sadness in his voice.

"Won't you get in trouble if you let me go?" Hakan asked suspiciously.

Moritz tilted his head thoughtfully from side to side, "maybe, but it'll be worth it if it snaps you out of this funk," he said before jerking his head in the direction of the door.

Hakan studied his friend's face. As much as he didn't want Moritz to get in trouble, he desperately felt he needed some time alone–away from prying eyes and ears– to figure out how to stop the attacks that were causing him to misuse his gift.

"What's it gonna be, Hakan?" Moritz asked after a few moments.

Hakan darted around him, quietly slipping out the front door and off into the night. He roamed the back streets, breathing in the warm, damp air as he enjoyed the calm. He wound his way through the city for over an hour, until he reached the furthest perimeter from the manor and gazed across the field to the treeline on the other side.

Hakan looked behind and around him for any sign of City Guards, before bolting across the grass and into the forest beyond. He continued his trek down the winding path, listening to the sounds of the creaking branches and small scurrying animals until he reached the destination his feet had subconsciously chosen.

Walking silently across the clearing, towards the cave he now despised on the other side, he let all the emotions of the past few months wash over him. He stepped inside the hollow space carved into the mountain and walked up to the waterfall, glistening like a liquid glass in the moonlight, sticking his hand out to let the cold water pour over his fingers.

"Why?" He whispered, as a tear streaked down his face.

As if in answer to his question, it began again. Memory upon memory appeared like a vision in Hakan's mind, filling him with sadness, fear, and hate. This time, though, he did nothing to fight it. On the contrary, he was determined to feel each emotion as deeply as possible in the hopes that he would finally gain control over the attacks if he experienced the worst pain the memories could provoke.

Hakan clutched at his head and dropped to his knees as he continued to relive the most heart wrenching moments since he last stood on the spot–the pain and anger almost unreal. Hakan howled with rage as he sat back on his heels and released an explosion like a bomb from his body, scorching the walls of the cave and interrupting the flow of the falls.

As Hakan gulped for air, he blinked his eyes furiously, trying to readjust them to the darkness. He glanced around at the blackened stone and what was left of his singed, smoking clothes. Just outside the cave, he

Chapter 13

noticed several plants had caught fire, and he quickly extinguished them before collapsing back onto the hot, stone ground, attempting to will himself into another attack. He thought of all the same memories, but try as he might, none appeared as vividly as before, nor did the emotions attached to them hit him as intensely. He tried again, and again, and again, but each attempt yielded the same result: bearable remembrance. Hakan's sigh of relief turned to a cry of laughter as he lay on the ground.

Satisfied that he had succeeded in taking away the overwhelming power the memories had held, he clambered back to his feet, and quickly made his way out of the cave and back to the manor.

"Cutting it a bit close, aren't you? It's nearly dawn!" Moritz whispered anxiously, surveying the prince's appearance as Hakan snuck back into the manor shirtless and looking as though his pants could crumble to ashes at any moment. "What happened to you?"

"Sorry," Hakan replied with embarrassment, wrapping his arms around his body to cover himself.

"What did you do?" Moritz asked, concern etched into his features.

"I... I think I finally made it so I won't have another accident with my gift ever again," Hakan explained, his face filling with relief.

Moritz stared apprehensively at the prince, "and this required you to come back half-naked and smelling like a campfire?"

Hakan rolled his eyes. "It'll be worth it in a few months when I haven't given the kingdom any more reasons to hate me and everyone calms down again," he insisted.

As they stared at each other, Moritz' gaze unfocused. "Another guard's coming this way. Hurry, we've gotta get you upstairs and showered, before someone sees or smells you," he quickly muttered, grabbing Hakan by the arm and leading him safely through the manor to the bathroom across from the prince's room. As Moritz grabbed the handle to close the door, he paused. "Hey Hakan," he whispered.

"Hm?" Hakan grunted back in confusion at the friend who had just insisted they hurry.

"Welcome back," he said softly with a small smile before quietly closing the door.

Chapter 14
UNAPOLOGETIC LOYALTY

Hakan told no one where he had gone or what he had done, only that he was convinced he was truly in control of his gift now, and after a month passed without further incidents Bror and Fannar were convinced as well. The rest of the capital, on the other hand, wasn't as trusting. The king was still wary and quick to scold Hakan for even the tiniest mistake, and strangers still ran in fear at the sight of him. Although he was sure people would warm up to him again eventually, it didn't stop the ache in his heart every time his smile or wave was met with glares and scurrying.

The one place in the capital where Hakan could go without the worry of being turned away was James' Bakery, and it had quickly become his favorite spot in the city. Fannar had started as a full-time apprentice to the baker following finals, and Hakan had taken to walking with his brother every morning to the shop, lingering out of sight in the kitchen or office for a few hours before returning to his lonely solitude at home.

"What's that?" Hakan muttered as he and Fannar approached the front of the shop early one morning,

"I think it's a fox," Fannar answered, his pace quickening.

As they walked closer, they examined the small, odd-looking animal tied up outside the bakery.

"It's definitely some kind of fox," Fannar insisted, softly clicking his tongue at the friendly creature.

"It doesn't look like the ones we usually see around here, though," Hakan replied, kneeling down and extending his hand towards it.

Fannar shrugged, and continued into the bakery, Hakan following close behind. They made their way back to the kitchen where they found James, already wearing a light dusting of flour as he prepared the bread-dough for the day.

"Good morning boys!" James called over the rattling and clanking appliances.

"Good morning, sir," the brothers replied, grinning ear-to-ear at the old man.

"Hey, what's with the fox?" Fannar loudly inquired, gesturing towards the front of the shop.

"Found him wandering around in the street on my way home last night. Poor thing seemed scared out of its mind; probably someone's pet who's got away–that's why I've got him tied up out front; trying to make it easier for his family to find him."

"Oh," Fannar mumbled, his face falling slightly, "So it's not staying, then?"

"Weeeeeelllll..." James said slowly, "not yet at least."

"What's with its ears?" Hakan asked, smiling as he remembered their disproportionate size.

"Not sure, but I think they give him a lot of character," James declared jovially, "honestly, I wouldn't be upset if no one comes to claim him."

Chapter 14

"You already have a rabbit, a ferret and that fuzzy, hopping animal you picked up at the convention in Avol this past winter. If you keep adding pets at this rate, you're going to need a bigger office Mr. James," Hakan told him with a snigger.

"Or a zoo," Fannar added, giggling along after his brother.

"Now that's an idea!" James exclaimed, bursting with laughter at the twins' shocked reaction. "Anyway..." he said, rubbing his hands together eagerly, "is today the day your brother and I get you to don an apron and join us in our baking endeavors?"

Hakan shook his head. "Sorry, I actually can't hang out very long today–I'm meeting up with someone this morning," he explained apologetically, pointedly avoiding his brother's suspicious gaze.

"Oh well, guess we'll just have to try again tomorrow, Fannar," James teased as he returned to his work.

Fannar returned James' mischievous grin before turning back to his brother. "Who're you meeting?" He asked in a low, hushed voice.

"Don't worry about it," Hakan answered as he plucked one of the bright-red strawberries from the basket on the counter and popped it into his mouth.

Fannar furrowed his brow and studied his brother's face, "But–"

"Aren't you supposed to be getting covered in flour right now?" Hakan asked playfully, nudging Fannar towards the nearest mixer. "I'm gonna go check on the zoo before I head out," he called over the din, waving as he darted up the rickety staircase. After an hour playing with

A Gifted Curse

the various fluffy creatures in the office, Hakan finally returned downstairs to quickly say his goodbyes.

"Here!" James said, tossing a paper bag to the prince, "can't send you off with an empty stomach!"

Hakan smiled and thanked the baker before slipping out the back door, and quickly making his way along the sparsely populated streets, the aroma of the warm muffins in the bag occasionally drifting to his nose as he squinted against the first rays of morning light.

"Finally!" Joule exclaimed from outside the Capital Guard Headquarters as he spotted Hakan.

Hakan raised the paper bag in the air, giving it a little shake, to show Joule what had kept him.

"We could've gone to James' *after* you helped me train!" Joule cried, thoroughly annoyed by his friend's priorities.

Hakan stopped and stared Joule dead in the face as he pulled out one of the large muffins and took an oversized bite.

Joule rolled his eyes and groaned in frustration. "Half of those better be for me," he grumbled, as he and a beaming Hakan entered the headquarters together.

Walking past the front desk, Hakan nodded to the guard behind it, who managed to become even more stiff from the gesture than she had been. He sighed and shook his head as he and Joule made their way down the main corridor and end-hallway to the sparring gym. Their footsteps echoed against the concrete walls and seating of the large, empty workout room as they walked over to place their things on the front row.

"You sure you're good with this?" Joule asked hesitantly as he set his backpack down.

Chapter 14

"Yeeeesssss," Hakan groaned, as he placed his bag full of muffins beside his friend's. "You said you wanted to get in one more training before City trouts tomorrow, right?" he asked, stepping onto the sparring mat.

"Yeah but–" Joule began, as he followed behind the prince.

"And Bror, Moritz, and Chasan are all working today…" Hakan continued, stretching his arms and legs out as he spoke.

"Yes," Joule confirmed sourly, "but you–"

"And you want someone who's going to be more challenging than New Honor Guard Iz or Battle Reserve Fannar?" Hakan asked, ignoring his friend's protests.

Joule fixed Hakan with a look of annoyed defeat. "Yes," he finally admitted, making his friend raise a triumphant eyebrow. Joule sighed as he studied Hakan's face. "You said you didn't want to use your gift anymore, though," he reminded the prince.

Hakan shrugged. "You're my friend… and I want to help however I can."

"Yeah, but, I…" Joule sighed and looked painfully around the room, "it's been two months since the warehouse thing, and we're already going to get in trouble for breaking the 'don't go around Hakan' rule. I just… I don't want to be the reason everything gets messed up again for you if something goes wrong," he explained, looking up at his friend, a glimmer of guilt in his eyes as he began to regret asking for his help.

"I'll be fine, Joule," Hakan warmly reassured his friend. "C'mon, let's get you ready to be the best recruit City's ever seen," he said, taking a ready stance, and gesturing for Joule to do the same.

An hour later, Joule had successfully pinned Hakan on the mat before flopping over himself, out of breath and soaked with sweat. "Now... I see... why you got... the food... first," he panted, his friend laughing as he kicked his way up to standing. "How are you not exhausted?" Joule whined, still sprawled on the mat.

"Not a whole lot to do in the Manor," Hakan mumbled with a grin, and jogged over to the step-seating to snatch up the bag of treats from James. As he perched himself on the front row, he called over to his still floor-bound friend, "you better get over here before I eat them all!"

Joule groaned from the effort it took to clamber to his feet, profusely muttering "ow" with every wobbly step he took over to his friend. As the two sat enjoying the fluffy, sweet morsels, the gym door swung open. Joule swore under his breath as he looked away from Adrig and the two City Guards who had entered with him, while Hakan did his best to ignore their existence entirely.

"This gym's only for Ladothite Capital Guards," Adrig said, more loudly than was necessary, given that he and his companions stood only a few yards from the tired teenagers.

The prince simply took another bite of his muffin as if he hadn't heard a word, but Joule had let himself become too annoyed to do the same. "King Eero trains here," Joule retorted, "He's not a guard."

"He's the king," Adrig scoffed, giving Joule a condescending look.

"Hakan's the future king," Joule quipped.

Adrig let out a mirthful laugh, "you think King Eero is going to keep *him* as the successor?" he questioned, shifting his incredulous look from Joule to Hakan and back,

Chapter 14

"Every fire-gifted in the kingdom's history has committed terrible crimes, and caused massive amounts of damage. The past few months have made it pretty clear that he's no different and the kingdom won't accept Eero handing him the crown. The second Hakan stepped through the falls, his brother became the heir – the rest of the kingdom's just waiting for his father to catch up."

"Bull," Joule growled, "everyone was fine with Hakan's gift isn't until the training accident, and if Bror had gotten hurt by any other gift, no one would have thought twice about it."

"What about the fireball he threw at me? I've never been attacked in the street like that as I was trying to help anyone else," Adrig said, cocking his head to the side.

"Save it," Joule snapped, "we both know whatever you were doing, you weren't trying to *help* Hakan that day."

"C'mon, Joule, let's get out of here. We're done anyway," Hakan suggested calmly, still refusing to engage with Adrig.

Joule seized his backpack as he and Hakan stood to leave, but as they stepped towards the door, Adrig planted himself in their way.

"Make up your mind; do you want us to leave or not?" Joule snarled, his temper quickly rising as Adrig continued to antagonize them.

"What I want is to keep the capital safe, but as long as your friend is allowed to walk around freely, it won't be."

Hakan rolled his eyes and raised his foot to step around the guards when Adrig lunged at him. He easily evaded the sudden attack, but the guard lunged again, this time forcing the prince to retreat onto the sparring mat as he evaded a kick sent at his midsection. Hakan continued to maneuver out of the way of every strike, wanting to avoid fighting against the strength-gifted guard. With each escape the prince made from an attack, though, Adrig's smug demeanor was slowly replaced with irate frustration, and his attacks shifted from taunting to deadly.

As Hakan twisted away from a punch that buckled the mat with its unnaturally heavy hit, he noticed one of other guards go after Joule, knocking him to the ground. As Joule fell, though, he sent a charge pulsing through his body, so when the speed-gifted guard started rapidly striking him, she was repeatedly electrocuted and quickly collapsed. The second guard wasted no time as she immediately began attacking Joule with her plant gift, and the exhausted electric-gifted struggled to defend himself as he made his way back to his feet.

Hakan tried to duck around Adrig, but he was determined to prevent the prince from helping his friend.

Joule struggled to keep up with the green tendrils as he repeatedly sent bolts of lightning to fry the onslaught of vines to ash before they reached him. However, he had expended an exorbitant amount of energy training with Hakan and was unable to sustain his defense. "Argh!" Joule let out a blood-curdling scream as one of the plants pierced his shoulder and threw him backwards into the air.

Hakan dodged another attack from Adrig and chanced a glance towards his friend. Joule was pinned against the wall of the gym, a vine as thick as his arm stretching from his limp friend's bleeding shoulder to the city guard.

"Joule!" Hakan cried, fear and anger bubbling up inside him, turning to fury as the image of his injured friend burned in his mind – this had gone beyond petty bullying.

Chapter 14

Without taking his eyes off Joule, Hakan shot a wall of fire towards Adrig, driving him backwards. The strength-gifted guard stumbled to the ground where the prince trapped him in a thick globe of flames before racing towards the plant-gifted. Desperate to save his friend, Hakan sent a large column of fire at the guard's outstretched arm as she shot another vine at Joule's heaving chest. The smell of burning hair and flesh filled the gym as the guard howled in pain, grasping at her blistered, blackened arm and side, the vines going harmlessly limp half-way up the steps. Hakan ignored her wails and screams as he rapidly scaled the step-seats, headed, tunnel-visioned, for his friend who had collapsed on the top row.

"Joule!" Hakan shouted again as he shook his unconscious friend.

The thud of hastening footsteps on the concrete step-seats made Hakan spin around. Adrig was advancing on him, his clothes singed and patches of burns dotting his face and arms; he had run through the walls of the fire-globe. Hakan sprang forward to meet him, a fireball rapidly forming in his hand. As the prince drew his arm back to attack, though, a sense of peace and calm washed over him, halting his movement.

Adrig too, seemed to be experiencing the same phenomenon as he stood a few steps down from Hakan, his eyes glazed and face blank.

A second later, Bror and several blue-and-black clad City Guards were rushing towards them from the door. While the city guards bent over to their fallen fellows, Bror raced up the steps to Joule.

"We need a teleporter in the HQ sparring gym," One guard shouted anxiously into a com.

"One of you, get up here and restrain Adrig," Bror ordered, as he hurriedly placed his fingers on his unconscious friend's neck, desperately hoping to find a pulse.

"City doesn't take orders from the Royal Division," the second city guard snapped, making his way up the steps towards Hakan, pulling restraints out of his belt as he climbed.

Bror jumped up, rushing down the steps to place himself between the city guard and the prince. "It doesn't have the authority to detain anyone in the Royal Family either," he hissed, his face inches from the guard.

"He attacked a group of guards, Bror," The first one argued from beside his electrocuted colleague.

Bror saw Amehllie noiselessly appear on the sparring mat, unnoticed by anyone outside himself and Hakan.

Her mouth fell open as she surveyed the scene, her eyes halting when they found Joule.

Bror took a sharp, exaggerated breath to get her attention before he turned to look at Hakan, then back to the city guard.

Amehllie nodded her understanding of his silent order and in another millisecond had teleported beside her friends, grabbing hold of the prince and royal guard and disappearing before the city guards had time to react to her presence.

As they reappeared in the courtyard of the Royal Manor, Bror turned to Amellie, his words quick and urgent, "get Joule, Bring him here."

Amellie nodded and vanished again, returning a few moments later with their injured friend.

Chapter 14

"Hurry, go to the Healer Corp, find Kesavan," Bror ordered, his voice strained, before kneeling down and cradling Joule in his arms. Amehllie disappeared again, and Bror turned to face Hakan, who he finally released from the influence of his gift. "What. Happened." he demanded, his expression a mixture of concern and anger.

"I–I was helping Joule train, and Adrig showed up," Hakan explained, trying to hold onto the sense of calm Bror had forced on him as he stared at his injured friend, "first he… he tried to kick us – well, me – out of the gym, but then he wouldn't let us leave, and he came at me. Then the other guards attacked Joule and one of them tried to kill him," he said, the calm quickly disappearing, replaced by anger as he replayed the events in his head.

"Is that the one you burned?" Bror asked tensely, and Hakan nodded. "Did you have another one of your attacks?"

"I–I don't know," Hakan croaked, "I don't think so. There weren't any flashes like before. Just… h-his face…" he faltered, his eyes glued to Joule's uncomfortably pale face, as Bror grew more cross with every word, "I couldn't stop thinking about the way his face looked when…I wanted, I *needed*, to do something."

"And there wasn't any other way you could stop her?" Bror exclaimed in frustration.

"She was going to kill him!" Hakan shouted back, his face incredulous, "She didn't need to send another vine at Joule, he was pinned against the wall! He wasn't even fighting back!"

Just then, Amehllie re-appeared with Kesavan, who immediately scanned his eyes up and down the sight of the motionless teenager.

"Hold him steady," Kesavan said urgently as he knelt down and wrapped his hand around the remnants of the vine still dangling from Joule's shoulder and extracted it.

To Bror and Hakan's horror, Joule didn't make a single sound as the plant exited his body.

The healer discarded the blood-covered tendril and quickly placed his hand over Joule's open wound.

"Is he–" Chasan yelled as he came rushing into the courtyard.

"He's alive," Kesavan loudly interjected.

Chasan anxiously ran his hands through his hair, tears of relief filling his eyes as he doubled over. "How did this happen?" He asked, looking up at Hakan, who once again retold the story. "You did what?" he bellowed.

"What's wrong with everyone?" He howled, looking down at Bror then back at Chasan, "What did you want me to do? Just stand there and let him die?"

Chasan let out a deep sigh. "Of course not, but… Hakan, that guard – on coms it sounded like you burned half her body! You took it too far!" he reprimanded.

"No, too far would have been treating her like she did Joule," Hakan hissed, "I only went far enough to make sure she wouldn't be able to try again."

There was a pause as his dark words hung in the air. "So that wasn't an accident then, you meant to burn her that badly?" Chasan asked when the shock had finally passed.

Hakan hesitated for a minute. "I meant to make sure my friend would be safe," he told them quietly.

"Even at the cost of worsening the kingdom's perception of you?" Kesavan asked, looking up from Joule to scrutinize the prince.

Chapter 14

"Yes," Hakan answered as he unflinchingly returned the councilman's stare, "and I won't apologize for keeping one of the few people who've stood by me alive."

Kesavan let out a sigh as he moved his hand from Joule's shoulder to the middle of his chest. "Well, your highness," he said to Hakan, "you were right about at least one thing: Joule was defenseless after he was struck with that vine."

Hakan's eyes flashed triumphantly between Bror and Chasan at the councilman's words – He *had* saved his friend.

"In fact, as depleted as his energy is," Kesavan continued darkly, "I'm surprised he was able to fight at all."

"Hakan!" King Eero roared as he stormed into the courtyard. "Upstairs. Now."

"What?" Hakan asked, confused by the order.

"You heard me," Eero snapped, the blue eyes he had passed on to his sons full of rage.

"But Jou–" The prince began to argue.

"He'll be fine, do as your father says," Kesavan interjected calmly, giving the prince a reassuring nod.

Hakan clenched his jaw, turned on his heels, and heatedly strode across the courtyard. He burst through the glass door of the sitting room and stormed up the stairwell towards his room. Slamming the door behind him, he paced, anxiously waiting for news about his friend.

He didn't understand why everyone was acting like he was the one in the wrong. The city guards had started this whole thing; Adrig and the others were the ones his father should be angry with, not him. All Hakan had done was protect his friend just like Joule would have done for him.

The minutes ticked by as Hakan circled his room again and again. Finally, he heard a creak, and spun to see his father stepping over the threshold. Eero closed the door, and leaned against the heavy slab of dark wood, his fuming gaze boring into his son.

"What part of 'you're forbidden from using your gift until further notice' did you not understand?" Eero seethed.

"I tried not to," Hakan insisted, unable to hide his irritation.

"Oh, you tried not to," Eero repeated sardonically, "What were you even doing at the guard headquarters with Joule, Hakan? As far I'm aware, Leal hasn't given him permission to be around you yet."

"I was trying to help him—" Hakan began to explain.

"Looks like you did a *great* job with that," Eero interjected callously.

Hakan paused, the sting of his father's words triggering a trickle of guilt. "It's not my fault," he said quietly, his eyes welling with tears.

"Maybe not completely, but you do bear some of the responsibility for what happened to your friend," his father replied coldly. "You know how the Capital Guards – really the entire kingdom for that matter – feels about you right now, yet you still went into their headquarters. Not only that, but you went there *intending* to use the gift that's the cause of all this."

"Nothing happened while we were training, though!" Hakan argued as the trickle turned into a rush of shame, "Even when Adrig attacked me I didn't use my gift until I had no other choice!" He shouted, the vein in his forehead rising to the surface, "Why am I the one in trouble and not the guard who tried to kill my friend?"

Chapter 14

"You already saw to it that she's been more than adequately punished," Eero replied evenly.

Hakan exhaled sharply. "So much for Fannar and I not getting treated any differently than anyone else," he spat, his anger festering towards its boiling point.

"Excuse me?" Eero demanded, incensed.

"When I used my gift to defend myself, Basilah and the others wanted me to be tried for breaking two kingdom laws," Hakan roared, "This guard tried to shoot a vine through my friend's heart, and the only reason she's gotten any kind of punishment is because I was there to make sure she wouldn't be able to kill him," he screamed, as a tear finally slipped free from his burning eye.

"If I remember right," Eero shouted back, making Hakan flinch, "someone made sure those charges never happened because, as you just pointed out, you shouldn't be treated differently than anyone in the kingdom!" They stared at each other in silence for a few moments, the king taking several calming breaths before continuing, "in the spirit of not treating you any differently, I've decided on the following consequences for this incident," he said in a quieter, albeit still furious tone. "Not only will you *never*, under any circumstances, use your fire gift again, but you will also be under the supervision of a Royal Guard at all times, both inside the manor and on the *rare* instances in the *distant* future that I allow you to leave it."

The muscle in Hakan's jaw twitched as he listened. "Either way they get what they want: I'm a prisoner," he whispered, filled with a mixture of anger and sadness.

"No, you are a son who's lucky to have a patient father who cares about you enough to not feed you to the wolves who are calling for your head," Eero replied with a pained expression.

Hakan turned his gaze to the floor. It didn't make a difference that he had stopped the memory attacks. He had still hurt someone with his gift, and that was all it took for any progress he had made with people to be washed away again–even though, as far as Hakan was concerned, the person had deserved it. Joule had been right to worry about them practicing together after all.

"Is he awake?" Hakan asked timidly, remembering Joule's earlier fear and wanting to reassure his friend.

"Yes... Kesavan told him he'll be tired the rest of the day, but he should be fine if he wants to go through with tryouts tomorrow," Eero told him, studying his son's expression.

"Can I go down and see him?" Hakan asked, his tone almost begging.

Eero sighed. "After what you just did, I doubt Leal would be okay with it."

"Please," Hakan whispered, his voice cracking as he looked pleadingly at his father.

Eero looked thoughtfully at his son, watching as Hakan fought back tears, questioning if they were sincere. He couldn't reconcile the tender-hearted child he had raised with the actions of the young man that now stood before him, and he wondered how much of his son's good heart had secretly faded away since his gifting. "Alright, you can go downstairs," he hesitantly answered, "but you *must stay* in the sitting room."

Hakan nodded eagerly and followed his father downstairs, peering out through the large windows. His brother, Ismat and Shammoth had also arrived since he'd been sent to his room, and the three of them stood with Chasan and Bror encircling their electric-gifted friend. The tension in Hakan's chest eased as he watched Joule arguing

Chapter 14

with the councilmen in the middle of the courtyard, his health clearly and completely restored. As he continued to stare, his father stepped through the glass doorway attracting everyone's attention. Chasan and the others caught sight of the prince, and Hakan tried to force a small, sad smile before turning and quickly rushing back up to his room as the pain of being separated from everyone overwhelmed him.

Chapter 15
DISCOVERIES IN THE DARK

It was two months before the king finally allowed Hakan to leave the manor with Bror, and only under the condition that they go at night and avoid being seen as much as possible. So, one warm, midsummer night, Hakan and Bror slipped quietly out of the manor, the hoods of their sweaters pulled down low over their faces and headed north for the foot of the mountain that wrapped from the southern tip of the capital around to its norther-eastern edge.

"Nice to get out, isn't it," Bror commented in a soft, cheerful voice, but Hakan remained silent. "C'mon Hakan, it's a beautiful night! Just imagine all the stars we'll be able to see once we get up into the mountain," he continued, almost child-like as he gleefully tugged at the prince's arm.

"I don't want to see stars," Hakan mumbled bitterly as he trod alongside his guard, staring at the ground, "I want to see my friends."

"One step at a time," Bror said slyly, "Tonight, stars. Next trip, friends," he said, a mischievous grin tugging at his lips.

Hakan's head snapped up in surprise. "Really?" he asked, a hint of hope returning to his features for the first time in months.

Chapter 15

"Mhm," Bror grunted, grinning at his friend, "we've been working on a plan to have Amehllie sneak everyone out to the mountain to see you for a little bit."

Hakan's face ached as a smile grew, working the neglected muscles in his cheeks, "and she agreed?"

"Yeah... you sound surprised," Bror said, a little puzzled.

"I haven't heard from her since the fight in the gym, so I assumed she hated me now too," Hakan said miserably.

"She doesn't hate you," Bror reassured him, "She's just in the same position as Joule and Shammoth."

"So, her mom hates me, great," Hakan corrected, the difference not making him feel much better.

Bror sighed. "You know, come to think of it, I don't really hear from her either," he grumbled a few moments later, his brows furrowing as he thought, "actually, I don't think she really reaches out to anyone except Iz."

Hakan sniggered at his friend's indignation from this realization. "So, if everything goes well tonight, I can see everyone next time?" he asked, a glimmer of happiness in his voice.

"Mhm," Bror grunted, a proud smile filling his face.

"So, how soon after tonight can we go out again?" Hakan asked eagerly.

"Not too long after I expect, maybe a few days–a week at most," Bror replied, pleased with the positive change in the prince's demeanor.

Hakan made a disgusted face. "That's so long," he said quietly, his cheer evaporating as he pouted.

"The other's have had to wait longer," Bror gently chided, "Joule, Shammoth and Iz were ready to storm the manor weeks ago after your mom..." he trailed off, his smile slipping as he mentally kicked himself for the blunder he'd just made with his words. "Anyway, I got them to hold off until I could come up with something outside the manor." He glanced over at Hakan; the smile he had been able to coax out of his friend had vanished at the mention of the queen. "Hey, I'm sorry, I didn't mean to–"

"Don't worry about it," Hakan interjected quietly, "you didn't make her like this."

"Neither did you," Bror said firmly.

"Didn't I?" Hakan asked sarcastically, returning Bror's compassionate expression with one of disdain, "She's like this because of stress… stress that's making her body fall apart faster than Kesavan and the other healers can treat it…stress that none of the emotion-influencer-gifteds seem to be able to stop… stress that she only has because *I* screwed up and caused it," he mumbled bitterly and his friend sighed, opening his mouth to speak before Hakan cut him off, "don't try telling me I didn't–she wasn't like this until the fight at the guard headquarters."

"Which is why I think us going out will be good for her," Bror said gently, trying to steer his friend away from his self-destructive thoughts.

Hakan raised an eyebrow at him, "How?"

Bror slowed to a stop, "I have to report to your parents how things go every time we leave," he explained, "I think it'll help your mom feel better if I were able to go back tonight and tell her and your dad that everything went great–especially if I can add that you didn't spend the whole time sulking," he added pointedly.

Hakan clenched his jaw, kicking at the ground for a moment as he thought. "Okay," he said as he pursed his lips.

"Alright," Bror said, throwing an arm around the prince and leading him onward once again. "So, tonight

Chapter 15

you and I go and admire the sea of stars in the sky, and next week the nine of us can have a midnight picnic in the forest at the base of the mountain. How's that sound?" He asked, furrowing his brows in confusion when Hakan's face twitched with irritation. "What's wrong?"

"I don't think it's a good idea having Fannar come," Hakan replied after a few moments.

Bror gaped at the prince. "Why?" he asked in bewilderment.

"If he comes..." Hakan said slowly, trying to think of a plausible excuse rather than admit the petty truth. "Dad might get suspicious and send other guards to follow us," he lied.

"No he won't," Bror said dismissively, scrutinizing Hakan,

"He might," Hakan argued, "it's just supposed to be the two of us going out, if he finds out Fannar came too... I don't want the others to get caught and get in trouble."

"Is there something going on with you and Fannar that I don't know about?" Bror asked quizzically.

"No," Hakan quickly replied, though his body language contradicted his words.

Bror pursed his lips. "You know," he sighed, "you're a terrible liar."

Hakan ground his teeth desperately wishing he could take back saying anything about his brother.

"I don't get it... what could you–*when* could you have gotten into an argument? I'm with you all the time, I mean, do you two only get into spats for the five minutes I'm in the shower?" Bror asked, slightly amused at the perplexities of the situation.

"No, we don't argue, it's nothing. Just forget it," Hakan grumbled, giving a stray pebble in his path a little kick.

Bror, however, did not forget it, and after a few minutes of puzzling, a dawning realization filled his face. "Ooooooh," he said, "this is because your dad started having Fannar sit in on council meetings and go with him on official royal trips and stuff, isn't it."

"No," Hakan firmly denied.

"Really? You're upset with him because of that?" Bror asked, sounding disappointed. "It's not like he asked to do it."

Hakan let out a frustrated sigh, as his worry for his mother and annoyance at his brother grew.

"You know, I haven't had to influence your emotions since this whole arrangement started, and I'd like to keep it that way," Bror cautioned, studying Hakan's expression as he used his gift to sense the prince's feelings.

"Me too," Hakan replied, taking a deep breath and trying to calm himself.

"Okay, so then why don't you stop getting in your own head, and let yourself have a good time for a few hours," Bror teased, giving him a little poke in the side, smiling as his friend jumped in surprise.

Hakan rolled his eyes at the trick, pursed his lips and held up a thumb in agreement.

"Good," Bror said with a satisfied smile.

As they continued along the road, Hakan tried his best to make good on his end of the agreement and focused on finding things to enjoy on their walk: Taking slow, deep breaths of the damp air as he watched the steam rise from the sun-baked pavement and kicking a puddle of water to watch the droplets fall like diamonds back to the ground.

Chapter 15

They wound their way through the northern residential district, occasionally stepping into the shadows between buildings to avoid being seen by other late-night strollers. As they once again heard voices approaching from ahead, Bror and Hakan hurried off the street, pressing their backs against the rough wall of a large apartment building.

"Still can't believe they let that kid onto the City Guard after what they did," A gruff man's voice said, the words gradually becoming more audible as he and his companion leisurely made their way down the road in the direction of Bror and Hakan's hiding spot.

"How many times are you going to go on about this?" came the nasally voice of the female companion, "Like you said, 'after what *they* did'... I'm sure the king had something to do with his acceptance. I don't see Chief Satna taking him after he and Hakan attacked the guards... not unless the king gave her no other choice."

Hakan's jaw dropped as he listened to the approaching conversation.

"That would make sense," the man scoffed, "I swear, he's gonna end up destroying the kingdom. He's gotta get past the fact that that ticking time-bomb is his son."

"Eero's not stupid, he won't let it get *that* far," the woman argued. "I mean, he's had him locked up in the Royal Manor for two months, and from what I've heard Hakan's not going to be leaving any time soon. I think the king finally realized the danger he was putting everyone in by letting a fire-gifted roam unchecked in the city."

"All he did was ground the kid," the man retorted spitefully. "What's he gonna do when his little fire-prince finally kills someone? How many people is Eero gonna let get hurt or die before he finally does what he knows he's gotta do?" The man asked, his voice urgent and full of malice as the pair walked past the alley

Hakan turned to look at Bror, anger and hurt filling his eyes, only for his friend to raise a finger to his lips imploring him to stay quiet.

The woman sighed. "I don't know, but at the rate that the boy is pushing his boundaries, I'd say we don't have long to wait before we find out," she somberly told her companion.

"I just hope it's one of those idiots that's still stupid enough to hang around him," the man said darkly, "they deserve to be his first victims."

A silent tear slipped down Hakan's face as he stared blankly into the darkness, his body beginning to tremble. Bror grabbed his arm, but Hakan closed his eyes and shook his head to stop his friend from using his gift.

"Well, If the king keeps him in the manor like he should, he won't have anyone else to hurt besides them," The woman pointed out, a hint of sadness in her voice.

"Maybe after his kid kills one of his friend's sons he'll finally come around," the man added callously.

Hakan listened as the disturbing conversation pondering which of his friends he might kill first faded into indistinct murmurs, and eventually disappeared. As another salty drop streaked down his cheek, he slid shakily down the side of the building, his face twisted with pain.

Bror knelt down beside him, his expression almost as strained as his friend's. "Hakan?" he whispered, barely able to get the word out.

Hakan moved his head slowly from side to side, once again refusing to have Bror use his gift, before dropping it forward as he let several soft sniffles escape.

Chapter 15

"C'mon, we're almost to the outskirts of the city. Let's get outta here," Bror said, tugging firmly on the prince's arm.

"No," Hakan said quietly.

"Yes, we're going stargazing," Bror told him in a firm whisper.

"No," Hakan repeated. "There's no point. It doesn't matter how many months I go without using my gift. Everyone's always just going to be waiting for the next time I mess up. They're never going to stop hating me no matter what I do," he rambled, gently hitting his head against the wall as he spoke, as hopeless thoughts flooded his mind.

"Look at me," Bror said, moving in front of his friend, and grabbing hold of his face, "You've only messed up because of those attacks, which have only happened when you got over-stressed and lost control of your emotions. As long as I'm around that won't happen. That's why Fannar asked me to guard you."

"What?" Hakan breathed, his shocked eyes snapping open to stare blankly at his friend, "this was Fannar's idea?"

"He didn't tell you?" Bror asked, surprised. "That day in the courtyard, Leal was insisting that your dad needed to hand you over to the City Division, and Fannar suggested you be placed under constant guard as a compromise, and that I'd be the best candidate since I'm your friend."

"So, it was Fannar's idea that I have a twenty-four-hour guard on top of being on house arrest?" Hakan spat angrily.

"It's not like that, Hakan," Bror replied, his patience dwindling.

"What is it then? Because it looks a lot like my brother doesn't trust me any more than those people do," Hakan said hotly, pointing a finger in the direction that the two night-stollers had disappeared.

"Now you're just being stupid. You know Fannar trusts you. So does Moritz, and Chasan and the rest of us," Bror snapped crossly. "I'm sorry you're upset that I'm giving up all my free time to keep you from crossing a line you can't come back from, but we can't just sit back and wait for you to figure out how to control yourself – not if you wanna have *any* shot of staying out of a detention cell let alone keeping your place as the heir," he said, his dark eyes boring into his friend's for several moments.

A wave of guilt washed over Hakan as Bror's words sunk in, but it did nothing to stem the growing urge to lash out at his brother and friend. Hakan dropped his head again and pressed his palm to his forehead as his mind drifted between the desire to hurt someone and the urge to disappear, each shift bringing a new wave of emotions cascading over him.

Bror, realizing what was happening, took a steady breath and reached out with the energy from his gift. He watched as Hakan's breathing slowly eased, disappointed that his friend had let himself spiral again rather than ask for help. As he removed the prince's feelings of guilt, fear, and anger, though, Hakan jumped up and took off running towards the edge of the city. Bror darted after him, quickly catching up to his distraught friend and grabbing hold of him.

As he felt Bror's hand close around his shoulder, Hakan spun and knocked it away, immediately returning to his desperate race for the forest at the foot of the mountain. Everyone had been wrong: Bror's gift couldn't help him.

Chapter 15

Even though his friend had filled him with a sense of calm, it did nothing to stop the urge to lash out with his gift. All Bror's influence had done was clear Hakan's mind enough to realize he needed to get as far away from his friend as quickly as possible before the part of Hakan that wanted to protect Bror lost control over his body. He flew past the last building, fighting the desire to turn and throw a fireball at his friend as he dashed for the green, towering plants ahead. He weaved through the trunks as quickly as he could, but Bror was mere feet behind, and Hakan was losing the fight within himself.

"Hakan, stop!" Bror called from a few steps behind the prince.

"No," Hakan groaned to himself, a fireball growing in his hand as he ran.

"C'mon Hakan! Stop fighting me!" Bror roared, nearly close enough to reach him now.

With the last ounce of mental strength Hakan had left, he swung his arm around and shoved the fireball into his own chest. He screamed with agony in the brief seconds he felt his skin burning away before losing consciousness as Bror tackled him to the ground.

Chapter 16
BREAKING POINT

Hakan opened his eyes slowly against the bright light flooding his room as he woke the next morning in his own bed, his body aching from the exertion to flee from his friend and fight the dark urges that had overcome him.

"How're you feeling?" Fannar asked softly as he sat on the floor beside his brother, his chin resting on Hakan's bed.

"Tired," Hakan croaked, squeezing his eyes shut and raising his hand to his sore chest.

"Kesavan healed the burn," Fannar told him as he watched his brother apprehensively, "but dad wouldn't let him restore your energy supply."

The memory of wanting to hurt his friend came flooding back, and Hakan's eyes flew open as he turned to look at his brother. "Is Bror okay?" he asked, his voice strained with concern.

"Yeah," Fannar answered, baffled by the question since Hakan was the one that had been treated by a healer, "yeah, Bror's fine… why?"

"I didn't hurt him again?" Hakan pressed, his face full of fear as he stared disbelievingly as his twin.

"No," Fannar replied, his face screwing up in confusion and concern. "You took off on him and then

Chapter 16

you... you hurt *yourself*," he explained with a frightened expression.

Hakan let out a sigh of relief and pressed his palms to his eyes – his friend was alright.

"Hakan," Fannar mumbled uneasily, "what's going on?"

The older twin slowly shook his head. "I don't know anymore," he finally admitted dismally.

At that moment, the door swung open, and their father entered, a grave expression etched into his features. "Fannar, go downstairs."

Fannar looked defiantly up at their father. "But–"

"Don't argue," Eero said softly, his face making it clear it would be unwise for his younger son to disobey.

Fannar pursed his lips and gave his brother an apologetic look as he stood up and quietly left the room, closing the door behind him.

Eero walked over to the window and crossed his arms, "You know, in all the thousands of years that the royal family has passed through the falls, not one of them has ever come out as a fire-gifted. Back when I went through with Tanlan and our other friends, everyone was afraid to get it–it'd been nearly two hundred years since we'd seen one, and people were convinced it was well overdue to be gifted again–but I wasn't scared. For some reason, I felt like it couldn't happen to the royal succession; that the falls knew how dangerous it would be giving a gift with a ruthless, power-hungry nature to the person responsible for so many lives," Eero turned and glanced around the room, his expression somber as he reminisced.

"But then you and your brother went through the falls, and instead of being excited, all I could think of was how could this have happened to one of *my* sons?" the king shook his head as he slowly crossed the room. "You know, of all the things you and your brother have done throughout your lives, of all the accomplishments, the thing you mother and I have always been proudest of was that you were both perfect examples of what it meant to have a good heart: Kind, generous, self-sacrificing. That good heart," Eero said, finally looking at his son, "is what gave me hope that maybe you'd be the one who would finally break whatever curse gets passed on with this gift..."

The king's eyes glistened as he stared at the older of his twins, "but I can't ignore what's been going on anymore, Hakan. You attacked your friend, you've gotten into dangerous fights and now you've hurt yourself; Bror said it was like you'd lost your mind last night! I–" He broke off, pinching the bridge of his nose as the conflicted feelings overwhelmed him.

Hakan swallowed hard. "You're handing me over to the City Guard now," he whispered over the lump in his throat.

"To be honest, I'm not sure what I'm going to do yet, Hakan," Eero answered sorrowfully, "I'm meeting with the council later tonight, I just... I wanted to make sure you knew, this isn't what I had hoped for, and if I could hold things off longer, I would, but... I just can't," he finished, shaking his head in defeat, refusing to meet his son's wounded gaze as he left the room.

Hakan stared numbly up at the ceiling, realizing that his father hadn't stopped the healer from restoring his energy as a punishment, but as a precaution. The more he thought about it, though, the more he considered that his father was right to. Hakan had no explanation as to why he had so deeply wanted to hurt Bror and his brother the night before. He knew in the moment it was wrong, but it still

Chapter 16

didn't stop his body from trying to act on it. *Whatever curse gets passed on with this gift.* His father's words echoed in his mind, filling him with dread as he rolled over on his side to face the wall, consumed by his thoughts.

The door creaked, and Fannar entered, returning to his watchful position cross-legged on the floor beside the bed. "Are you hungry?" he asked gently.

The older twin paused for a minute before he answered, "no."

"C'mon, it's almost noon, you should eat something," Fannar insisted, the gentleness replaced with concern as he stared at the back of his brother's head.

"Maybe later... I'm too tired right now," he told his brother hollowly, pulling his blanket up to his chin and closing his eyes.

"You sure?" Fannar persisted in vain as Hakan continued to lay on his bed in silence. After several long moments in which Fannar's heart filled with sadness and frustration, he stood and exited the room, once again closing the heavy door behind him.

Hakan lay there, letting the sense of emptiness engulf him as he watched the shadows on the wall change during the sun's unstoppable march across the sky. As evening approached, anxiety over the imminent council meeting began intruding on the numb-quiet Hakan had succumbed to. Images of the councilors insisting the successor be changed and the dangerous fire-gifted prince be locked away in a remote detention facility, forever separated from the people he cared for, plagued Hakan, suffocating him as he tossed and turned on his bed.

Then a thought, like a whisper, came to him: *They can't turn you over to the guards if you're not here.*

Hakan's heart raced as he considered the idea for a moment, then shook his head. It was stupid, after all, to think of running. Even if he could avoid all the people in the kingdom who wanted to see him imprisoned, Moritz would be able to track him down in a matter of hours.

Would he track you down though? His thoughts whispered. *Moritz is your friend, maybe he'd let you get away. You could hide in the mountains; snow valley's never let go of the grudge from being absorbed into the kingdom, maybe they'd let you hide outside their village.*

Hakan pictured living his life as a hermit in a cave deep in the mountain range, his uneasiness over his unknown fate making the prospect look more than a little appealing.

You'd be far away from anyone you could hurt, the whisper added, and the memory of burning Bror months earlier resurfaced, followed by the events of the previous night.

Hakan threw the blanket from his body and sat up on the edge of his bed, taking slow deep breaths as he tried to keep himself calm. The effort was fruitless though, as the memory of Chasan's shocked face following Hakan's declaration that he had meant to hurt the city guard in the gym filled his thoughts. Hakan clutched his head as he saw all the frightened and disappointed looks of his friends and family over the past year and half, and his restless worry grew too strong to bear.

He tiptoed over to the wardrobe and changed out of his ruined, burned sweater and into a hooded jacket. Trying his best to move without a sound, he crept first over to his bed then his brother's, removing the sheets and blankets and tying them together. Once he had secured the makeshift rope to the frame of Fannar's bed, Hakan returned to his

Chapter 16

side table, grabbing his mini-tab to type out a short apology note before setting the device down gingerly on his brother's pillow. Then, heart heavy, he went back to the window, cautiously leaning over the sill to check above and below for signs of guards.

Satisfied that the coast was clear, Hakan scooped up the blanket-rope, and began slowly descending the side of the manor, praying Moritz and his heightened sense of hearing weren't on duty. Pulse racing, he quietly repelled down from the third floor to the grassy ground between the building and the sheer face of the mountain without incident. Thrilled that he might actually succeed in his escape, Hakan cautiously made his way to the end of the manor and peered around the corner to check the small street between his home and the next. He almost couldn't believe his luck when he found the street deserted. He pulled his hood over his head, took a deep breath, and darted for the other side of the street. Not stopping to check if he'd been seen, Hakan kept running along the space between the city's edge and the mountain.

After passing several alleys, he made a sharp left and an immediate right, deciding that if he had been spotted escaping the manor, it would be smarter to weave through the maze of backstreets. Half an hour later, making his way as fast as he dared, Hakan began to re-think his decision to run away. There was still a tiny part of him that was reluctant to let go of the future he had been working towards his whole life.

No, Hakan told himself firmly, *that's all gone now. That future disappeared the second you tried to hurt one of your best friends.* His thoughts drifted to the memory of Bror lying on the ground, an angry burn in the middle of his chest.

"Whatever curse gets passed on with this gift", his father's words again echoed in his thoughts, and he slowed to a stop, pressing firmly on his temples. The memory of his mother standing over his bed after his incident at the warehouses drifted back. Running away from his impending imprisonment meant his friends and family would never be allowed to see or help again, and with his mother's unstoppable deterioration, she most likely wouldn't survive long enough if the day ever came that Hakan regained control of his cursed-gift and his father permitted him to return. A torrent of emotions consumed him as more painful memories raced through his thoughts, and he leaned against the rough wall of a nearby building as his body began to tremble.

"Well, look what we have here," Adrig droned arrogantly as he slowly approached from the cross-street ahead.

The guard's voice seemed distant and muffled as Hakan tried to fight through the onslaught of memories taking over his consciousness, but the sound was still enough to ignite the prince's anger alongside the swirl of fear and sadness he was already combating.

"I thought they had finally come to their senses and locked you up for good after what happened last night," Adrig continued.

The guard's tone of dark satisfaction pushed Hakan's temper over the edge, and the prince pelted the nearest piece of rubbish at him with all his might.

Adrig caught and crushed the debris, clicking his tongue menacingly at Hakan. "Come now, your highness," he chided in a would-be-friendly tone as he took another cautious step towards the fire-gifted, "let's not make this difficult."

Chapter 16

Hakan's mind froze. "Difficult?" he parrott incredulously.

For eighteen months he had put up with Adrig's denigration. For eighteen months he had at least tried to maintain some self control whenever there was a conflict with him. But now, as he stood there watching the city guard stalking him like prey–the guard who had played an instrumental part in bringing Hakan's world crashing down around him–the prince broke.

Hakan lunged at Adrig, who stumbled backwards in surprise as the prince encased his arms with fire, incinerating the jacket sleeves that had covered them. Adrig tried to block Hakan's blows, but each successful defense meant more of the guard's uniform was burned away. Finally, Hakan shot a plume at Adrig's leg, sending him tumbling to the side as the smell of burning hair filled the alley. The same time the fire connected, the enraged prince struck the guard hard on the throat, preemptively silencing the scream of agony that would have followed the leg injury. Adrig fell to the ground, gasping for air, his eyes squeezed tight against the searing pain as the fire-gifted glared down at him.

He could run. It would be a few minutes before Adrig would be able to speak, and if he hurried, he might have enough of a head start to make it to the foothills of the mountains. As he pondered, though, Adrig took a swipe at the prince's legs. The fury inside him boiled over again, and Hakan surrendered to his impulses, unleashing his gift on the guard's other leg. As Adrig writhed on the ground, gripping his bloody and blistered limb and croaking in anguish, more images flashed through Hakan's mind. Each time Hakan was forced to revisit a memory, he yielded to the desire to burn more of Adrig's body, continuing until he was nothing more than an unconscious, smoking heap. When he finally stopped, tears of fury were streaming down his face as he stared down at the shallowly breathing guard.

Before Hakan had time to fully process what he had just done, dozens of thick vines shot up from the ground, quickly wrapping around his arms, legs and waist. The plants immediately pulled him to his knees, and through the panic as he struggled against the plants, he heard another familiar voice.

"Don't try it, Hakan," Chasan yelled pleadingly from behind him.

Hakan craned his neck around and saw Chasan, Moritz, and Councilman Naukaron standing in the alley–all in uniform. Hakan's heart ached as the idea of fighting his way out crossed his mind and was immediately dismissed. He turned back to stare down at Adrig, the reality of the depth of his mistake crashing down on him.

"Hakan," Moritz called, his voice riddled with concern as he stood there, desperately hoping his friend would cooperate.

"More guards are on the way, your highness. Even if you get away from us, you're not going to make it very far," Tanlan said, his voice even and firm.

As if on cue, several more city guards arrived in the alley from the opposite direction, but their expressions were far less encouraging as they were teleported to the location – filled with fear and hate.

Hakan took a shaky breath before he hung his head and sat back on his heels in defeat.

Moritz and Chasa rushed forward, each grabbing hold of an arm as Chasan released the vines. For a split second, Hakan got the urge to run.

Chapter 16

"Don't," Moritz warned, as his grip on Hakan tightened.

Hakan exhaled sharply, realizing Moritz' heightened sense of touch had noticed his muscles tense in anticipation. Once Chasan had secured Hakan's wrists in metal restraints behind his back, his friends gently pulled him to his feet and turned him towards the teleporter that had brought the other guards.

As his friends nudged him forward, Hakan whispered, almost inaudibly, "I'm not going back to the manor... am I."

"No," Moritz grimaced.

Chapter 17
FIGHTING FATE

Hakan was teleported to the Capital Guard headquarters, Moritz and Chasan still holding tight to him as they approached the reinforced door of the detention wing. Chasan nodded to one of the sentries flanking the entrance, who pressed his thumb on the scanner set into the wall. As Hakan's friends wordlessly escorted him down the corridor lined with holding cells, he heard the whirring and clicking of the locking mechanisms turning back into place, securing the only exit.

They halted in front of the empty cell at the end and Chasan placed his thumb on another scanner to unlock the door of the transparent-faced room, watching as it pulled back from the frame with a hiss and slid to the side. Moritz nudged Hakan forward, following him into the cell before turning back to face the door.

"No," Chasan said as Moritz extended his hand expectantly towards him.

"Give me the key, Chasan," Moritz said evenly.

"It's safer for him if he keeps them on," Chasan replied, his expression full of compassion.

Moritz sighed. "You're really going to make me do this?" he asked, his voice and expression full of disappointment. He drew himself up to his full height and stared down resolutely at Chasan. "As a member of the

Chapter 17

royal family, and until King Eero revokes those privileges, Hakan falls under the jurisdiction of the Royal Guard, and I say the restraint is coming off," he told him, once again holding out his hand for the key.

Chasan took a deep breath, and reluctantly handed a small metal square to his friend, "I still say it's a bad idea."

"Your opinion has been noted, Chasan," Moritz said as he stepped behind the prince to remove the restraints.

"I'm not going to do anything," Hakan insisted quietly as he rubbed his wrists.

"You mean anything *else*," Chasan corrected, his expression incredulous, "have you forgotten why we had to bring you here? What you were caught doing?"

"Enough," Moritz snapped as he walked the restraints back to Chasan, eying him apprehensively, "you know as well as I do that keeping his hands bound isn't going to make any of them less afraid," he said curtly, jutting his chin the direction of the sentries, "it'll just make it harder for Hakan to defend himself if they decide to do something stupid."

"Hey," Hakan interrupted, "who figured out I was gone?"

"Fannar," Moritz replied, turning to face the prince, "he took some food up to your room to try and get you to eat but you were gone. He called in a panic, hoping I could track you down and bring you back before anyone else realized you had snuck out."

"But it was already too late for that," Chasan added bitterly. "Someone must have overheard Fannar's call and told your father because we ran into Naukaron as we were tracking you and he knew you'd taken off and assumed we'd helped," he explained, his voice resentful.

"If he hadn't slowed us down, we might have been able to get to you before..." Moritz trailed off, his frustration with their failure quickly turning to sorrow.

"Before I crossed a line I can't come back from," Hakan said, quoting Bror's words as he finished the thought. "I'm sorry," Hakan told them softly, looking up with somber, watery eyes, "I really am."

A dark silence hung over them for a few moments before one of the city guard sentries banged on the entrance door and waved for Chasan, who let out a sigh. "Come on, let's go see what they want."

Moritz pursed his lips and let out an exasperated breath as he stepped out of the cell and Chasan pressed his thumb to the scanner again to slide the cell door back into place. Hakan leaned against one of the smooth concrete walls, watching the last warm rays of sunlight fading outside the single, slender window of his cell as he waited, hoping his friends would be able to return.

Several silent minutes later, he heard the noises of the entrance unlocking, and Fannar appeared on the other side of the cell door, anxiously wringing his beanie.

"Where're Chasan and Moritz?" Hakan asked, his words being carried through a speaker that sat above the cell's scanner.

"I wanted to talk to you alone," Fannar replied, his voice similarly being projected through several small speakers in the ceiling of the small holding space.

"Why alone?" Hakan asked apprehensively, unsure what his brother could say that he wouldn't want their friends to hear.

Fannar paused. "Because...I just do," he began nervously as a pained expression crept across his face. "I heard the guards telling dad what happened...did you really

Chapter 17

torture a city guard with your gift?" He asked disbelievingly, his eyes begging his brother to deny it.

Hakan turned his gaze to the floor and swallowed hard. "Yes," He admitted somberly.

Fannar gaped at his brother. He had wanted so badly for the guards to be exaggerating because the incident involved Hakan, that the admission cut through his heart like an icy knife.

"Is that all you wanted?" Hakan asked hollowly as he tried to disconnect from the wave of shame the question had unleashed.

"How could you do that?" Fannar roared, his eyes gradually filling with tears.

"It doesn't matter," Hakan grumbled, annoyed at his brother's indignation. "You definitely get to be the successor now, congratulations," he snapped, reminding Fannar how much the situation benefitted his younger twin.

"What?" Fannar bit back, growing more confused.

"I'm curious, when did you realize you actually *did* want to be king someday?" Hakan pointedly asked.

"The hell are you talking about?" Fannar shouted, bewildered by his brother's statement, "if I didn't care about being on your council, *why* would I want the responsibilities of being the king? I was perfectly happy working for Mr. James."

"You also looked perfectly happy to go to all the council meetings and on all the trips with dad," Hakan retorted.

"What was I supposed to do?" Fannar demanded incredulously.

"Tell him no! Tell him you don't want to be king," Hakan yelled, his anger peaking. "Tell him that you haven't given up on your brother," he croaked, finally saying out loud the part that had hurt him most.

"And cause mom and dad even more stress while they were trying to do damage control from your fight at the gym?" Fannar exclaimed, exasperated, "and it's a good thing I did since you've gone and made sure I don't have any other choice anymore!"

A pained silence came over them as they glared at each other. "So you did give up on me," Hakan muttered, every trace of anger gone from his voice as his eyes filled with sorrow.

"I've never stopped hoping you were going to be different from the other fire-gifteds, Hakan. I still hope you will be," Fannar replied as he stared disappointedly at his twin, "but the kind, caring brother I love could *never* torture someone."

Hakan let out a short laugh, his eyes growing glossy, "You'd be surprised how tempting it is after spending almost a year and a half being tortured yourself," he said sardonically.

"This! This is what I'm talking about!" Fannar exclaimed, desperate to make Hakan understand. "You've changed. It's not like before when you had those attacks and things were out of your control. You're knowingly hurting people now, and you're not even sorry anymore when you do."

"You have no idea what I'm feeling, Fannar," Hakan said with a miserable smile, finally letting a tear escape as he leaned his head back against the wall and stared through the ceiling. "Was there anything else you wanted to ask me? Because if you're just going to stand there and lecture me about all the things I already feel terrible about, you can go."

Chapter 17

Fannar paused, taken aback by his brother's response, unable to decide if Hakan's regret was genuine. "Why did you run?" He finally asked, but his brother said nothing. "I found the message you left on your tab. You apologized, but you never said why you were leaving," Fannar added, hoping mention of the note would prod Hakan to respond, but again, his brother remained silent. "What were you planning on doing?" he asked.

The worry in Fannar's voice stung too much to ignore. "Not what you're thinking," Hakan finally answered.

"You hurt yourself last night," Fannar pointed out in an attempt to justify his concern, "you ran away from Bror, and you hurt yourself."

Hakan momentarily turned back to his brother with a bemused expression before letting out a derisive laugh and returning his eyes upwards.

"What? Talk to me!" Fannar demanded angrily.

"Why? You're not going to believe me," Hakan scoffed.

"Try me," Fannar implored stubbornly.

Hakan looked back at his brother as he considered whether or not to answer. "You asked Bror to guard me because of his gift–"

"–he told you?" Fannar interjected in surprise.

"BUT," Hakan continued, "what you didn't know, was my emotions weren't the cause of the problem–they were the effect."

"Stop being a cryptic asshole already," Fannar snapped impatiently.

"Dad thinks the fire gift comes with a curse, and he's right–and I can't keep control of it yet. I was running away to be alone, so the only person I could hurt was myself," Hakan explained.

"So last night..." Fannar said slowly as he thought over Bror's description of the previous night.

Hakan nodded his head somberly. "Whatever the fire-gift does to people, it started happening to me again last night. I *wanted* to hurt Bror – and you too actually when he told me the twenty-four-hour supervision was your idea – but I also *didn't* want to hurt anyone," he said, his voice full of derision as he thought back. "When Bror used *his* gift to help me calm down, it didn't take away the want I had to use mine on him; it just cleared my mind enough to realize what was happening and gave me time to try and get away. When I realized I wasn't going to be able to stop myself from attacking him, I..."

"You used your gift on yourself," Fannar finished, his eyes wide and mouth open, and his brother nodded. "And tonight–the guard?" Fannar prodded.

"Adrig cornered me while I was trying to escape the city. It was a lot harder to resist the urge to use my gift on him than it was with Bror, and I gave in. I wish I hadn't, but I did," Hakan answered mournfully.

"What about in the gym, did the same thing happen then?" Fannar asked, as guilt for allowing himself to doubt his brother crept into his chest.

"I think that's actually the only thing that was just me," Hakan said thoughtfully, trying to compare how he had felt during each incident.

"There's gotta be a way to stop it," Fannar insisted, resting his hand on the transparent door.

"I can only come up with one so far," Hakan replied darkly.

Chapter 17

"Absolutely not," Fannar said firmly, giving Hakan a scathing look. "Maybe you going to the detention facility will be a good thing. You won't be able to hurt anyone, and it'll give me and the others time to try and find something to help you take back control of your gift... hopefully before I have to be king," Fannar said, thinking aloud.

Hakan studied his brother's expression, his heart softening slightly as watched Fannar lose himself in thought. Whatever doubt his twin had entered the detention wing with, it had been effectively dissolved and replaced with the familiar, loving determination that Hakan now realized he greatly depended on.

As Fannar refocused on the present, he noticed Hakan staring at him, not with ire or indifference as he had at the beginning of their conversation, but with gratitude. He smiled at his brother and finally saw a glimmer of hope in the older twin's eyes. Suddenly a soft thump came from the entrance to the wing, and Fannar turned just in time to see a blue and black clad figure fall away from it.

A moment later, Moritz burst through the entrance, one of the sentries slung unconscious over his shoulder as he quickly closed the door behind him. "Fannar, seal it!" He ordered.

"What? Why?" Fannar asked, shocked and confused.

"Just do it!" Moritz bellowed as he shoved Fannar back towards the entrance and dropped the sentry down in front of Hakan's cell.

Fannar steadied himself and quickly created a thick wall of ice, sealing the exit, while Moritz grabbed the guard's limp hand and pressed the thumb to the scanner of Hakan's cell.

"We have to get Hakan out–now," Moritz said hurriedly as he flopped the guard off to the side.

"Why?" Hakan asked, his expression confused as Moritz entered the cell.

"Better question is How? You just had me seal the only exit," Fannar reminded as he joined them.

"Fannar make the window as cold as you can as fast as you can," Moritz said, the urgency in his voice worsening, making Fannar move to obey without question.

"The windows are made of ladite," Hakan pointed out as Fannar pressed his hands to the smooth surface and mist began sinking to the floor. "It's unbreakable, that's why they use it for the front of the cells and the windows."

"Not unbreakable, just very strong–stronger than any of the *common* gifts," Moritz quickly explained as Fannar worked, "but its integrity gets compromised under extreme temperatures. Usually that's not really a concern since there are only two exceptionally *rare* gifts that can create those extremes," Moritz said with a smirk, "I'm pretty sure if we use your gifts back-to-back, we'll be able to break the window."

"*Pretty* sure?" Hakan echoed apprehensively.

"I think that's the best I can do," Fannar said as he stepped aside from the now ice-cold window.

"Your turn," Moritz said firmly, gesturing his head towards the window.

Hakan took a deep breath as he stepped forward and began blasting the hottest fire he could create, quickly making it feel as though they were standing in an oven. After several seconds, the transparent material shattered, and the three of them rushed forward.

"Fannar, can you get us down there?" Moritz asked, gesturing to the alley below.

Chapter 17

Without a word, the younger prince placed his hand on the window frame and ice crystals instantly spread and grew from the spot, quickly creating a steep slide from the cell to the ground.

"Good job, Fannar," Moritz said proudly, patting him on the back as the ice-prince wiped the beads of sweat from his brow. "Make sure you leave your mini-tab here," he instructed Fannar before nudging the other twin towards the window. "Hakan, you go first," Moritz said, dropping his own mini-tab on the floor before climbing on the slide behind Hakan, Fannar following close behind as they all zoomed several stories down to the ground.

One by one they flew off the slide, clambered to their feet, and raced off down the dark alleyway, disappearing from view of the guard headquarters before the sentries could come to.

The trio ran several blocks before Fannar finally spoke. "Moritz, what's going on?" he panted as they ran.

"Adrig's dead," he said flatly.

"What?" the twins spluttered as they slowed to a stop.

"No," Hakan said, shaking his head in shock, "no, he... he was alive. He was breathing when you took me. I hurt him, but I didn't do enough to kill him–I didn't *want* to kill him."

Moritz quickly pulled everyone out of sight between two large dumpsters. "I know, his heart was beating steadily too. I don't know what happened with him after we left, but he's dead now," he hurriedly explained, his expression grave, "and the council convinced the king that Hakan is too much of a threat to be left alive."

"That can't be right," Fannar protested.

"They were going to execute him as soon as the Royal Guard had located all of Hakan's friends," Moritz explained patiently. "They wanted to make sure none of us would be able to interfere when the guard leadership came to execute him."

"I don't believe it," Fannar said, still refusing to accept that his father was capable of giving such an order.

"Wait, how do you know all this?" Hakan questioned.

"Iz. He went to the manor after Fannar messaged everyone that you'd run away, and he overheard the council talking," Moritz hurriedly explained, "He came to the headquarters and because he correctly guessed I'd still be using my heightened hearing, he was able to warn me from down on the street without alerting any guards"

"Where is he now?" Hakan asked, worried.

Moritz shook his head, "he's fine, he's going to meet us outside the city."

"What about Chasan?" Fannar added uneasily, "He was in the hall when I went in to talk to Hakan. Why didn't he come in with you to help us escape?"

Moritz clenched his jaw for a moment before answering. "Because I didn't tell him what Ismat said. I made up an excuse to get him to leave," he added, when he saw Fannar's eyes popping from their sockets with the assumption Moritz had knocked their friend out.

Hakan's heart twinged as he realized Moritz' reason for not telling Chasan. "You didn't think that he'd help, did you?" he asked, dejected.

"I wasn't willing to take the chance, and I didn't have the time to take on the two sentries *and* Chasan if he took their side," Moritz told them, his eyes briefly betraying the hurt his doubt caused. "Now, we need to split

Chapter 17

up," he continued, shaking his head, "Fannar, I want you to head north towards the mount–"

"We need to go back to the manor," Hakan interjected, his expression hard.

"What?" Moritz blurted, looking at the prince as though he'd lost his mind.

"Are you crazy?" Fannar demanded, his brows furrowed as he glared at his brother, "we just broke you out of the guard headquarters and now you want to turn yourself in?"

"No," Hakan said quietly, "I want to say goodbye to mom."

"No," Moritz answered flatly, "I'm sorry, Hakan. It's too risky."

"You said dad was sending the royal guard to find everyone," Hakan reminded him, "that means there will be less guards at the manor because they'll be out looking for Iz and the others. Your hearing should be able to help us avoid anyone that's left."

"No, I am getting you out and as far away from the city as I can," Moritz argued.

"Once you get me out, I won't ever be able to come back," Hakan pointed out, fighting back tears as he continued, "and when I left the first time, I didn't think about the fact I'll probably never see her again. I *need* to say goodbye... please, Moritz."

"Hakan," Fannar said quietly, grabbing his brother's arm, "Moritz' right, you can't risk being caught. If dad had decided to just lock you up, I'd say go for it, but..."

"You told me one of the worst things when your parents died was that you didn't get to say goodbye to them. You said they left for your mom's tournament before you'd woken up, so you never got to say it," Hakan reminded his friend, "please let me say goodbye to my mom."

Moritz stared at the prince, eyes watering before reluctantly nodding his head in agreement. "Okay, Hakan," he said weakly.

Chapter 18
PAINFUL GOODBYES

"If we're going to do this, I want us all to trade clothes and have Fannar start heading south– make sure you get spotted but keep the hood up," Moritz instructed, as he removed his uniform shirt and passed it to Hakan.

"So, you want me to be a decoy," Fannar asked, pulling off his own shirt and handing it over to his friend.

"Yes, but don't do anything stupid. The guards will probably come at you with lethal force; don't wait too long to fight back," Moritz implored, and Fannar nodded his understanding as he pulled his brother's shirt over his head. "Hey, try and tuck as much of your hair in as you can," Moritz added to the older prince as he watched Hakan tightening the Royal Guard cap over his blonde locks.

Once everyone was dressed in their last-minute disguises, they set off their separate ways. Hakan had been correct that Moritz' heightened senses would be sufficient to avoid detection, and the two successfully made their way through the dark streets relatively unnoticed. As they approached the manor, creeping along the back walls of the buildings to the south, Hakan's eyes lit up.

"They didn't take it down," he said, nudging his friend and pointing to the shadow of the blanket-rope he had made, swaying like an enormous tail from his window.

"I guess we found our way in," Moritz said, closing his eyes in concentration. "I can only hear one person in the residential wing–that'll be your mom. Everyone else is concentrated in the councilroom," he added, surprised.

"No one's patrolling the roof?" Hakan asked suspiciously as his friend listened.

"No," Moritz confirmed, a touch of amusement in his voice. "I guess they don't think you'd try and come back here...they really do underestimate your stupidity," Moritz teased.

Hakan pursed his lips and gave his friend a gentle whack on the shoulder for the quip, before bracing himself to run across the small street between their hiding place and his home. "Say when."

"Go," Moritz whispered, and the two darted for the rear of the manor, and Hakan's make-shift rope. They quickly scaled the wall and climbed through the window of Hakan and Fannar's bedroom before quietly making their way over to the heavy door, where they paused for Moritz to re-check everyone's locations. "Shit," Moritz breathed.

"What?" Hakan asked anxiously from beside him.

"They've got Fannar," Moritz told him, the muscle in his jaw tensing. "We need to hurry," he whispered, pulling the door open and slipping into the hall.

Hakan followed closely behind his friend as they quietly made their way down the stairwell to the floor below. They stepped off the landing into his parents' study, and Hakan darted across to the door that led to the bedroom, hurriedly swinging it open. His mother lay still and pale on the bed, her breath labored and the features of her face taut with pain.

"Hakan," Moritz whispered as his friend stood at the foot of the bed, frozen in shock.

Chapter 18

"I... they haven't let me see her since she..." Hakan whispered back as tears welled up in his eyes.

"We don't have much time," Moritz gently reminded him, "They've already teleported Fannar back to the councilroom for your dad and the others to question him."

Hakan nodded and walked around to the side of the bed before kneeling down and gingerly taking his mother's hand in his own. "Mom?" he said softly.

The queen's eyes fluttered open. "Hakan," she whispered weakly, her eyes sparkling as she realized who had woken her. "My sweet boy... I have missed seeing your face."

"I've missed you too mom," he croaked in reply as tears streaked down his cheeks.

"Oh, my poor baby," she said, giving his hand a small squeeze. "Don't cry."

"I'm so sorry, mom," Hakan whispered, his features twisting with sadness.

"I know," she said warmly, giving him a tiny, encouraging smile, "I know how hard all of this waiting must be for you," Irina said kindly, struggling to keep her eyes open as she spoke, "It must feel like it's taking forever, but I'm sure it won't be too much longer until things go back to normal again. You'll see, soon enough you and your friends will be back training and laughing together. Just be patient."

"I'll try," Hakan told her somberly, "if you promise to get better."

"It's a deal," Irina said as confidently as she could. "I already feel stronger now that I've seen you," she added happily, "your father should have listened to me sooner about letting you come down. I told him: I needed to see *both* of my boys to be able to recover."

"Maybe we can convince him to let me and Fannar come down and say goodnight every day," Hakan suggested, his heart aching as he said the words, knowing that he would not be able to follow through, "how does that sound?"

"Perfect," she said, her weak eyes briefly fluttering open to beam up at him.

"Hakan," Moritz quietly interrupted.

"Moritz?" Irina asked curiously, turning her attention to the foot of the bed. "I thought *Bror* was supposed to be watching over Hakan," she said, confused.

"Hakan's doing so well that His Majesty is letting us trade off now," Moritz lied, giving the queen a warm, compassionate smile before turning to Hakan with a warning expression, "We should head back upstairs now, though."

Even though to the queen it had sounded like nothing more than a dutiful instruction, Hakan knew it was Moritz' way of saying he had run out of time. He nodded solemnly to his friend as a fresh wave of tears streamed from his eyes and turned back to his mother.

"I'll come back as soon as I can," Hakan whispered, unable to find his voice, "I promise."

"Tomorrow," Irina whispered back hopefully, her eyes glistening with her own tears as she gave his hand another feeble squeeze, "I love you sweetheart."

Hakan gently laid his head against his mother's shoulder, rubbing his thumb over the back of her cold hand. "I love you too, mom," he said with a small sniff, "goodbye."

"Good night, Hakan," Irina replied, "sleep well."

Chapter 18

Hakan nodded, doing his best to smile for his mother as he stood and followed Moritz from the room, quietly closing the door behind him. As he turned to follow his friend back upstairs, Moritz suddenly wrapped his arms around Hakan.

"I'm sorry, Hakan," he said quietly as he hugged his friend.

"I didn't know she had gotten so bad," Hakan whispered, his voice cracking, the image of his once strong, vibrant mother now reduced to a shadow lingering in his mind.

"Neither did I," Moritz replied sympathetically, releasing Hakan and turning an ear in the direction of the council room. "Let's go, we're about to lose our escape route," he said, grabbing hold of Hakan's arm and dragging him to the stairwell, "Fannar's not answering their questions, so your dad is sending him to his room with a guard."

The two hurried up the stairs and back to the twin's room, quickly retreating out the window. As their feet landed on the soft, dewey grass, they raced to the corner of the manor as Moritz listened for movement.

"Go," he whispered urgently, and for the second time that evening, Hakan ran northward across the small street between his home and the next, continuing along the space between the buildings and the mountain as fast as his legs would carry him. They raced along the dark space for several minutes, the hair on the back of Hakan neck prickling anxiously.

"Argh!" Hakan exclaimed as a web of vines sprang up from the ground, wrapping tightly around his legs and feet, sending him crashing forward onto the soft green ground while a muffled thump told him Moritz had come to the same, abrupt halt behind him. Hakan twisted around, quickly scorching the vines and freeing himself before jumping up to help his friend who was hurriedly hacking at the tendrils with a knife.

As Hakan moved to attack the vines that had entrapped Moritz, a new one shot up from the grass, grabbed hold of his arm, and pulled it down to the ground, sending the ball of fire into the side of the mountain.

"Give it up, Hakan," Chasan called from atop a nearby building.

Hakan gave his trapped friend a questioning look as the plants around their limbs tightened. Eyes full of determination, Moritz gave the prince a tiny nod, and a moment later, Hakan released several small explosions from his arms and legs, destroying the vines that had held them. He bounded to his feet, deftly avoiding the new onslaught of plants from Chasan as he worked to free Moritz. The prince destroyed the last vine around his friend's ankle, and the two arduously pressed on with their escape along the border of the city, Hakan reducing the vines to ash while Chasan repelled down to the ground to pursue them.

"We don't have time for this," Moritz huffed, as he sliced through another vine that had gone for his midsection. "We're gonna have to fight him," he growled, and Hakan spun around, sending an enormous fireball flying in Chasan's direction.

Chasan jumped out of the way of the flaming sphere, rolling several yards before springing back to his feet to continue the fight, but his opponents had disappeared.

As Hakan's attack passed him, Moritz had run for the nearest street, grabbing the prince along the way and

Chapter 18

quickly dragging him out of view. They raced along one of the old, cobblestones alleyways between buildings, before being dumped out onto a main road.

Moritz hastily looked around, trying to get his bearings. "That way!" he shouted, pointed up the street, and took off at a run, Hakan following close behind.

Suddenly, several vines burst through the pavement, quickly growing and winding around each other, creating a cage around the fugitives.

"Stay close," Hakan hurriedly murmured as he began filling the cage with fire.

Moritz pressed his back to the prince's and watched as he fed the flames, until he felt the adrenaline from the chase evaporate and a sense of calm wash over him. "Bror," he breathed, a hint of defeat in his voice.

"C'mon guys, don't do this," Bror called over the crackling of Hakan's fire as he and Chasan cautiously approached the vine-cage.

"They're going to kill him," Moritz said in an eerie-calm as he and Hakan wrestled to resist the influence of their friend's gift.

Bror halted mid-step. "What?" he questioned, his expression a mixture of horror and disbelief.

"The council convinced dad that I'm too much of a threat," Hakan said in the same, unnaturally calm tone as Bror's gift repelled all of his emotions.

"He even ordered the rest of the Royal Guard to keep us from interfering with the execution," Moritz added, a taste of satisfaction in his tone.

"You must've misunderstood something," Bror insisted, "Eero wouldn't do that to you."

"He did," Hakan replied, sadness creeping in as he fought the emotion-gift.

"We promised to protect the lives of the Royal Family, Bror. All of them. I'm going to continue to do that, even if it's protecting them from each other," Moritz called, his voice growing stronger as Bror's influence slipped little by little.

"He killed a guard, Moritz," Chasan replied, a hint of sorrow in his voice, "we can't just let him take off."

"And there's more you don't know," Bror added sadly.

"I could say the same for the two of you," Moritz retorted, glaring at his friends.

"I can break the cage," Hakan whispered over his shoulder.

Moritz grabbed hold of Hakan's wrist and squeezed to let the prince know he'd heard the message. "Whatever you think Hakan may have done or why," he said evenly to Bror and Chasan, "do you really believe he deserves to die?"

"That's not for us to decide," Chasan resolutely replied.

Moritz then turned his gaze to Bror, who looked less certain. "Is that how you feel, too?"

"I think we need to get to the bottom of things the right way: by you two turning yourselves in and coming with us before you make things even worse for yourselves," Bror answered, his voice and expression pleading.

Moritz nodded somberly at them. "I'm sorry," he said, his eyes glistening as he stared painfully at his friends. "NOW!" He said to Hakan, covering his face with his arms.

Hakan forced the sea of fire outward like a firework, incinerating the cage and knocking Bror and Chasan backwards several feet.

"Go!" Moritz ordered.

Chapter 18

"Not without you," Hakan argued defiantly.

"I'll buy you time, we're not far from the northern forest–Iz should be there by now. Follow that street, and just stick to the warehouse area until you're out of the city. Don't stop for anyone or anything! Go, go!" Moritz urged as he turned and sprinted to attack Chasan, who was already recovering from the blast.

The prince hesitated, reluctant to leave his friend behind to face imprisonment or worse for helping him escape. As Bror began to stir on the ground, though, Hakan choked down his guilt and took off the direction Moritz had indicated. A few minutes later, he reached the pocket of the warehouses among the homes and apartments.

Almost there, he thought, a flicker of hope igniting in his chest

As his shoes pounded against the ground, though, he heard a growing 'woosh' from behind. He glanced back in time to see a large mass of water zooming towards him with the force of a tsunami and threw himself sideways out of its path. He scrambled back up to his feet as the glimmering, swaying waterform changed direction and again rushed towards him, this time meeting with a large column of fire. Within seconds, half of the water had evaporated, and Hakan watched the attacking mass retreat, returning to the water-gifted who was purposefully striding towards him. The prince's blood turned cold as the attacker passed under a streetlamp, illuminating the face of the king.

Chapter 19

FIRE AND WATER

Fear surged through Hakan's veins at the sight of his father walking determinedly his way down the road. He swallowed hard, the bitter taste unsettling his stomach as he sped off down the road. Making a sharp turn at the first cross-street he reached, he hurriedly tried door after door as he snaked his way around the warehouses attempting to lose his father. As he rounded another corner and tried what felt like the hundredth handle, his heart leapt as it turned, and he ducked inside.

Hakan's shaky hands were a fraction of a second too slow to close it, though, and the water slammed against the thin steel door with a deafening roar, pouring through the inches wide opening that the prince was trying desperately to close. His efforts were futile though, as his father's gift soaked the warehouse floor, causing his shoes to slowly lose traction. Hakan's foot slipped, and he was flung backwards as water surged through the open door, consuming and throwing him across the warehouse. Hakan's eyes flashed with stars as his father's attack pinned him against a rough stack of plywood, making him lose precious breath as he struggled to escape the relentless assault.

He really does want me dead, he realized. As the water pounded against his body, Hakan's heart shattered,

Chapter 19

his lungs screaming for air. *And if you don't do something soon, you will be,* he told himself.

Forcing away the heartache, Hakan focused, drawing and concentrating the energy from his gift as fast as he could into his upper-body. Finally, as the familiar sense of quiet darkness started to creep in and threaten unconsciousness, he released the collected energy from his chest, filling the warehouse with a blast that shattered the windows. The force of the explosion sent the king, who had been advancing on his son, careening backward into the wall. Hakan eagerly gasped for breath as he clambered to his feet, the charred remnants of Moritz' now soaked royal guard shirt clinging to his arms and torso. His eyes darted around the warehouse, anxiously searching for another way out.

The space was in the midst of renovations; new rooms had been erected along the walls and the materials to construct more had been scattered around the warehouse after his explosion. Canvas drop-cloths, buckets of paint and cleansers, and other stacks of plywood and scaffolding were strewn around and had become fuel for small fires.

Finally, Hakan spotted another door on the other end of the building opposite where he had entered. Before he could run more than a few yards though, the ominous whooshing sound returned. He rounded on the spot, once again sending a column of fire to meet the attack.

"How long do you think you can keep this up, Hakan?" Eero called harshly over the roar of their colliding gifts, advancing on his son as steam filled the air.

Hakan said nothing, concentrating all of his efforts on sustaining the column while he created a fireball behind his back. Once the opposing gifts had created enough fog to block them from each other's view, he threw it in a curve at the place just ahead of where the king had disappeared as one of the burning piles exploded.

Distracted by the noise of the explosion, Eero almost missed the glow of Hakan's second attack speeding through the haze. He dove out of the way as the fireball zoomed past and struck another pile of wood. The column of fire tore through the remnants of the king's water attack and poured onto the wall behind the king, joining the rapidly growing number of things that had been set ablaze. Eero sprang up, beads of sweat collecting on his forehead, and ran for the last place he had spotted his son.

Hakan strained against the crackling and pops of the numerous fires, listening for movement. He heard the footfalls as his father rushed him, and sent another blast of fire towards the sound, groaning in frustration when he saw it too hit the wall.

Breathing hard from the effort to dodge his son's attack, Eero drew the vapor from the air, clearing their view of each other, and condensing it into two spheres off to Hakan's side. As the king sent the water streaking at his son like spears, Eero rushed him head-on.

Hakan shot a plume of fire from his hand, evaporating one of the spears before awkwardly dodging the other, and spun around just in time to block a strike from his father. Arms trembling, exhausted by all the fighting throughout the night, Hakan pushed his father back, and spun into a kick. The king, who was showing no signs of tiring, easily blocked the attack and landed a kick of his own in Hakan's stomach. As the prince stumbled backward, Eero drew more vapor from the air, forming it into a whip. He flicked it at his son, but missed, instead knocking over a bucket of solvent that sat on the scaffolding behind him. The liquid poured out of the bucket

Chapter 19

and onto a burning heap of canvas below, sending the flames blooming upwards and catching another wall on fire.

The warehouse had quickly become an oven, both father and son dripping in sweat as they continued to attack each other while more of the walls and building materials turned into fuel for the raging fire. Finally, one of Hakan's fireballs connected, striking his father in the shoulder. The prince bolted for the door as the king doubled over in pain, but once again, didn't make it very far before the threatening woosh-sound returned. Like deja-vu, he turned, and the stream met with a plume of fire, refilling the warehouse with mist.

As Eero lost sight of Hakan through the dense vapor radiating from their opposing gifts, he used the cover to create arrow-like streaks of water. They flew silently through the air at the prince, all but one narrowly missing.

Hakan felt the sting as the water-arrow grazed his left arm, and afraid his father was going to try again, expanded the column of fire spewing from his hands. Throwing every scrap of energy he had left into the burning flow of fire, he overpowered the king's attack. Hakan stood, his chest heaving as he listened intently for the sound of his father's gift, but all he could hear was the roar of the flames around the warehouse. Trying not to think about what he may have just done to his father, he made another attempt for the door.

"Stop!" The king yelled as the haze began to subside, but the sound hurried steps only picked up their pace. Eero drew all the water from the floor and air together, clearing his view once again and creating a thin, glistening snake-like form. The snake turned into a spear as the king sent the water streaking through the air. It shot through the prince's shoulder, and Hakan tumbled forward to the ground. "You're not leaving this City, Hakan," he yelled, slowly making his way towards his son.

Hakan scrambled painfully onto his hands and knees, as blood dripped from the half-inch-wide hole left by his father's attack. As he tried to stand, he saw a glint of something flash by his leg; his father's water-spear had delicately sliced along his inner thigh, making him fall once again onto his hands and knees.

"Give it up son," Eero bellowed as another burning pile exploded inside the warehouse, sending smoldering ashes floating through the air, "don't make things harder than they have to be."

Hakan let out a pitiful laugh as he turned his gaze back towards the king. "Why should I make it easier for you to kill me?" he yelled back horsley.

Eero froze, a trace of shock flitting through his eyes as he stared back at the prince. "What makes you think I'm trying to kill you, Hakan?" he asked, failing his attempt to make the accusation sound unthinkable.

Hakan closed his eyes, brows briefly twitching upward. "Guess I get it from you," he scoffed, his face filled with glum amusement as he strained to bring himself into a kneeling position to face the king.

"Get what?" Eero asked cautiously, taking another step forward.

Hakan tilted his head to the side. "Being a terrible liar," he replied confidently, wincing from the sting of his injuries, "I know you and the council decided to execute me."

Eero clenched his jaw. Hearing the words from his son, in a voice of deepest betrayal, was far more difficult to stomach than he had guessed it would be... words his son

Chapter 19

shouldn't have known to say. "How do you know about the execution?" He asked curiously.

"Doesn't really matter how I know," Hakan groaned, lifting himself upright with his good leg and gingerly adding weight to the other, "I didn't want to believe it until now," he added, his eyes reflecting his devastation.

"You didn't really give me a choice, Hakan," Eero told him irritably, his voice growing raspy as smoke filled the warehouse, "since it took you less than a day to prove to the entire kingdom how dangerous you can be."

"Why not just lock me up?" Hakan demanded.

"Yeah, because that worked so well earlier tonight," Eero spat back sarcastically, "No one'd trust any cell to be strong enough to hold you after you broke out of the headquarters."

"You're lying again–that had nothing to do with your decision," Hakan argued, exasperated, his eyes filling with tears, "You decided on the execution before Moritz and Fannar helped me get out of the headquarters."

Eero studied his son's face, his own filled with concern. "How do you know all of this, Hakan?" he asked pointedly, but the prince simply shook his head, "what are you hiding, son?"

Hakan flinched at the last word, "how could you agree to execute me?" he asked bitterly.

"Just stop it," the king snapped, "It's not going to work anymore."

"What?" Hakan muttered, confused.

"This," Eero said, waving his hand at Hakan, "this act–as if you're all hurt and guilt-ridden; I'm not buying it anymore."

Hakan stared blankly at the king, his mouth silently opening and closing several times as he struggled to form his now chaotic feelings into words. "What am I supposed to be? My dad just admitted he's going to kill me, and basically saying it's my own fault... how else do you expect me to feel?" he cried, his voice shaking.

"You know, you acted all innocent and sorry at the manor this morning too, but then you snuck out and killed a city guard," Eero sniped back.

"I didn't kill him!" Hakan exclaimed in frustration, the remorse for not fighting harder against his curse washing over him as tears slid down his face.

"So, he set himself on fire and died, is that what happened then?" Eero offered sardonically, refusing to believe the regret Hakan displayed was sincere.

"I didn't do enough to kill him! I don't know what happened!" Hakan yelled in desperation.

"Well, I'll tell you what happened then: Adrig left headquarters for his shift in one piece, ran into you, mysteriously got covered in severe burns and died before Tanlan and the others could stop it," Eero rattled off savagely.

Hakan shook his head in disbelief. "Moritz said he was alive when he and Chasan took me to the headquarters," Hakan argued.

"Well, we wouldn't know that since Moritz never returned to the manor to give Basilah a report like Chasan did," the king shouted over the steadily raging fire around them, "not that it makes much of a difference; Adrig's still dead and the only thing that could have caused it was you torturing him. If anything, it's *worse* because now that means he suffered longer from the burns before he died."

Chapter 19

Hakan's stomach dropped as the fire raged around them. More than half the walls were covered with flames now, and the scaffolding was creaking ominously as the piles at their bases blazed red-hot.

The prince turned the possibility over in his head that Moritz had been wrong; that Arig had been in a more critical condition than his friend had realized, and that he – Hakan – had in fact done the unthinkable. Despite how much he had detested the guard, he never meant to end his life; he had only wanted the guard to suffer a small portion of the pain he had caused.

"I... I didn't mean to..." Hakan began, his voice cracking as his throat burned, more from guilt than the acrid smoke that was steadily thickening.

"No, no more manipulations!" Eero growled, shaking his head, creating a glittering sphere of crystal-clear water in his hand,

"When have I ever been manipulative?" Hakan cried, tears streaming from his red eyes as his father prepared to attack again. "Every time I have messed up with my gift, I've owned up to it! And every time no one has been more angry than I am at myself! If I killed Adrig, it was a mistake–I didn't mean to, but that's why I had to run away, but he just wouldn't leave me alone!" Hakan disconnectedly exclaimed, glancing around hopelessly at the intense fires quickly destroying the warehouse as his thoughts began to spiral once again.

Eero hesitated, confused by Hakan's words, "what do you mean that's why you had to run away?"

"I needed to go somewhere where I'd be away from people, but he–he stopped me and wouldn't let me go," Hakan rambled quickly, his expression panicked and sorrowful.

"What are you talking about," Eero asked anxiously.

"You were right. The fire gift is cursed," Hakan moaned, pressing his palms to his watery eyes as he finally confessed the whole truth to his father, "it keeps making me want to hurt people, and I've been trying for months to stop it, but I haven't been able to figure out how!"

"That's why you tortured the guard?" Eero asked suspiciously.

Hakan nodded miserably, "and why I hurt Bror the day of the gifting ceremony… It happened again with him last night, but I–I couldn't let it… I couldn't let it hurt him, so I ran, but he followed me."

"And you're saying that's the reason you used your gift on yourself?" Eero asked, doubtfully.

Hakan nodded again, his feelings overwhelming him, "but I couldn't tell anyone what was going on. I was afraid no one would understand. I was afraid of ending up exactly where I am now: all alone."

Eero sighed. "I really wish I could believe that Hakan," he said, his eyes glistening as he stretched the sphere into another long, deadly cylinder.

As the king made to strike, though, a large section of the wall behind him broke away from its framing, descending towards a large set of red-hot scaffolding in front of it. Hakan, seeing his father was unaware of the danger, reflexively raced forward.

There was a loud *bang* as the burning wall made contact with the metal frame, and Eero finally spun around to see the falling debris. Before he could react though, Hakan slammed into his back, sending him tumbling out of the way of the scaffolding as it crashed to the floor.

Chapter 19

Eero pushed himself upright and spun around. Hakan could have–should have–made a run for it. Instead, his son had run towards the danger and saved him.

Hakan lay stretched out on his stomach on the soot-flecked floor, pinned from the waist down by the fallen scaffolding. He slowly lifted his face from the ground and looked over to his father, his expression exhausted and defeated.

Eero gaped at him for several long moments before scrambling to his feet and hurrying over to firmly grasp the hot metal that trapped him.

"On three, I lift, you crawl, got it?" The king instructed.

"What?" Hakan mumbled back, confused.

"One... Two..." Eero began counting as he braced himself to try lifting the heavy frame, "THREE!"

As his father strained to free him, Hakan crawled as quickly as his beaten, exhausted body would move, tucking his legs out of the way as the king lost his grip on the scaffolding. He looked up at his father, his features still riddled with confusion as to why the king hadn't taken the opportunity to kill him.

"You know," Eero said compassionately, turning to kneel down beside the prince, "even a king can make mistakes." He looked thoughtfully at his bruised, broken son as he continued, "I think I may have been too hasty deciding how to handle things today."

"What?" Hakan breathed in shock.

"Cooperate," The king told him sternly. "Come back with me, and I'll send you to the high-security detention facility. As long as you don't break out again, I don't see any reason for things to go beyond that. While you're there, I'll do what I can to find a way to stop your gift."

Hakan stared in disbelief at his father, debating whether or not to trust the compassion in his expression. "Wha– what changed?" He whimpered.

Eero shrugged, looking back over at the fallen scaffolding, "you just gave me a pretty good reason to believe my son's good heart is still in there somewhere." He turned back to the prince with apologetic eyes, "and that maybe there's more going on than I realized."

As Hakan stared up at his father's serious expression, there was a deafening bang that sent their eyes anxiously darting around for the source.

Every wall and flammable supply had caught fire. Smoke poured out through the broken windows while another set of scaffolding crashed to the floor, buckling under the heat. Another loud bang exploded through the warehouse, and they looked up to find several of the metal beams above bowing ominously downward.

Hakan fought the exhaustion and agonizing pain as he struggled to lift himself up from the ground. As his father took the prince's arm around his shoulder to help, the ceiling let out a loud and terrible groan, followed by several pops.

"Dad?" Hakan asked, fear filling his features as he glanced over at his father's suddenly soft expression.

Without warning, the king created a swell of water that swiftly carried his son towards the rear door and away from the collapsing roof.

Hakan hit the ground, the water splashing down haphazardly around him as he rolled several more feet, skidding to a halt near the exit. He picked his head up, looking desperately to the place he had left his father and

Chapter 19

his body went numb as his gaze met with the tar roof. "DAD!" He shouted horsley, his face screwed up in a mixture of denial and grief. "No... Dad?... DAD!" he called again and again.

As Hakan rolled over and began trying to crawl his way over to the fallen roof, he saw several guards rush through the entrance on the other side of the collapse; a moment later, he heard more entering the door behind him.

Hakan was trapped.

He abandoned his desperate attempt to return to his father, and laid his blackened face down on the ground as he placed his hands on his back in defeat, silently crying as the reality of his father's sacrifice set in. Consumed by grief and despair, the prince didn't register what was being said around him as the guards moved cautiously closer... until someone suddenly shouted 'stop'.

"I'm not doing anything!" Hakan weakly cried back.

A second later a hand wrapped around Hakan's shoulder, and the warehouse and fires vanished, replaced by a quiet forest.

Chapter 20

AFTERMATH

"What the–" Hakan murmured, taking in a mouthful of grass before someone tugged roughly on his arm. "Aah!" he exclaimed, squeezing his eyes shut from the pain.

"Sorry," came the voice of his rescuer beside him.

"Amehllie?" Hakan asked, craning his neck and squinting at the two shadowy figures crouched beside him.

Amehllie released her grip and sniffed at the dark, sticky residue that had transferred to her hand. "Is this your blood?" She asked anxiously.

"Yeah," Hakan breathed as he slowly rolled over to his side.

"How badly are you hurt?" Ismat asked, as he began searching the pockets of Hakan's borrowed pants.

"Uh," Hakan mumbled, trying to bring his anguished mind back to his injuries, "um.. I, uh, my legs… they..." he stuttered, groaning as he struggled to sit up.

"Shit," came a third voice behind him.

"Moritz?" Hakan breathed in relief as Ismat finished rifling through the pockets, turning on a small flashlight and illuminating his friend's faces. "How did you get away?" he questioned as Moritz took the light.

Chapter 20

"That'd be me," Amehllie said proudly as she watched Moritz examine the dirty, blood and sweat-covered prince.

"And me," Ismat added, impatiently.

"Yes, Iz helped too," Amehllie admitted, giving Ismat a quick pat on the shoulder.

"When Bror came-to, I tried to keep the two of them busy as long as I could," Moritz explained, widening the tear in the pants along Hakan's cut, "when they finally overpowered me, they called for a teleporter–"

"Too bad for them the wrong teleporter heard it," Amehllie interjected, pointing to herself with a satisfied smile. "After Iz warned Moritz, he came and found me. He told me about the execution and asked me to help rescue you. He and I were waiting here in the north forest when the call went out that they had caught Moritz and needed transport, so I flashed over there and pretended I was taking him to headquarters."

"Instead, she brought me here," Moritz added.

"A few minutes after they arrived though, Chasan called for water-gifteds over the city comms saying a warehouse was spewing smoke," Moritz said with a scolding glare at the prince.

"When Amehllie teleported her and I there," Ismat continued explaining, "Bror was working on getting the guards organized to breach the warehouse and then the roof collapsed..." he trailed off, studying his injured friend's suddenly glazed expression.

The image of the debris had floated back to Hakan's mind...and what lay under it. "Are you all okay?" he asked, anxiously looking at each of them with watery eyes, "none of you are hurt, are you?"

"Moritz is pretty beaten up from his fight," Ismat grimaced.

"Nothing too serious," Moritz said dismissively, as he continued to assess the damage to the prince's shoulder. "We need to figure out what we're going to do about his injuries," Moritz announced, frowning down at Hakan.

"I can go back and grab a healer," Amehllie quickly offered.

"No one from the Healer Corps. is going to help me," Hakan replied despondently, wincing as Moritz prodded at his ribs.

"Sure they will; I can be very persuasive," Amehllie chided back.

"It's too risky," Moritz said, shaking his head, "we'll have a better chance on the run if we have your teleportation gift. We can't take the chance that you might get caught."

"I won't get caught!" Amehllied argued, her brows furrowing, offended by the lack of confidence in her capabilities.

"Even if you don't get caught," Ismat patiently explained, "whoever you bring here will see where we've gone. We'll have half the guards in the city on top of us as soon as you bring the healer back."

"No problem – I just won't take them back," Amehllie said coolly.

"No… anyone you bring here has to be taken back," Hakan said quietly, sounding dazed, "…unhurt."

The teleporter rolled her eyes. "Fine, look, I'm pretty sure there's one I can grab who won't screw us over."

"If it's the one I think you're thinking of," Ismat said slowly, his face scrunched up in thought, "she was just

Chapter 20

really professional before when it came to our friendship with Hakan; I doubt she'll have any sympathy for him, especially if she knows about Adrig."

"Well, we can't stay here too much longer, and we can't move him in this condition, so what else do you suggest we do?" Amehllie snapped, her temper rising.

"Okay, okay, okay," Moritz exclaimed, quieting the others before he closed his eyes and sighed. "Amehllie, go and *ask* the healer if she'll help."

"Got it–give her the choice to come before resorting to kidnap," Amehllie happily replied.

"That's not–" Moritz began admonishing before she quickly vanished. "Hey," he snapped, looking back down at Hakan, "did you not hear the part where I told you 'don't stop for anything'?"

The prince hung his head, unsure how to explain to his friends what had happened. As he stared unfocused at the ground, Ismat gingerly wrapped an arm around him, letting out a small sniff as he pulled Hakan close.

"He's just hurt, Iz; he's not dying," Moritz mumbled irritably.

The prince glanced up at Ismat – his friend's face was inexplicably twisted with grief. The puzzling reaction reminded Hakan of something that had nagged at him back in the alley after his escape from the detention cell, "Iz…how did you overhear the council talking about the execution? They would have been shut up in their room at the manor with guards posted outside the door. If you had heard they were going to detain all my friends, the guards would have heard too… there's no way you'd have been able to get away."

"Uh," Ismat stuttered nervously as they stared at him.

"Iz," Hakan said warmly, surprising his younger friend, "you didn't just hear, did you? You saw what was going on."

"What?" Moritz mumbled, confused, as Ismat nodded nervously. "Were you in the council room?" he asked suspiciously.

Ismat shook his head, his gaze fixed on the blades of grass around his knees.

"How far away were you?" Hakan asked, his eyes brimming with kindness and admiration.

"Umm," Ismat said thoughtfully, "not too far– a few blocks maybe? I was working my way through the market district searching for you, and I picked up a guard getting the message they'd caught you. I refocused on the manor because I thought they would take you back there, and that's when I picked up the council talking about what to do with you."

"Wait, refocused what?" Moritz anxiously demanded, still confused by the bizarre conversation he was listening to.

"His gift," Hakan answered proudly.

"Gift?" Moritz gaped. Then the realization hit him, "you're a telepath?"

Ismat nodded his head solemnly, "yeah."

Hakan sighed, "why didn't you tell us?"

"Why do you think? I was afraid everyone would push me away; I didn't want to get shunned like the other telepaths," Ismat explained, before glumly meeting Hakan's eyes, "If you could have, wouldn't you have hidden your gift?"

The muscle in Hakan's jaw twitched guiltily, "I would never push you away, Iz."

Chapter 20

"So, you read the thoughts of the council during the meeting?" Moritz asked.

Ismat nodded, his expression growing dark, "it wasn't pretty–especially after Bror's dad told them Hakan had killed Adrig. Even Councilwoman Damra was insisting that Hakan be executed."

"What about the others?" Hakan asked hollowly.

"The decision was unanimous," Ismat told him quietly, "Leal and Haldis convinced the others it was too dangerous to even let you be tried by the courts–that your dad had to exercise his powers as king to eliminate the 'imminent deadly threat' to the kingdom *immediately*."

A cold silence fell over the three friends as they waited for Amehllie to return, Moritz and Hakan turning over Ismat's information as they listened to the leaves rustling in the breeze. After nearly twenty minutes, and a great deal of worry that she had been captured, she finally appeared with a dark-haired young woman who looked just a little older than them. She glanced nervously around at the small group, spotted Hakan sitting on the ground, and timidly moved to take Ismat's place beside him.

"May I?" She asked nervously, her hands hovering over the prince's shoulder injury.

Hakan gave her a small nod. "Thank you for coming," he mumbled as he felt the healer's palms gently press against his skin.

"I got the feeling your friend wasn't going to take no for an answer," she said drily.

"Amehllie," Moritz growled, shooting the teleporter a disapproving glance.

"Hey, I didn't join your little rogue rescue operation just to let Hakan die of an infection." Amehllie chided, crossing her arms in front of her chest testily as she glared back at the royal guard.

Hakan sighed and shifted on the ground, painfully pulling away from the healer. "I'm sorry," he said through gritted teeth, "you don't have to help if you don't want to. Amehllie'll just take you back to the capital."

"No, Amehllie will not," Amehllie snapped back defiantly, her eyebrows shooting skyward.

"Yes, you will. I don't want you kidnapping people, and I'm not going to force anyone to help me," Hakan argued, as he tried to breathe through the pain.

"You'd really let me go back?" She asked skeptically, wincing as the prince gave her a pained nod. She paused, studying his soft, apologetic expression. "...did you kill the king?"

Stunned silence fell over the others at her question, and everyone's eyes turned to Hakan, who swallowed hard and looked down at the ground, his expression full of guilt and remorse.

"No," Ismat answered firmly, reaching over to grasp Hakan's hand. "King Eero died saving Hakan from the collapsing roof," he croaked, struggling to keep his voice calm and even through his own grief as he described the memory he saw in Hakan's mind.

"It's my fault he died. I caused the fire that made it collapse," Hakan argued dully. "You weren't trying to set those fires," Ismat insisted, "you just wanted to get out of there alive."

"What about the queen?" The healer asked hesitantly.

Hakan's eyes darted to meet hers. "What do you mean the queen?" he questioned, his face filling with terror. "What happened to my mom?" he begged, desperately

Chapter 20

hoping he had misunderstood the meaning behind her question.

The healer watched the tears welling up in his eyes, unsure if she believed his ignorance. "She... Councilwoman Basilah said you killed them both," she finally answered.

"What?" Moritz asked hollowly, reluctant to believe her, "what do you mean 'both'?"

"No, she... she was fine when I left...my mom's fine," Hakan spluttered, shaking his head in denial.

"It wasn't you," The healer mumbled as she watched the prince falling apart.

"What... happened... to the queen?" Moritz asked slowly, trying to maintain his own composure.

The healer shook her head mournfully, afraid to say any details out loud that might cause Hakan more distress.

"Moritz," Ismat interjected as his friend opened his mouth to press the healer further, shaking his head warningly at him before projecting the horrific scene from the healer's memories to Moritz' mind.

"No, sh–she can't be gone," Hakan whispered, the words breaking the damn that had restrained his grief. His lip quivered as he slowly shook his head from side to side, tears streaming down his face. A moment later, he slumped forward, overcome with sorrow.

The healer's face filled with pity as she watched the orphaned prince mourning his loss. Taking a steadying breath, she shuffled forward and replaced a hand on his back, wordlessly resuming her work; first closing the hole in the prince's shoulder before healing not only the gash in his leg, but also the handful of fractures caused by the falling scaffolding. "I'm sorry I can't do more," she said wearily, taking a step back from the grief-stricken prince.

"Thank you," Moritz said hoarsely to the healer, who nodded somberly in reply. "Amehllie, take her back to the capital."

Amehllie moved over and placed a hand on the healer's shoulder, and the two disappeared, leaving Ismat and Moritz alone among the creaking trunks and branches to watch over their softly crying friend.

"Ismat," Moritz said, cautiously, "were those the healer's memories I saw a little while ago?"

The young telepath nodded, a sickened look on his face as he recalled the sights and sound before Amehllie noiselessly returned, her face blank.

"Hakan, I know you're hurting right now, but I need you to stand up," Moritz said, holding a hand out to the prince.

"She said she's not going to tell anyone she saw us— we can let him rest a little longer," Amehllie quietly insisted.

"Hakan, up... now." Moritz said sternly, pulling the prince to his feet and extracting a knife from a hidden spot on the belt around the prince's waist.

"What the hell?" Hakan exclaimed as Moritz placed himself between the prince and the others, pointing the knife at Ismat.

"Yeah, what the hell, Moritz?" Amehllie added, shocked at the hostility towards their friend.

"I don't think it was *your* gift attacking you the last few months, Hakan," Moritz said over his shoulder, still not taking his eyes off Ismat, "I heard you and Fannar talking about the attacks in the detention cell. What happens during them, and when did they start?"

Chapter 20

"What does that have to–" Hakan questioned, bewildered as he watched his friend's grip tighten on the knife.

"Answer!" Moritz growled, cutting him off.

"I–I see flashes of all the bad memories that involve my gift," Hakan quickly explained.

"And they started the night you burned Bror, didn't they?" Moritz asked pointedly, his head tilting to the side as he raised his eyebrows at Ismat.

"Yes," Hakan confirmed, tugging at his friend's arm. "Put the knife down Moritz, this is crazy!" he exclaimed.

"Think about what else happened that day, Hakan," Moritz instructed, his tone turning dark.

"You think it's me," Ismat lamented, reading Moritz thoughts.

"The first attack didn't happen until *after* your gifting," Moritz pointed out, "and I'd describe what I just experienced with your gift as flashes of the healer's memories."

"Gift? What gift" Amehllie asked, stunned.

"He's a telepath," Moritz told her coolly.

"Iz has nothing to do with it! I also told Fannar the attacks were making me want to hurt people, remember? It wasn't just memories," Hakan argued, trying in vain to reach around Moritz to take the knife away.

"See, it can't be Iz, then. Telepaths can only read and project thoughts and memories, Moritz," Amehllie insisted, stretching a protective arm in front of the telepath.

"No, Amehllie, that's only what most telepaths are *limited* to. It's extremely rare, but there have been telepath-gifteds who were strong enough that they could control others. And the falls have been handing out a lot of rare and powerful gifts the last few years," Moritz reminded her, his eyes still deadly set on the youngest member of their group.

"If I was using my gift to hurt Hakan, why would I warn you about the execution?" Ismat asked patiently, "why would I help *rescue* him? What would be the point?"

"I don't know, but I already saw one of my best friends admit that they'd let Hakan die tonight. So sorry, but I'm not taking any chances," Moritz explained, a trace of sympathy trickling into his voice.

Ismat stared back at him with a wounded expression and sighed. A moment later, both their eyes glazed over as Ismat projected more memories into Moritz' mind, showing the determined guard his most cherished moments connected to Hakan since becoming a telepath:

Moritz heard Hakan's thoughts after the dismal gifting ceremony expressing his sincere desire to make Ismat feel special; saw Hakan spending his free time helping Ismat better his fighting skills, the prince's inner thoughts reflecting how much he admired Ismat's hard work and dedication to improve; saw messages of Hakan checking up on Ismat leading into finals and offering to help him with his studies however he could.

Each time, Moritz saw everything from Ismat's perspective, including the telepath's own thoughts of how grateful he was to have Hakan as a friend.

"Still think I'm messing with him?" Ismat asked evenly, as a tear slid down his cheek.

Moritz lowered the knife, and shook his head, "I'm sorry, Iz."

"It's okay," Ismat replied compassionately, "I'd probably do that same thing if I was in your position."

Chapter 20

"Ssssssooo..." Amehllie said, looking back and forth between the two, her face screwed up in confusion, "you two good now?"

"Yeah," They answered together, and softly chuckled.

"Okay... so what's the plan?" She asked, looking around.

Moritz looked over to Hakan, "how much did she heal you?"

"She healed the injuries, but she didn't restore much of my energy," Hakan answered.

"She's only been in the corp a couple of years, she probably hasn't strengthened her gift enough to fully restore it like Kesavan can," Amehllie explained, her voice tinged with disappointment.

"Either way, we should probably get some distance between us and the capital; somewhere remote," Moritz said, glancing anxiously around the forest.

"I think I know a good place," Amehllie said, "when my family moved to the capital, we camped our way across the kingdom. I think I can take us to a bunch of out-of-the-way spots, come to think of it."

"Okay, let's get out of here then," Moritz replied as Amehllie extended her arms out for everyone to grab hold of.

An instant later, they were standing in a meadow clearing surrounded by unfamiliar thick-trunked, smooth-barked trees.

"You're sure we're a safe distance from any cities here?" Ismat asked uneasily.

"Yeah, we're pretty deep into the Euluana Forest," Amehllie answered, "only people we might run into are super-intense campers or hikers."

"Okay," Moritz said thoughtfully, surveying the surroundings, "we should probably move into the trees though, just in case Fannar sends any flyers out searching for us."

Amehllie gave him a puzzled look. "Fannar?" she questioned.

"Yeah," Moritz replied, his expression sullen.

Ismat's mouth dropped as the realization hit him, "Eero's gone…" he muttered, his voice trailing off as he looked over at Hakan, who hadn't been paying attention to the conversation since Moritz had lowered the knife.

"What?" Hakan asked when he realized his friend was staring at him.

"When King Eero made the decision to execute you, he also agreed to name Fannar the successor," Ismat told them.

"Which means the council will have recognized Fannar as the new king as soon as they learned about your dad's death," Moritz explained morosely as he turned and began leading them towards the trees.

"Wait, if Fannar is the king," Amehllie pondered as they followed, "then why did we come here? We don't have to hide if Fannar's in charge."

"Yes, we do," Moritz insisted, his mood sour.

"Why?" Amehllie asked, frustrated.

"Because we can't be sure Fannar is on our side," Moritz impatiently explained, "this whole thing looks really bad from the outside. Fannar knows I took his brother to see their mom just before she was killed, and Hakan was the only one in the warehouse when the roof collapsed on their dad. After the conversation I heard him and Hakan having back in the detention wing, it's not outrageous to

Chapter 20

think Fannar would believe his brother's the cold-blooded killer everyone's making him out to be."

"Iz could show him Hakan's memories and prove he didn't do anything though," Amehllie argued.

"No," Hakan said, his voice distant as he stopped mid-step, his gaze unfocused as he thought.

"What do you mean 'no'?" Amehllie gruffly inquired, as everyone halted.

Hakan sighed. "I don't think Iz showing him my memories will make a difference," he said darkly, his face anxious as he looked over at Ismat, "are you sure my mom was killed? She was really weak when I saw her, she could have just–"

"Hakan," Ismat interjected, his brows furrow sympathetically as he shook his head.

Hakan nodded silently and took a deep breath, forcing down the new wave of grief that threatened to derail his thoughts. "I wasn't the last one in that part of the manor," he said despondently, turning his gaze to Moritz, "dad sent Fannar to our room when he wouldn't talk, remember?"

"Wait," Amehllie breathed, her eyes widening, "you think Fannar killed Queen Irina?"

Ismat looked horror-struck from her to the prince, recalling the healer's memory. "Fannar's the one who found her," he told them numbly.

"You didn't happen to read Fannar's thoughts when he was at the headquarters, did you?" Moritz asked sardonically.

"No," Ismat answered, "I just made sure you got my message and then went to track down Amehllie."

"This is crazy!" Amehllie exclaimed, "there's no way soft, squishy Fannar killed anyone."

"We've been thinking someone overheard him call me, but he could have gone to tell your dad himself after he hung up," Moritz told the prince, his voice tense from the sickening thought.

"Why though?!" Amehllie argued, still wrought with disbelief.

"To be king," Hakan answered shortly.

"Okay, even if he wanted to be king, I can only see him taking advantage of Hakan's crazy moments to switch the succession. You're talking about him *killing* his *mom* – that's a whole other level that I just can't see Fananr being capable of."

"Everyone who turned on Hakan said 'maybe we don't know him as well as we thought," Moritz retorted testily, "...maybe *we* don't know Fannar as well as *we* thought." They glared at each other for a few moments before they heard the snap of a branch in the distance.

"Come on, we need to get under some cover," Hakan said urgently, gesturing for them to keep moving.

"And get some rest," Moritz added, looking pointedly at the prince as Ismat's stomach gave a loud growl

"And once the sun's up, maybe figure out what we're going to do about food and water," the telepath said, sighing.

The four walked seval feet into the cover of the thick canopy and decided to settle in among the exposed roots of one of the larger trees.

Hakan lay, eyes wide open, staring at the shadowy branches above, as he listened to his friends' breathing steadily slow. While the others drifted off into their own uneasy sleep, he sat there going over everything from the moment he and Bror had stepped foot out of the manor for

Chapter 20

their abysmal midnight walk. Twenty-four-hours ago, he had felt like a prisoner in his own home, desperately wishing for things to change. Now Hakan wanted nothing more than to go back to that point when the people that meant the most to him were all still in his life; he had lost both of his parents, his brother, and probably more than half of his friends. Words could not describe how much Hakan wished he could go back and refuse to leave his room when Bror had come to collect him for the walk. He began beating himself up over the thought that if he had just stayed home, maybe his curse wouldn't have been triggered.

Hakan shot upright, heart pounding. His thoughts raced as he realized he was now with *three* of his friends out in the middle of nowhere, miles from help if his curse reared itself again like it had done with Bror. Panic steadily rose in him as he debated what to do, unable to decide if he should wake Amehllie and have her take him to Snow Valley like he had originally planned, or if he should just slip quietly off himself and not risk waking the others.

"Don't," came Ismat's soft voice.

Hakan sighed. "You shouldn't keep reading people's thoughts without their permission," he quietly hissed, irritated by the intrusion.

"Sorry," Ismat apologized, "I heard you sit up suddenly and got worried."

Hakan ground his jaw for a few moments as he thought.

"You're doing it again," Ismat said knowingly.

"Doing what?" Hakan asked, annoyed.

"Your stupid-silence," Ismat said, smirking.

Hakan scrunched up his face, peering over at the dark figure beside him.

"You've been doing this weird thing with your breathing and go silent when you're thinking about doing something stupid," Ismat explained, smiling so wide Hakan could hear the grin.

"I can't stay, Iz," Hakan insisted.

"Ah, there it is," Ismat whispered triumphantly.

Hakan let out a frustrated breath and shook his head. "I was barely able to stop myself from hurting Bror the other night. I don't want to risk that I might not be able to stop it the next time it happens."

"It might not even happen anymore," Ismat replied calmly, "Moritz had a good thought–it's possible that a telepath has been messing with you all this time, and if that's the case, you won't have any issues with your gift now that we've gotten you away from them."

"Thank you, Iz, I'm glad you liked my idea," Moritz murmured impishly from Hakan's other side.

"And what if it's not a telepath?" Hakan argued, his voice riddled with fear, "I don't want to take any chances; none of us are healers."

"If you have another meltdown – and we can't handle it – I'm sure Amehllie will happily go back and ask that healer for help again," Moritz reassured the prince.

"If he shuts up so we can get some sleep, I'll grab a hundred healers," Amehllie groaned from the other side of the tree.

"Like it or not," Moritz grunted as he repositioned himself among the roots, "you're stuck with us, Hakan."

Hakan stared out into the darkness, a flicker of warm comfort seeping into his heart. He didn't deserve their kindness and loyalty, and yet Ismat, Moritz and even Amehllie were clearly dead set on staying with him.

Chapter 20

Worried as he was for what may lie ahead for them all, he was grateful that he wasn't going to be alone.

He leaned back, resting his hands behind his head as he closed his eyes, focusing on that small warm feeling; on the friends who had given up everything to save and help him. As he slowly drifted off to sleep, Hakan promised to do whatever it took to protect and care for them in return.

Chapter 21

HAPPY BIRTHDAY

Fannar stood in his old room, staring at the delicate golden diadem on the dresser that had been his, thinking back to the gifting eighteen months earlier. It hadn't been that long, but it felt like a lifetime away. Images of his parent's smiling faces floated to the forefront of his thoughts as he reminisced over the happy, dream-like memories of his unbothered life before the ceremony; of care-free wanderings around the capital, late nights filled with laughter and mischief with his friends, and the loving warmth of his parents' arms. It was almost unbelievable how quickly and radically his life had changed.

"Your Majesty," came the voice of a royal guard behind him, "Your father's council members have all arrived, sir."

"Alright," Fannar replied hollowly, still staring at the delicate, twisted metal, "I'll be down shortly." he listened as the guard's footsteps faded away and raised his head, meeting his reflection in the mirror.

It wasn't supposed to be me, he thought bitterly as he stared at the silver bands adorned with diamonds stretched across his forehead. He clenched his jaw and fought the urge to throw the diadem out of the window, opting to instead slam his fist into the hardwood dresser. A

Chapter 21

soft knock came from the doorway, and Fannar turned to see Bror standing in the opening.

"That help?" Bror asked, pointing to Fannar's now throbbing hand.

"No," Fannar sulked as his friend stepped over the threshold and pulled a small box from behind his back.

"Happy Birthday, Fannar," he said with a weak smile, holding the box out to the prince.

Fannar sighed and stared pointedly at the box, "I told you I didn't want to be reminded what today is."

"Yeah, I know," Bror said sympathetically, setting the box down on the dresser beside the golden diadem, "You can think of it as a coronation present instead if that would be better."

"I don't want to be reminded of that either," Fannar grumbled, glaring down at the box.

Bror pursed his lips. "So does that mean you still haven't decided who you want on your council, then?" he asked patiently, and Fannar shook his head. "I know you don't want to think about it, but your coronation is in a hour, and you're going to have to announce your council by the end of the ceremony... it'd be nice if we could let all the members know who they are beforehand, instead of having them find out when you tell the rest of the kingdom."

Fannar walked over and sat on the edge of his old bed, staring down at his hands as he gently rubbed them together. After a few moments, he looked pleadingly up at his friend, "who do you think I should have?"

Bror gave a little shrug as he replied, "I have no idea."

"That's very helpful, thanks," Fannar scoffed, rolling his eyes.

"Just... choose the people you trust to be honest with you," Bror told the soon-to-be king as he sat down beside him, "people who won't be afraid to tell you when they think you're wrong, and who care about the kingdom."

There was another pause as Fannar thought. "What about you?" he asked, glancing over at his friend.

Bror's eyebrows shot up in surprise, "you want me on the council?"

"You already ignored my request that everyone forget about my birthday, I think you could handle telling me when I'm wrong about something as king," Fannar said, a small hint of happiness in his eyes.

Bror scrunched his nose, his ears turning pink as he considered the idea. "You sure you don't wanna ask someone older?" he asked, his pitch noticeably higher than usual.

"Nah," Fannar said, a mischievous smile touching the corners of his mouth, "you'll be twenty-one next month, you're practically middle aged," he added with a chuckle.

Bror closed his eyes and sighed, relieved his friend's mood had improved even if it came at his expense. "If you think I can be helpful, then yeah, I'd be honored to be a part of your council."

"Good," Fannar nodded, his shoulders dropping slightly as some of the tension left them, "as the first member of my council, what do you think about keeping Kesavan, Basilah, and your dad on as well?"

"I think keeping a few members from the old council on is a good idea since you're taking over so young," Bror answered, then his face lit up as another idea occurred to him. "Hey, you know who you should ask?"

Chapter 21

"Who?" Fannar asked, curiously searching his friend's gleeful expression.

"Mr. James," Bror told him, nodding proudly at his own suggestion. "He has a good heart, he'd bring the same level of life-experience to *your* council that Haldis did for your dad's, and he's definitely not going to have any problems setting you straight if you ever need it," he said, chuckling as he pictured the baker telling Fannar off during a future meeting.

"I don't know if I could ask him to do that," Fannar replied shyly.

"See, now this is one of those nice perks of being the almost-king: you can delegate someone else to do it for you," Bror pointed out, nudging his friend with a sly smile.

"Yeah, I guess so," Fannar said, scrunching his nose at the thought. "Hey, d'you think Shammoth and the others would be on the council too?" he asked hesitantly.

"Probably," Bror replied, grinning broadly as he fought back laughter, "I'm sure Joule'll give you loads of grief first for waiting so long to ask him though."

"Probably," Fannar agreed, letting out a small laugh along with his friend.

They sat in silence for a few minutes as the fleeting moment of happiness faded, and Fannar resumed the anxious rubbing together of his palms.

"Have we heard anything about them yet?" Fannar asked as he looked over to the unoccupied bed on the far side of the room.

Bror's jaw tightened. "No. Nothing since Iz and Amehllie were spotted at a market in Elibet a few days after the escape."

"They have no idea who they're protecting," Fannar hissed through gritted teeth.

"We haven't had any reports of healers going missing," Bror reminded him, studying his friend's dark expression, "It's been almost a month, and as beaten up as he looked, there *is* a chance he didn't survive his injuries."

"Chance isn't good enough," Fannar replied coolly, "I need to see his body. I need to know he's paid for what he did to them."

"Don't start this again," Bror pleaded, his face filled with pity, "what happened to your mom and dad isn't your fault."

"I helped him escape, Bror!" Fannar exclaimed, "I wanted so badly to believe that my brother was still in there that I bought all the lies and tears, and now my parents are dead because I helped him!" He growled, his lip quivering as he glared at his friend.

"Moritz is really stubborn and resourceful, he still might've gotten your brother out even without your help," Bror insisted.

Fannar's jaw tensed as he considered the argument. "Why didn't Chasan just kill him when he had the chance?" he asked as his eyes began to fill with angry tears, "if he had, I'd still have dad at least; I'd have had more time to learn how to be king."

"Because you weren't the only one fooled that night, Fannar," Bror replied bitterly, "Hakan fooled everyone–he's still fooling Moritz, Iz and Amehllie…" his voice trailed off, and he took a deep, calming breath. "Trust me, no one regrets his getting away more than Chasan."

"He didn't fool everyone," Fannar corrected dolefully, "dad saw what he'd become." He chewed his tongue for a moment in agitation as a tear slid down his face, "I tried to refuse when he ordered me to start going to

Chapter 21

meetings and on official trips with him... told him that it would just make things worse if he felt like he'd definitely lost the crown. I told dad I couldn't do that to my brother, but dad said he didn't want me to be unprepared if the day came where I had to be the successor... he didn't realize it was already too late... I'm about to be king and I'm *overwhelmingly* unprepared."

"I think you're more ready than you're giving yourself credit for," Bror said encouragingly, "you've been working really hard to learn a job you thought you'd never have... cut yourself some slack." He sighed as he watched the prince shake his head before adding, "After all, according to your mom, you have the thing that is most important for the kingdom."

"A good heart?" Fannar asked doubtfully,

"Mhm," Bror mumbled, standing up and offering a hand to his friend, "and I think they'd both be proud of how well you've handled everything so far." The prince took his hand, and Bror pulled him to his feet before turning to head for the door.

"Bror," Fannar said, staring down once again at his old diadem on the dresser.

Bror turned back to his friend, his expression quickly growing concerned as his eyes fell on Fannar. "What's up?" he asked, following the prince's startlingly dark gaze down to the dresser.

"After the ceremony, I want you to change the orders for Hakan's capture," Fannar softly answered, his tone deadly, "...I want him alive."

Bror shook his head doubtfully as he replied, "He's too strong of a fighter, that probably won't be possible."

"It's not up for debate," Fannar said evenly, turning his gaze to his friend, "no one touches Hakan."

"Why the change?" Bror cautiously questioned, filling with worry at the unexpected depth of hatred reflected in his friend's demeanor.

Fannar's eyes bored unflinchingly into Bror's as he spoke, "...because I need to be the one who kills the monster that destroyed my life."

~~~~~~~

Hakan stood at the edge of the crowd gathered in the small-town square, a thick scarf wrapped around his neck and piled high to hide the lower half of his face. As he watched the live broadcast from the capital on the large screen, a mixture of anger, resentment and sadness coursed through him. The crowd erupted in cheers as his brother recited the final part of his oath as King of Ladothite, and Hakan anxiously tugged the brim of his hat lower. It was done. Hakan had officially lost the crown to Fannar, and the kingdom was thrilled to have their new Ice King.

"You shouldn't be here," Moritz suddenly whispered in his ear from behind him, "If you're spotted, we'll have to—"

"Yeah, I know, I know," Hakan grumbled mournfully. "I just wanted to see if he'd actually go through with it," he whispered, his tone and expression reflecting the bitter acceptance of the moment.

Moritz glanced uneasily around at the crowd roaring in celebration of their new leader. "Come on, let's go," he implored his friend, tapping the prince's ankle with his foot.

Hakan nodded and the two turned and began making their way out of the small, aged town. Once they were a safe distance out, the exiled prince unwound the

Chapter 21

scarf and sighed as the cool autumn air gently blew against his face.

"I thought we agreed it was a bad idea for you to go into any of the towns we camp near," Moritz scolded, glancing disapprovingly at his friend.

"Yes," Hakan acknowledged dully, staring at the ground as they continued their walk.

"In fact, I think it was *your* idea, wasn't it?" Moritz asked pointedly.

Hakan heaved a deep sigh. "Yes," he repeated.

Moritz let out a frustrated groan, and glanced back over his shoulder towards the town, "We should have Iz come back and check that no one recognized you."

"Everyone was too busy watching my brother get crowned to notice me," Hakan mumbled, kicking at the grass, "especially after you had Amehllie cut and dye it."

"Still..." Moritz said as they crunched their way into the treeline, turning sharply off the path several yards in. "So... I'm guessing you still haven't had any attacks if you felt brave enough to go around people again."

"Nothing," Hakan answered in a prickly tone.

Moritz' head tilted to the side as he looked curiously at his friend, "why are you upset about that?"

Hakan simply shook his head, his brows furrowed.

"If you haven't had any more attacks since we left the capital, then there's a good chance that I'm right and they had nothing to do with your gift. You should be relieved that you're not actually an uncontrollable danger," Moritz said with a slight chuckle.

"I've gone multiple months between attacks before," Hakan replied with a shrug, "I don't want to get my hopes up that things are going to be different this time."

"I could understand that," Moritz replied, staring thoughtfully at him, "but your heart-rate is telling me you're lying."

Hakan slowed to a stop and looked around. "Why should I be relieved? If someone else was making me hurt people, then I didn't just *lose* everything I cared about–my life was *stolen* from me," he explained bitterly, his face twisting with hopelessness, "and I can never get it back."

"After everything that's happened, how can you stand there sounding so sure of what can or can't happen? You know, two years ago, we were all sure it would be another thirty or more years before there was a new king, and we were sure it was going to be you…look how that turned out," Moritz criticized, fixing the prince with a harsh stare for a few moments. As he scrutinized his friend, he sighed, his features softening. "We can't bring back your parents," he admitted softly, "but if a telepath was behind your attacks, then we might be able to get you your crown again."

Hakan gaped, dumbfounded, at the ex-royal guard. "What about my brother? What if he won't give up being king?" he demanded.

"First, we find the telepath," Moritz told him patiently, "if they're working together, we need to take him or her out of play first… then we can deal with Fannar."

Hakan bit his tongue as he considered the idea before nodding his agreement, the thought of having something to work towards settling his agitation. "Okay, but how are we going to find them?" he asked as the new problem occurred to him.

"That," Moritz announced, walking behind the prince and placing his arms on his shoulders, "is a problem for tomorrow." He gave his friend a gentle push and they

Chapter 21

resumed their walk back to camp. "Oh, and Hakan…" Moritz added, "happy birthday."

Pronunciation Guide

NAMES:

Hakan Aimakos: hŭ-KĂN Ā-mŭ-KŌS
Fannar Aimakos: FĂN-är Ā-mŭ-KŌS
Bror Naukaron: BRŌR NOW-kŭ-rŏn
Chasan Bedraget: CHĂ-sĕn BĔD-rŭ-gĕt
Moritz Mohkem: MŌR-ĭts mō-KĔM
Joule Bedraget: JŪL BĔD-rŭ-gĕt
Shammoth Adimena:
   SHĂM-öth ĂD-ĭh-MĔN-ä
Ismat Pyaara: ĬZ-măt PĒ-YAR-ŭ
James: Jāymz
Eero Aimakos: Ē-rō Ā-mŭ-KŌS
Irina Aimakos: ĭ-RĒ-nä ĀY-mŭ-KŌS
Tanlan Naukaron: Tăn-lăn NOW-kŭ-rŏn
Leal Bedraget: LĒL BĔD-rŭ-gĕt
Kesavan: KHĔ-sä-văn
Haldis: HŎLL-DĬS
Basilah: Bŭh-SĬL-äh
Sythe: Sīth
Utara: Ū-tär-äh
Setna: Sĕt-näh
Afi: Ä-fē

LOCATIONS:

Ladothite: LĂD-ō-th-ī-t
Avol: Ā-v'l
Cerra: SĔ-rä
Lynna: LĬN-ŭh

Elibet: ĚL-ĭh-BĚT

OTHERS:
Derbala: dār-BÄLL-ŭh

Gift Guide:

Common Gifts

Water
Plants
Wind
Speed
Strength
Animal Communication
Healing
Heightened Sense of Sight
Heightened Sense of Hearing
Heightened Sense of Smell
Heightened Sense of Taste
Heightened Sense of Touch
Electricity

Uncommon Gifts

Influence emotions
Shapeshift
Telepathy
Bioluminescence
Teleport
Intangibility
No Gift

Rare Gifts

Telekinesis
Flight
Invisibility
Fire

Ice
All Heightened Senses (only 1 on record).
Foresight
Illusionist

Made in the USA
Coppell, TX
07 October 2024

38273791R00177